THE GIRL AT THE BORDER

THE GIRL AT THE BORDER

A NOVEL

LESLIE ARCHER

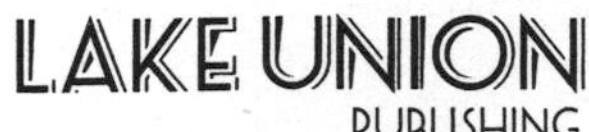

This is a work of fiction. Names, characters, organizations, places, events, and incidents are either products of the author's imagination or are used fictitiously. Any resemblance to actual persons, living or dead, or actual events is purely coincidental.

Published by Lake Union Publishing, Seattle

www.apub.com

ISBN-13: 9781503904774 (hardcover)
ISBN-10: 1503904776 (hardcover)
ISBN-13: 9781503901384 (paperback)
ISBN-10: 1503901386 (paperback)

Cover design by Kimberly Glyder

Printed in the United States of America

First edition

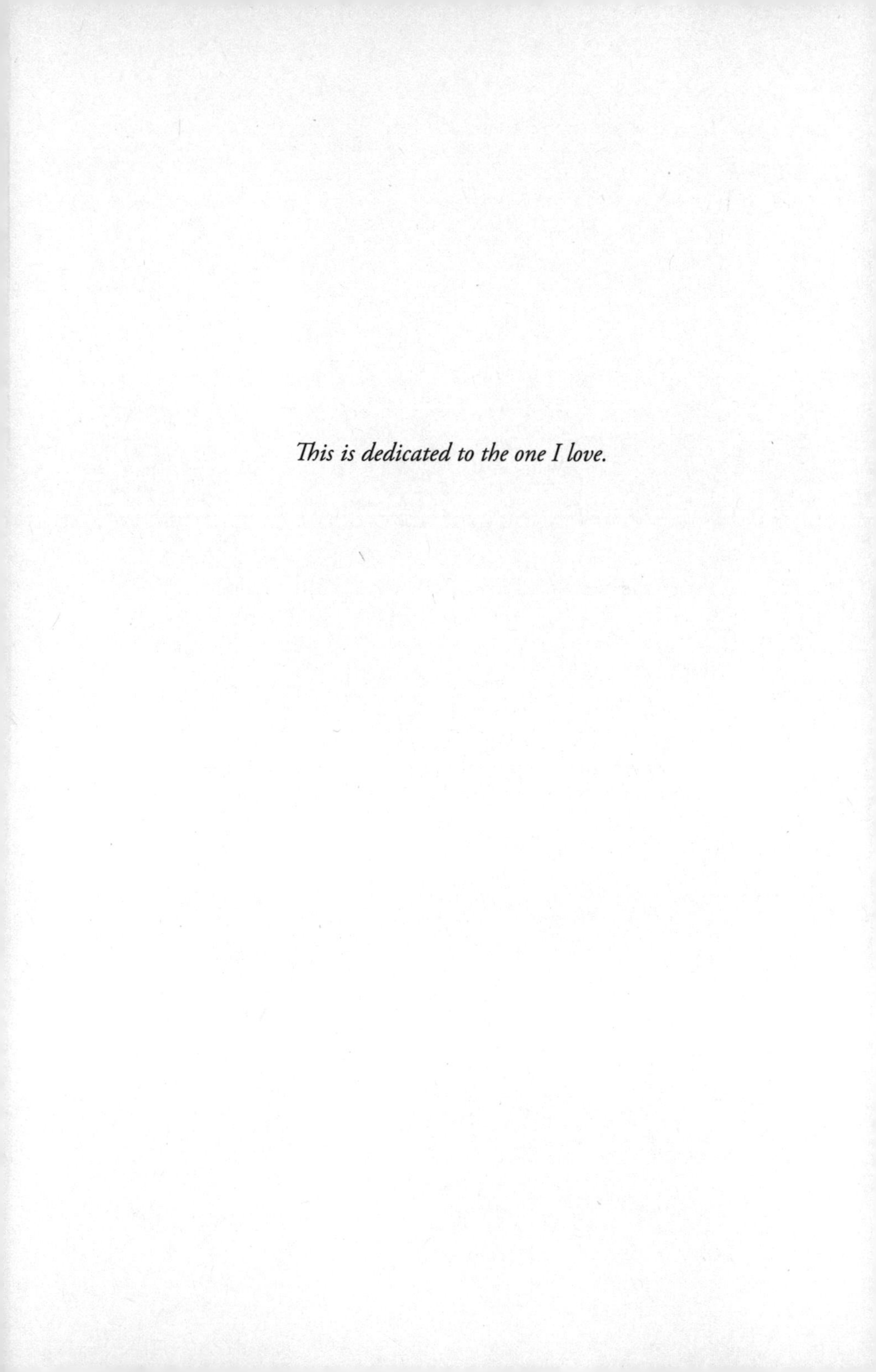

This is dedicated to the one I love.

My death waits there among the leaves

In magician's mysterious sleeves.

—"*My Death,*" *by Jacques Brel,*
Eric Blau, Mort Shuman

We are the resurrection and the light.

AUTHOR'S NOTE

I have been fascinated by the Etruscan civilization ever since my father took me to the Metropolitan Museum of Art in New York City, where I first saw artifacts made by the Etruscans, an ancient pre-Roman people. It's true that their origins are shrouded in controversy. That they eventually settled in the Tuscany region of Italy around 800 BC, lending the area their name, is beyond doubt. I have traveled there often in search of their remnants. But in the time before Tuscany and Etruria, a slightly wider area of settlement, where were the Etruscans? All over the Mediterranean, certainly, for they were most probably seafarers, but whether they began in another part of Italy, the islands of the Tyrrhenian Sea (as far back as the fifth century BC, Greek historians referred to them as Tyrrhenians), or regions farther east, it is as yet impossible to determine with any degree of certainty.

They remain hidden—a mystery. Just one of the reasons I fell in love with them and why they make an appearance in this novel.

THE EXILE

ONE

The morning Bella disappeared, Angela was with Bella's father on a boat off the coast of Crete. It was an island that under Richard's expert archaeologist's hands had slowly but surely been giving up its secrets. They had taken a break from the painstaking work that Richard was certain would help illuminate the mysterious and contentious origins of Etruscan civilization.

Bella, thousands of miles away, walked out of her house on a Saturday morning that was like all other Saturdays in what kids called Deadborn—the Michigan city abutting Detroit better known as Dearborn—but was in retrospect like no other Saturday in her life. At dinner the night before, she had told her mother, Maggie, that she would be off the next morning to study at the library, then have lunch at McDonald's.

Maggie wasn't likely to have heard; when Richard was away, mother and daughter barely spoke. After school, Bella would secrete herself in her room. On weekends, she attended a small study group. She never watched TV, rarely went to the movies, and after the first time, never went back to the mall, where many of the girls in her class hung out after school. No doubt another mother would ask herself what exactly her daughter did in her bedroom all afternoon and evening. Maggie didn't care.

On that particular Saturday morning, as Bella stepped out into the morning, Maggie was still in bed, the thick curtains of the upstairs bedroom drawing a veil across the rising day. Maggie, under the blankets, a satin sleep mask covering the top half of a face as crumpled as a used tissue, was oblivious to the world around her. Not even the herbal scent seeping from the mask could disguise the medicinal fug that had colonized the bedroom for the past six weeks.

Bella, small boned, somewhere between plain and pretty, bounced down the front steps. Her black hair, drawn back from her broad forehead, shone like a helmet. Her large gray-blue eyes took in the quiet street. A woman pushed a baby carriage down the sidewalk, heading away from her, toward the park. A kid on a shiny red bike appeared along a cross street, head down, legs pumping, and then was gone. The morning remained nearly deserted, serene, unremarkable.

Dressed in lightweight jeans, a blue-and-white-striped T-shirt, and old-school Keds, Bella adjusted her heavy backpack so that it sat precisely between her narrow shoulder blades before she set off at a brisk pace.

Richard Mathis and Angela, half a world away: the breeze wafting over the water, the clouds tumbling overhead, the water's rhythmic slap against the boat's wooden hull. They stood side by side, watching the trailing spangles of Mediterranean moonlight, like an enchanted wake, as the boat headed toward the Cretan shore. After what had happened, it was such a relief simply to be alive, to drink in the beauty of the night, to breathe the salt air, and to know everything was going to be all right.

Late the next morning, Richard's cell phone rang. He was not alone. Angela was with him, and so were the press vultures that had lately descended on the instantly famous dig. She would never forget the look on his face while he listened—consternation, concern, a grim struggle against an invisible tide.

"What is it? What's happened?" she asked against a rising fear. But he didn't answer, and then it was too late.

Twenty minutes after he received the call, he was gone. Forty-eight hours after that, he was dead.

TWO

Six weeks earlier, Angela, watching a seaplane swinging low over the jewel-tone Mediterranean, felt the anxious gut clutch that accompanied each arrival of the dig's only physical connection with the mainland. Gulls screeched out of its way, complaining bitterly against this metal-winged mutant as it glided onto the water's skin with minimum wake. As soon as it had come down, they swirled around it with greedy anticipation, searching for a morsel or possibly a meal dropping out of its gargantuan mouth. Disappointment harrowed them when all that emerged was another human being who with seeming deliberation ignored their constant hunger; they wheeled away in a huff. In stark contrast, Angela's heart rate accelerated as the seaplane's sole passenger was ferried ashore in the dig's shabby blue tender.

It was her first glimpse of Richard Mathis, but even at that distance, through the shimmering heat haze, she could see how handsome he was, feel his charisma. Everyone loved a star, even one in the once-syncretic world of archaeology. But telegenic Richard Mathis had made archaeology both popular and fun. PBS had anointed him, and the proliferation of individualized cable channels had made him famous. Because everyone loved him—or, more accurately, his image—she was bound and determined not to.

He stepped off the gently rocking tender, his gray-blue eyes wide apart and roaming, and Angela went down the sloping shingle to meet him, cursing Kieros for sticking her with this assignment. She imagined Mathis would be an ego-driven, privileged martinet, prickly, stubborn, imperious, who would expect everyone around him to march to his tune. Not her, not her. He was in for a surprise.

He was dressed for work: many-pocketed khaki shorts and short-sleeve shirt; sturdy boots, well worn, scratched here and there by briars and rock outcrops at previous digs. He carried a soft-sided suitcase along with what appeared to be an oversized physician's satchel made of pebbled pigskin.

Angela had taken a clandestine peek at his impressive CV while the team leader, Kieros, had his back turned. Mathis was a professor at the University of Michigan in Ann Arbor and a ranking member of the American Association of University Professors, and he had supervised digs in Jerusalem, Sinai, and Ephesus. Then there was all the TV bullshit. Most notably, so far as she could see, he had been part of the team formed by the Vulci archaeological park that had unearthed the Tomb of the Silver Hands, the burial place of a noble Etruscan family, seventy-five miles northwest of Rome. Since almost nothing was known of the Etruscans or their empire, this find caused quite a sensation in the archaeological and ancient history spheres. Even before that triumph, though, he had been as close as the archaeological world got to a rock star. He lectured at universities, consulted with museums all over the world, even in Russia and China. There had even been intermittent talk of doing a film of his life's work. Each time the rumor resurfaced, Richard shot it down as nonsense. In the perverse calculus of the tabloid world, paper and internet both, these denials only served to fuel the rumors and further burnish his reputation.

But as sensational as the find at the Tomb of the Silver Hands had been, the team's bounty here on Crete had the potential to top it, which was why the museum funding Kieros's work had enticed Richard Mathis to join the dig. There was a strong possibility that what Kieros and the team had unearthed was an Etruscan tomb. What the Etruscans were doing on Crete was anyone's guess. No written histories of the Etruscans had ever been found, so anything that was known about them came from the archaeological digs in and around Rome. They were apparently indigenous to the area, and though later on in their history they ruled the sea-lanes of the Tyrrhenian Sea, there was no evidence yet of them having colonized Crete.

"Are the rumors true?" Richard Mathis said after the necessary introductions.

"You have to understand," Angela said as she accompanied him back to camp, "we're in the earliest stages of excavation. The more we found, the slower Kieros ordered us to go."

Richard nodded. "A good man, Kieros. By all accounts prickly, stubborn, imperious." He eyed her. "Did I say something amusing?"

"Only to me," Angela said.

"Care to share?"

"I don't think you'd find it funny."

He stopped, turned to her. "Try me."

She looked into his gray-blue eyes and somehow felt herself to be the surprised one. "Prickly, stubborn, imperious—those were the three traits I was sure would define you."

He threw his head back and laughed. "I think I'm going to like you, Angela Chase."

They continued on toward his tent.

"I find it interesting that Kieros sent you to meet me instead of coming himself."

"He's on his daily call to Athens."

"I'm sure. He's not in the least happy I'm here. He's insecure, as well—so I've heard." He stopped abruptly again. "I have offended you, haven't I?"

"Not really. I've become accustomed to my place here."

He looked at her, his pale eyes penetrating while at the same time revealing nothing of himself. "Well, you shouldn't." He smiled. "So I'm asking you—all the speculation swirling around the dig: What's true, and what isn't?"

Angela licked her lips, for a moment at a loss for words. It had been years since a man had spoken to her with such candor. Long ago and far away. She felt something hidden, obstinate in its rebellion, reluctantly shift inside her. "What we know is this: We set out to find what seemed to be clues to the real-life Minotaur. What we found was an Etruscan tomb. At least that's the prevailing thought."

"Not Kieros's thought. His theory would be upended." Richard shook his head, sunlight spinning off his thick hair. "Imagine if you've discovered a doorway to the lost."

Angela shuddered. *A doorway to the lost.* The personal meaning for her bore nothing but dire consequences. Coming out into the light, being found again, would almost certainly be the end of her.

They had reached the tents, but after setting down his bag in the tent assigned to him, Richard was in no mood to settle in.

"I want to see the dig," he said.

"No problem," she said. "I'll get Kieros. He should be finished with his call."

"Don't bother. He's lost his chance. And you're here. You know the site, don't you?"

"Sure, but—"

"You take me."

"I'm thinking Kieros will be pissed."

A conspiratorial laugh. "I'm thinking the same thing."

They crossed the five thousand or so meters to the dig site. Fabric snapped in the hot, dry wind as if they were entering a marina, boarding a sailing vessel. No one was about; the sun was surrounded by white, as if it had bleached all color from the sky.

"Truthfully," he said, "I don't want to hear Kieros's biased opinion on what this dig is—which is what he wants it to be."

"I don't know enough to be biased one way or the other."

"There, you see? How much do you know about the Etruscans?" he said in a conversational tone of voice. This was the first thing she had noticed about him—well, the second thing, after his eyes—he talked to her as an equal. She was used to being talked down to by the archaeology professors on the team. Not that she minded so much; she hadn't their credentials, after all. Nevertheless, it was a change, another demarcation, a latitudinal crossing from *there* to *here*.

"Not nearly enough," she said.

He showed her a half smile, enough for her to tell that her answer pleased him. Not that he felt it either right or wrong—intuition told her he was not that kind of man—just that he appreciated her candor. She was, of course, affected by his charisma, as, she had read, was everyone with whom he came in contact. But she was surprised by his warmth, the way he listened to her even when his gaze was on the dig. He was, not to put too fine a point on it, aware of her as a human being. That was something that hadn't happened—that she hadn't wanted—since she'd left America. On the contrary, she had strived to blend in, to be invisible, to disappear as completely as possible. Her goal had been to be a nonperson. For the first time in four years, as she walked next to Richard Mathis, she realized what a superb job she'd made of it. She had been grayed out. Now color was slowly flowing back into her.

"Here's what you came to see," she said, moving toward the dusty plank ramp of section 17K.

"Look." Richard pointed to the side of the dig closest to them, the layers of sedimentary soil, each a different shade of ocher. "I think of digs as being like books, you see? Each layer of earth a chapter to explore, a new perspective on history unfolding. Another bit retrieved, another lost bit found." Then he laughed softly. "I'm afraid you can take the professor out of the classroom, but you can't take the classroom out of the professor."

She didn't mind that in the least. She was here to learn, and Richard possessed the knack all the best teachers had of making their subject fascinating.

Richard, standing beside her, said, "The composition and discipline of the Roman legions we're so familiar with from films and books were Etruscan in origin." He turned in an arc, pointing. "You see this dig is on a north-south axis. This was specified in Etruscan sacred books. All Roman legion camps were set up the same way. Though, to be honest, Kieros is skeptical of this theory. He's holding out for the Minotaur and the origins of the Cretan myths."

He spoke like a professor, but when they reached the lowest level of 17K and he breathed in the dust of ages, his demeanor changed completely. In Kieros's unconventional methodology the excavation was divided into physical grids, marked off with string they needed to duck under in order to access the squared-off sections. Every square was numbered, lettered, or both. Though he moved carefully and expertly around the site, Richard's expressions and little gasps of joy were those of a young boy circling the tree on Christmas morning.

"See here. Most definitely Etruscan," Richard said, kneeling beside a pithos, a large storage jar three-quarters buried. "But not an indication of an Etruscan burial site." He sat back on his haunches. "The Etruscan civilization rose between the tenth and the eighth century BC." He possessed that great gift of speech; he could make the phone book fascinating. "They had an enormous influence on the Roman Empire that in many areas of Italy, particularly Tuscany, survived to the present day. It was the Etruscans who drained the swamps and transformed what had been a loose agglomeration of tribal sheepherders' huts into Rome, whose armies would eventually dominate large tracts of Europe, Asia, and North Africa. From the Etruscans, too, came the antecedents of Latin and the Roman gods."

"Do you think they were indigenous to Tuscany—Etruria—or migrated from Asia Minor?"

"What do you think?"

That's what she got for trying to impress him. "I'm afraid I don't know enough about them."

"Most don't, even the so-called experts." He nodded. "And that's why you're here. Why we're both here, really. To learn more about what was lost." He looked all around him. "There's so much more here," he murmured, as if to himself. Then, to Angela, "How did you come to be on Kieros's team? You're pretty young to be on such a senior project."

"You're right. And I have no academic creds. I told Kieros I was whip smart and likely the fastest learner he had ever seen."

"And?"

"He told me to stop wasting his time. He told me to get out of his office."

"Did you?"

"What d'you think?"

"Well, you're still here."

She nodded. "I said, 'What d'you have to lose? What you'll pay me is shit anyway.' That made him laugh. He said, 'How d'you feel about cleaning out the latrines?'"

Richard lifted an eyebrow. "That bad?"

"Not quite, but almost. I'm a female with no academic background. Ergo, to these eggheads I'm a moron. I'm ordered around like a third-world employee."

"Well, let's see if we can fix that," he said. "You're my assistant now."

~

They worked down in 17K, one of the deepest parts of the dig's southernmost axis. 17K was the largest of the rest of the dig's squared-off sections. It was also the newest. A tunnel had been found. It led them downward. LED lamps had been set at intervals on the left, where floor met wall. The farther they proceeded, the more steeply the tunnel descended. At the same time, the tunnel's ceiling pressed down, obliging Richard to duck his head, curve his back.

For seven days straight, they worked side by side in the cramped quarters, Angela watching every move Richard made, absorbing every word he said as he described to her what he was doing and why. For seven days straight they found nothing of value, and she began to wonder whether the pithos was the only Etruscan artifact in the dig, whether the dream of an Etruscan necropolis on Crete was just that: a dream. They daily emerged from one twilight world to another, aching and frustrated. "Don't lose hope," he'd say to her like a prayer. "Never lose hope." At dinners they exchanged barely a word. Richard was plunged into thought, distracted, as if he was trying to work through a whole subset of his world of which he had not made her aware. To distract herself, she took to bringing books to read, first Eric Cline's brilliant *Three Stones Make a Wall: The Story of Archaeology* and then more often her beloved companion, *Moby-Dick*, immersing herself in the minutiae of life aboard the *Pequod*.

Afterward, walking back to their tents, he might offer her a drink. She felt a tidal pull of wanting to know what was troubling him, but she sensed that asking him would be to cross a line. She already knew enough about him to understand that she needed to take her cues from him.

Those nights they would sit up in his tent drinking and talking about the day's work. She felt his intensity, his dedication, his optimism like a ray of morning sunlight. And the next day, she would join him in the morning sunlight for a quick breakfast before they returned to 17K and set up shop all over again.

But once, at dinner, when he noticed the book she was reading, he said, "How do you find Melville's writing? Most people can't get through it, or if they do manage to struggle to the end, they don't understand what he was getting at."

She looked up. "It's a wormhole to another time, another place, that elates and terrifies me. The strands of revenge, punishment, madness, God's will, the nature of evil, mysteries that are beyond human comprehension."

"Ah, a fellow lover of *Moby-Dick*," he said with soft smile. "What are the odds? It seems to me some form of sign or portent." His gaze drifted away for a moment. "I gave my copy to my daughter: a legacy of wonders, you might say. But the sad thing is I have no idea whether Bella has even read a word of it."

After that, they spent their nights reading their favorite portions of the novel to each other in the slow, hushed tones of storytellers Melville would have recognized and approved.

~

On the fifteenth day, as he did each day, Richard carried with him to the work site the pigskin satchel that held his own tools. He wouldn't touch any of the team's tools, an idiosyncrasy that Kieros could at least grumble about under his breath without too much fear of retaliation. Richard would simply smile a Cheshire cat smile, an expression Angela felt sure he had spent an inordinate amount of time perfecting. In any event, that placid, goofy smile produced in Kieros visible angst and poorly suppressed anger. The tension between her boss and Richard was slowly increasing to the level of an overclocked computer. She could not help but feel that in his neurotic way, Kieros was spoiling for a verbal argument with Richard over something he could actually document. Clearly, Richard was amused by Kieros's increasingly Rube Goldbergian machinations.

Richard unpacked his tools, unrolling the length of chamois in which they had been carefully wrapped. He switched on his headlamp. He took out a brush and dusted off what seemed to be a rock outcropping. Almost at once, the area darkened, and Richard said, "Bingo!

You see? Black fired clay. I do believe we have ourselves a bucchero, an example of Etruscan funerary pottery."

Slowly and methodically, Richard unearthed the leading edge of a piece of finely etched bucchero. "Depending on the carving, this could be a very important find," he said excitedly. He was rarely wrong, in Angela's short experience of him.

Pocketing the brush, he took up a pick, small as a dentist's instrument and just as sharp, and a hammer of approximately the same dimensions and began to work around the area, never coming anywhere near the slice of bucchero he had exposed. After perhaps forty minutes of this, he moved aside, handed the tools to Angela, and said, "Okay, your turn."

Her heart thumped heavily in her chest. "You must be kidding."

"Not at all." He pushed her down on the stool, pressed the pick and hammer into her hands. "There's only so much you can learn by watching. In archaeology, as in all human endeavors, learning comes by doing."

She looked up at him. "What if I make a mistake?"

"All we can hope for, then, is that you learn from your mistake."

"But you're trusting me with your bucchero. I don't—"

He gestured with his chin. "Begin at the beginning, as the Red Queen told Alice." He smiled reassuringly. "You've observed me long enough. Have faith."

She returned her attention to the rock surrounding the precious Etruscan artifact. A bead of sweat snaked its way down her spine. Her upper lip was damp, her armpits suddenly swampy. Nevertheless, she took a deep breath, let it out slowly. Focused on the spot where she would start to the point where everything else faded to gray. Drew on her own training to calm herself, steady her nerves and thus her hands. Set the point of the pick to the spot she had chosen, the one where Richard had left off. Raised the hammer back, then struck downward.

She hardly heard the impact. A fistful of dust flowered outward, then subsided to the space between her boots.

"Too tentative," Richard said softly, not unkindly. "Put more of yourself into it."

She did as he ordered, heard the resounding smack, felt it through the bones of her hands, into her wrists. Willed herself not to flinch. A silent explosion of dust, a satisfying chink in the stone. She moved the pick, hammered down, again and again, finding a rhythm, moving in a clockwise direction as she had seen Richard do.

"Good," he said. "As I suspected, you are indeed a quick learner."

She returned her full concentration to freeing the bucchero from its centuries-old entombment, and when bit by bit it began to emerge, her elation was almost too great to contain. She set her implements—Richard's—on her thigh, concentrated again on taking deep breaths.

"You felt it, didn't you," he uttered softly.

She nodded, for the moment unable to speak.

"What did she feel?" Kieros, in his usual manner, had come upon them with the stealth of an owl hunting its prey.

"The ecstasy of discovery," Richard said without turning around or, in fact, acknowledging in any other way Kieros's unexpected presence. It was the flip side of his Cheshire cat smile, intended to belittle Kieros, to keep him at a remove.

Kieros wasn't having any. "What d'you think you're doing, Richard?"

"Uncovering what appears to be an exceptionally fine piece of bucchero. What have you been up to, Kieros?"

The Greek slapped away his question with the hairy back of his hand. "No, what you're doing is taking advantage of an assistant—a dig novice without a degree—to do your work for you."

"I'm teaching her."

"Whispering in her ear? Bullshit."

At this, Richard stood up, but even now he did not turn around, obliging Kieros to move if he did not want to keep talking to Richard's back. When the Greek hove into view like an overladen ship, Richard said, "Kieros, my dear sir, you are paying this girl a salary, penurious though it might be."

"Blame the museum, not me." Richard's habit of turning conversations against him clearly irritated Kieros, but just as clearly he didn't know how to untangle himself.

"All right then. If a salary is being paid, a service must be rendered. Am I right?"

"Of course you're right," Kieros snapped, "but—"

"But nothing. With every strike of the hammer she is learning her trade, which means each day she becomes more valuable to you. Since her salary is fixed—I assume that's true . . ."

"It is." Said grudgingly and with not much volume.

"Exactly. Then the more she learns, the more expert she becomes, the greater her value to you and this team, and the bigger bargain she becomes." Richard impaled Kieros with his stare. The Cheshire cat grin appeared like sunlight through clouds. "Am I right?"

Kieros, unable to meet Richard's penetrating gaze, shifted his own gaze to the blooming quadrant of the bucchero. He frowned, as if deep in thought. "If she so much as chips it, Richard, she's gone. And it'll be on your head." Then he turned on his heel and strode away.

THREE

In the dead of night, Angela awoke with a start, her heart hammering in her breast. She shook like an alcoholic detoxing, drenched in sweat that had nothing to do with hormones and everything to do with her dread of her former life. It had been this way for four long years—so long, in fact, that she had more or less gotten used to these symptoms, rarely remarked on them to herself. But now she felt them acutely; now they pained her greatly; now she suspected that she could no longer tolerate them. And why?

Richard Mathis had come winging into her life fresh from the Turkish coast, the dust of Ephesus, of lost civilizations on his boots, in his hair. Richard Mathis with the twinkling eyes, the ironic lopsided smile that made him seem boyish. Richard Mathis, twenty years her elder, with a wife named Maggie and a daughter named Bella; he was forbidden. And though the forbidden was not unknown to her—the gate to the path others would not take had always stood open for her—she knew that wasn't what she wanted from him. Someone who listened to her, someone with whom she could talk. My God, how she had missed that! When she was with him, the deadening tension she lived with day and night melted away. She relaxed. Her self-sufficiency—the bedrock upon which she had based her vanishing act—was shifting. Richard had spun that coin, the other side coming into view, the dark side: the bleakness of being alone. Now, when she wasn't with him, she felt the near death of being alone, without trust, without faith. Without joy.

Excited and frightened in equal measure by these thoughts, she brushed aside the flap of her tent, stood staring at the dim outline of Richard's tent. She very badly wanted to talk with him, even if it was only to say, *I can't sleep. How about you?* But she couldn't get her feet to move in the right direction. Reluctantly, she did an about-face, picked her way across the rocky terrain to where it sloped down steeply to the shingle where Crete met the Mediterranean. A half-moon, cool as milk, followed her, dripping its light onto the water, a bridge on which she imagined walking out and away, farther away than Crete, farther away than any foreign land.

She sat, arranging herself with her knees up against her chest, arms wrapped around her shins. Staring out into the water, she wanted to hear a sound other than the slap of the wavelets against the shore—a bird's cry, even a cricket's chirp—but there was nothing. Just the water and the wind stirring her hair against her cheek.

Drifting in reverie, she was unaware of time passing. But thinking about the past was for her never a good idea, and inevitably tears burned her eyes, ran down her cheeks. She felt the disturbance of the air by her side, felt his heat just before Richard sat down beside her without even a simple "May I?" Of course he may; that was how he approached life. Wiping her eyes with the back of her hand, she flung herself back into the present.

"You looked very alone out here," he said.

"I *am* alone," she said, but she thought she heard a subtext in his statement, a larger meaning that might constitute a concern.

"What are you doing here, Angela?"

"Learning about the history of the lost."

"Not at the dig," he said. "I mean here on Crete."

"Where else should I be?"

He was silent for a moment. Then he shrugged. "I don't know. Somewhere where there's nightlife, music, dance, people your own age."

"You talk as if I'm sixteen."

"My daughter, Bella, is sixteen. You're what? Seven, eight years older?"

"I'm twenty-five."

"Ah, youth!"

"Going on forty."

He laughed. But then the laughter cut short when he saw she wasn't joining in.

"I don't get along with people my age," Angela said curtly. "I never have."

He turned to her. "What are you running away from?"

His question chilled her.

"I hope it's your past," he said, "because you can't run away from yourself." Picking up a small stone from between his feet, he cast it into the sea. "Take it from me: I know."

This interested her. "You're running away too. From what?"

"You first."

When she shook her head, he inhaled deeply, then said, "When I was fourteen, my parents died. Their car was T-boned by a drunk at the wheel of a semitruck." He paused for a moment, searching for another stone to throw, but he couldn't seem to find one of the right shape. "We were all supposed to be going to a family birthday party. By rights I should have been with them, but I pretended I was sick. Stuck a finger down my throat and vomited. My mother didn't want to leave me alone, but I persuaded her I'd be okay. Even then I had a gift of saying the right thing in the right tone of voice. After they left, I made myself popcorn, dug into a quart of chocolate ice cream, and settled down on the living room sofa to watch *Clue*. I remember all I was interested in was Lesley Ann Warren's boobs. I must have been watching them in her low-cut dress when they died. Maybe not the exact moment, but close enough." He gave her a frightening smile of a skeleton; his voice had changed, become thick and clotted with emotions dredged up from the swamp of his past. "I've been trying to escape that moment all my life."

"Survivor's remorse."

He nodded. "Their death hit me like a cannonball." Raked fingers through his hair. "I'm what you might call off-axis."

"Not according to all your awards, your discoveries. The press treats you like a superstar."

"Uneasy lies the head that wears an identity, to unpardonably mangle Shakespeare's *Henry IV*."

She laughed at the joke made by this charming and erudite man with a wicked sense of humor who wasn't afraid to make a stand against authority. He treated her like a human being; he did not condescend to her as the others at the dig did. He stood up for her with Kieros. But at the dark heart of his words lay a truth for her as well as for him. She knew more about slipping into a new identity than he could even suspect. Beneath Angela Chase, the identity she had adopted when she'd fled New York, lay Laurel Springfield, silent, unmoving. Waiting, perhaps, for this very moment to stir and return to life. Still, there was uncertainty.

"Why are you telling me all this."

"Because you asked."

She shook her head. "You don't seem to be someone who responds to intimate questions."

He looked at her levelly. "I don't. Under normal circumstances." He gestured. "But here we are on Crete—enisled, you might say. I see you down here, and you seem sad. You were crying." His head tilted. "Yes?"

He waited and waited. Someone inside her opened her mouth and said, "Yes," startling her.

"I hate to see you sad." He stretched his long legs, dug the heels of his sandals into the scree. "That's no crime, is it?"

"That depends on how many sad girls you know."

He laughed softly. “Your turn,” he said.

“Truth or consequences.”

His smile was soft, almost dreamy, the hard edges of his public persona continuing to round off. “Oh, nothing as severe as that.” He shrugged. “But, you know, if you’d rather not . . .”

It was a dare; if she backed down now, she was sure she’d lose respect—and his attention. “All right then.” She pursed her lips to keep them from trembling. For a moment, she felt poleaxed. The past bound her in its winding cloth. Giants in her chest were using her heart as a bowling ball. “I left New York under something of a cloud.” Breathless, scarcely believing that she would admit as much to someone she had known little more than a week. “That was four years ago. I guess you could say I’m in exile.”

“What happened?” he asked.

No, that wasn’t going to happen, not even with him. It was too devastating for her to go there. A lie, then. But to be believed, all lies must be interwoven with a truth, preferably a universal truth: “My boss wanted something from me. When I refused, he accused me of embezzling, said he had evidence against me.” And now a bit more of the truth slipped out: “But I guess I would’ve left anyway. I loved my father so much, but he was never around.”

“Like me,” Richard said with a far-off look in his eyes. “I’m never around for my daughter.” Then his expression cleared. “What about your mother?”

“She left us.” She wanted to go on, but the words stuck in her throat like a thistle. There was an empty space where her heart used to be. That she’d told him this much was causing her stomach to churn. Why? She had lied early and often to everyone she met who knew her as Angela Chase. Why should lying to Richard be any different? Because, like it or not, he was different. His concern had awakened something in her she had thought dead. Could ashes be reignited; could something phoenixlike arise from the dread of her past? His concern for her was precisely the same as it was for the Etruscan artifacts he was searching for. And why not? A lost civilization, a lost girl. It had been so long since trust had not turned into betrayal that she had lost faith in its existence. And yet she had to admit to herself that she was beginning to trust Richard, to believe in what he said, to consider the fact that he had her best interests in mind—that he, in fact, not only respected her intelligence, her ability to learn at light speed, but also liked her as much as she liked him.

But he was pressing her now, and surprising herself, she responded, "My mother was gone by the time I was sixteen, suddenly, in the middle of the night." And that was as far as she was prepared to go. "Why do all awful things happen in the middle of the night?"

"I don't know, but it certainly seems to be the case."

"Anyway, a year later, my father died—of a broken heart, I have no doubt."

"So we were both orphaned at an early age." He took a breath, let it out slowly. "It's a terrible thing to have your parents die when you're young. I don't think you ever recover. Your capacity to love is . . ."

"Broken," she finished for him. "Stricken from the book of life."

FOUR

The night before Bella disappeared, Maggie was sitting at the kitchen table, hands wrapped around a mug of tea heavily larded with Irish whiskey, now her alcohol of choice. She had swallowed a couple of Vicodin, along with something else; she couldn't remember what, except that it numbed her mind. Where was Bella? Up in her room, as usual, which suited Maggie just fine; she wouldn't have to look at her. Her hands trembled; the great serpent in her belly, lodged there at the moment of Bella's conception, uncoiled, spitting its poison through her system. As a naive little girl in Maine, she had dreamed of falling in love, marrying, living happily ever after. This was what she thought had happened to her when Dr. Richard Mathis had come along and swept her off her feet. Her heart had opened, expanding toward him, and everything had been fine—better than fine, perfect. That was how deluded she had been, to think anything could be perfect in real life. Real life was a bitch, filled with disappointments, coercion, betrayal.

Richard was always leaving. At first, it was only for a week, nine or ten days at the most. She supported him, like any good wife would, as his fame grew and his world expanded, as he became more and more in demand. She was justifiably proud of him, rabbited on about him incessantly to any of the other wives who would listen. One by one, they all got bored, preferring to discuss the PTA, playdates for their two- and three-year-olds, carpooling. Subjects that made Maggie's eyes cross. In time, the women drifted away.

Then Richard had told her he wanted a child. At first, she had rebelled, but in the end she gave in. She always wound up giving in to him. The pregnancy was fraught, as if her body continued to rebel against the inevitable, as if it knew some sort of tragedy was coming. Then, after it all, she was all alone with just Bella. Richard was away for first a month, then several months at a time. He left her all alone with this wet, whimpering bundle of flesh that yowled, attacked her swollen nipples at all hours like an insatiable vampire, deprived her of sleep, of relaxation, of quiet. Bella never stopped crying, never, it seemed, slept. She was assailed by an endless chain of maladies: colic, strep throat, ear infections. High fevers, scarlet face, inconsolable: every illness terrified Maggie, anxiety for her and for the child making sleep a state of being she could scarcely remember. When Richard did return, the baby nestled into his arms as if she were a part of him. Not a cry, not even so much as a whimper, sending Maggie into a drugged sleep, where she tossed and turned on the rough seas of resentment. And then he was gone again, and she was bound to the house, joined with this needy thing whose insatiable desires would never allow her a minute's surcease.

As if that wasn't nightmare enough, each morning she would stand in front of her full-length mirror, staring disapprovingly at someone she didn't recognize. Her breasts were swollen, her nipples darkened, her hips wide enough to support a tank. About her buttocks, flat as a Mercator projection, the less said the better; after the first time, a furtive glance thrown over her shoulder, she did not care to return her gaze to them ever. To cheer herself up, she went shoe shopping, but the two styles she loved most didn't fit her, though they were the right size. When she blamed the lasts, the salesman said, "Madam, your feet are flat. You can't wear these styles anymore." This enraged her more than anything else that had come before, and she pitched an impressive fit at the store.

Sloshing more whiskey into her empty mug, she drank half in one go. This kitchen was so dismal, just like the rest of the house. Was it any better than the hospital room from which she'd been released a month ago? Finishing off the whiskey made her feel no better. In fact, it had turned her melancholy into despair. She and Richard had been happy once, hadn't they? It was getting more and more difficult to remember, as if those memories belonged to someone else, some character up on the silver screen where happy endings were assured. Where was that girl now? Gone, gone, gone, sucked up into the violent twister and, like Dorothy, deposited somewhere strange, with no ruby slippers to get her back home.

FIVE

17K: Angela and Richard resumed the delicate excavation they had left off late yesterday. Working alternately, sometimes in tandem, they spent the next six hours in nerve-tingling, back-breaking intimacy—a kind of intimacy Angela had never before experienced and that she began to treasure—at the end of which they had completely freed the bucchero. As fine an example of Etruscan handiwork as Richard swore he had ever seen: a handleless jar mounted with the magnificent bas-relief of a regal sphinx. Lion's body, eagle's wings, and the impassive face of an Etruscan, whether female or male it was impossible to tell. Perhaps, Richard opined, it was both, for though the traditional sphinx had a female head, with the Etruscans, he said, one knew only enough never to take anything for granted.

"One thing is for certain: the Etruscan sphinx is a guardian of the interred," he said, his voice vibrant with elation. "Here we have solid evidence that we've stumbled upon the tomb of a member of a high-ranking family." He turned to her, grinning. Then he kissed her lightly on the cheek. "You see, Angela, it seems you've brought me the greatest good fortune!"

Holding the bucchero gingerly between her two palms, Angela traced the Etruscan sphinx with her eyes, as if the intensity of her gaze could bring it to life.

"The dead are here," Richard said. "I can feel it." He was on his feet, fingertips running along the rock face of the inner wall. Leaving her, he moved off to his right. "And I want to see their dead, Angela. It's vital because so little is known about them. It's as if they disappeared into the early Roman Empire, as if they assumed a new identity."

He moved farther to his right. "You see, the wall here describes a slight curve that runs into the current end of the 17K tunnel." He turned back to her. "I'll need to get Kieros to lengthen this tunnel."

"Through the solid rock?"

"Maybe." He turned back to the rock face. "But maybe, if we're very, very lucky, this is nothing more than a wall."

"The entrance to the main Etruscan tomb."

He whirled, grinning. "Yes!" Then his expression darkened. "But to get him to do that . . . Kieros is a pragmatic man. He guards his budget like Cerberus. I suppose I don't blame him, the budget he's been allotted. No verbal argument is likely to sway him." He tapped his fingertip against his lower lip. "Besides, another issue has raised its head."

"What's that?"

"If Kieros was unhappy before, he's now totally pissed."

"Ever since he came by and saw the bucchero."

"He was expecting to find evidence of the Minotaur. Instead he stumbled across the Etruscans."

"Not his field of expertise."

"Precisely. It's fear that's making him so unhappy."

She gave him a sideways glance. "What d'you mean?"

"He's worried that I'll replace him as team leader."

She hadn't considered this, but she thought he might be right. "Would you?"

He stood so close to the rock that he might have been a corpse dog sniffing out the dead. "That's a good question."

She considered further. "It's a matter of power, isn't it? Purely a male thing."

"You mean you wouldn't do it, given the opportunity?"

"I very much doubt I'd be given the opportunity."

"Why d'you say that?"

"First, archaeology, like most disciplines, is male dominated. Second, women aren't heard the way men are."

He frowned. "How do you mean?"

"When a man voices an opinion, it's taken into consideration. If a woman voices an opinion, she's either ignored or told to calm down."

He turned, watched her staring at him. "You may be right." Then he waved a hand. "Anyway, Kieros has nothing to fear from me. I have to be in Sinai soon."

She felt her heart skip a beat and thought, *What the hell?* "How soon?"

He shrugged. "Not sure. I'm not my own master."

"No," Angela said. "I suppose you have many masters."

He grunted. "Back to the problem at hand. Getting Kieros to do what we want."

She liked that he said *we* instead of *I*. She liked it very much.

She lifted the bucchero up as an offering. "How about this for a start? Kieros can't very well ignore what's right in front of the entire crew's eyes."

"Right you are," Richard said. "The bucchero's a good start. But for him it won't be enough." He came back to where she knelt, the artifact cradled like a baby in the crook of her arm. "We need to find more evidence that we're near an Etruscan tomb, that the bucchero isn't merely part of a small find." He took up his implements and set to work: tap-tap, tap-tap, tap-tap-tap. "No time like the present."

~

One-two. One-two. One-two-three. The banging of the shade against the sides of the open bedroom window, where the butter-yellow walls met the inset metal frame. This was the sound that Laurel, who would one day in the future become Angela, had associated with the screaming from her parents' bedroom next door from the time she was nine years old. Many nights she would be awakened by the window shade or the arguing. She would lie in bed, waiting, while the rhythmic banging and raised voices continued unabated. The ferocity of their arguments, the pitch of their voices, hurled at each other like knives, defied space and drywall alike. For over half a dozen years she had been paralyzed by those voices, by the venom they carried. She would imagine a pair of spitting cobras she had seen on a National Geographic special. Then scrabble beneath her pillow for her iPod, stick the earbuds in, and press play. She would leave the iPod on shuffle. Lenny Kravitz's "Again," which was a joke either on her or her raging parents, then Pearl Jam's "Last Kiss," which also might be irony heavy, if she were in the mood for such things. She would fall asleep to Eagle-Eye Cherry's "Save Tonight."

But now, as for the past many months, a silence, heavy as smog, hung in the kitchen as father and daughter solemnly ate the breakfast he had prepared: scrambled eggs, toast and butter, coffee.

"Great stuff, Dad," she said, her voice bright, inviting him in, as she wolfed down her food. "Where'd you learn to cook eggs like this?"

Her father, toying with his food, said, "When you're alone, you learn . . ." But he stopped there, his voice drifting off to some other time or place he might wish to be in.

She tried to talk to him, tried to rally him, but it was no use, and finally she gave up. After rinsing her plate off in the sink, she bent, kissing her father on the forehead.

"Love you, Dad."

"Love you, too, Rabbit," said so mechanically it broke her heart all over again.

Down the gritty brownstone steps, out into the rumpled West Village morning. A crushed 3 Musketeers wrapper spun along the gutter like a tumbleweed, chased on the breeze by the warm, yeasty smell from the bakery wafting around the corner on Seventh Avenue; kids and their mothers, a smattering with their fathers, skipped past, laden with Hello

Kitty or Batman backpacks. Laurel was in high school, too old to have a parent walk her to school, although the idea of it was beyond her ken.

Truth be told, school had always bored her, and at sixteen she felt high school was no better. Of late, her incessant reading had taken on a voracious edge. She devoured books the way kids ate those pyramids of cherry turnovers, bear claws, and chocolate cigars displayed in the bakery window. She was a ferocious self-learner who needed neither teacher nor mentor. The library was her universe. She harbored an almost desperate need to learn, as if some passage in the most arcane tome would provide the means for her to fix her parents, to remake them into what she wanted—needed—them to be. That the natures of her parents were unfixable by her or by anyone else save themselves was brought home to her again and again through her reading of psychology texts. Yet it was one thing to learn something and quite a bit different to feel it in her bones, to accept it as truth. For a while, at least, hope sprang eternal, and she continued her assault on wide-ranging knowledge. And even after the truth had sunk in, she never lost her thirst for learning. She was like T. E. Lawrence staggering out of the desert into an oasis of unending water. For her, the library was that life-giving oasis.

Often, she would hide out at closing time, eluding the staff, waiting until the vast space was locked up, utterly silent. Then, flashlight in hand, she'd roam the stacks, searching for more books that would stretch her knowledge far past its normal age limit. She had been known to read all night. But there were other nights when, meaning to do so, she would instead fall asleep at the table, head on crossed forearms, only to start awake to the sound of her own desperate sobbing.

The sidewalk had emptied of kids. Parents now far away, starting their adult rounds. Classes were about to begin—history, chemistry, language lab. Of what use would they be to her? She turned around, hurried the other way.

At the library, she once again dove into the latest textbooks on computer programming, the subject of which more and more fascinated her. When she could, she worked on one of the library's computers, which she found as winded as a runner about to have a heart attack. One evening she had spent several hours cleaning out the hard drive and defragging it, clearing the browser caches of cookies.

When she'd had enough of C++, C, and Java, she took down a copy of *Moby-Dick* to clear her head. Making herself comfortable at a table, she commenced to lose herself in Herman Melville's thrilling prose: "Whenever I find myself growing grim about the mouth; whenever it is a damp, drizzly November in my soul . . . then I find it high time to get to sea as soon as I can."

She looked up from the page and thought, *Get to sea.* Be in the world, not in the classroom, where dusty ideas and the weariness of teachers were all to be had. She returned to the novel but could no longer concentrate. It was time, Ishmael had thought, to get to sea before he stepped into the street and deliberately knocked people's hats off.

Quitting the library, she walked east and entered Washington Square Park. It was a damp and overcast day in late May, the sky low and flannel gray. The plane trees were fully budded out, the ground covered with an undulation of newspaper pages crackling in the wind like sails. She sat on a wood-slatted bench, watching with critical alertness the men play chess on the park's inlaid concrete-aggregate tables. The slats were painted grass green. Each table had a little wooden box with a metal post on top, which the players slammed down every so often with the flat of their hands. Timing the moves.

On the other side of her, a junkie, no more than seventeen or eighteen, lay half sprawled, mouth open, closed eyelids fluttering with dreams of a better life. One of the chess players, an Italian with a natty panama and neat goatee, glanced up. He had a wandering eye that made it seem as if he could see everything at once.

"What're you doing here all by your lonesome?" he said, not unkindly.

He was younger than the other players by, she judged, a good decade. "Hanging," she said.

"On a school day, huh?" He grunted, lifted his hirsute chin toward the junkie. "That there could be you, *piccola*," he said, again not unkindly, "you don't watch yourself."

She snorted. "I'm too smart for that."

He eyed her for a moment. "I'll just bet you are." He shooed away his playing partner with a practiced flip of the back of his hand. "This isn't the first time I've seen you here. You know how to play chess, *piccola*?"

"Some. Maybe." She shrugged. "I don't know."

"Well, come on over here, and let's see what you got." He watched her take the seat opposite him. There were some hee-haws and guffaws from his fellow players, which he shushed with a sidelong glance. His nimble fingers moved over the chessboard, arranging the pieces to start a new game. Out of courtesy, he gave her white. "Your opening move. I'll show you."

"If it's all the same to you, I'd rather do it myself."

His hand, which had been hovering in the air over her rank of pawns, withdrew. "Be my guest." He observed her with a mixture of curiosity and a certain proprietary amusement as she made her first move: pawn to king 4.

"You sure you want to do that?" he asked, a skeptical tilt to his head, the front brim of his panama dipping low.

"I'm sure."

"Two moves from now I'll take your pawn with my knight."

"And I'll take your knight with my knight." She looked across the board at him. "It's called a pawn sacrifice, right?"

A slow, almost ecstatic smile spread across his face. "You're a ringer, aren't you?"

She wrinkled her nose. "What's a ringer?"

"Someone who knows more than she lets on." He held out a leathery hand, crossing the no-man's-land between the ranks of black and white pieces. "My name's Orfeo, *piccola*," he said. "What's yours?"

SIX

Night into day. The eastern horizon cracked the fiery sun open like a raw egg, spreading yolk-yellow rivulets across the water. Angela came awake instantly, her heart pounding, her throat filled with dread. Again and again and again. Imagining one of Dey's people tracking her down, killing her, or worse, dragging her back to face what she had done when she had worked for him.

She sat up, swinging her legs over the side of the bed, rubbed the sleep out of her eyes with the heels of her hands. Then she stood, stretched hugely, crossed to the tent flap, and stepped outside. She stared out across the raw Cretan morning toward Richard's tent. She felt the pull of him, like a lodestone, drawing her toward him. Loneliness ate at her like a tapeworm.

She wasn't aware that she had moved until she found herself, blinking, at the edge of his tent. As if of its own will, her right arm lifted from her side, her hand pulled aside the flap, and she peered inside.

Richard was crouched on the edge of his bed, hunched over, body tense as he peered at the glowing screen of his mobile, below which his thumbs were busy pressing keys as he texted someone. She didn't mean to move, but as she did, her knee cracked, loud as a twig snapping in the forest, and his head sprang up, eyes staring. But it was the look of silent pain on his face that staggered her, sent her emotionally back on her heels.

"I'm sorry, I—" She started to back away, stumbled over a stone, twisted, and fell. Another stone, sharp edged and vengeful, seemed to hurl itself at her, struck her temple as she hit the ground.

Tossing the mobile onto the rumpled bed, Richard jumped up, ran to where she lay. She had already risen up on one elbow.

"You're hurt," he said as he helped her to her feet.

"No, I'm . . . really, I'm fine."

"You're not fine; you're bleeding."

She pressed fingertips into the hair at her temple as he led her into his tent. They came away red and sticky. He sat her down on the bed, went to get a first aid kit. Beside her, his mobile lit up.

"You've got a text message coming in," she said as he snapped open the lid, pulled out cotton balls, Betadine, and a fistful of different bandages.

He crossed back to where she sat. "It can wait."

"It's from . . ."

He began to wipe away the oozing blood.

"I couldn't help noticing." She winced as he applied the Betadine. "The text is from Bella."

Parting her hair, he peered at the wound. "You've got a little gash. The head always bleeds a lot. This comes first."

Angela frowned, not understanding his curt tone. "You must have been in the middle of texting her when I stumbled in."

"Without announcing yourself." He continued to work on her lacerated scalp.

"Sorry." She winced again as he put pressure on the wound. "Stupid of me."

"It wasn't stupidity," he said firmly. "Fear drove you."

"Fear? What d'you mean?"

"Keep quiet. You'll ruin my work." He hummed to himself. "You know precisely what I mean. Your heightened fear . . . damn it!" A new burst of blood, immediately damped down as he applied pressure. "It's a well-known medical fact that cortisol levels in the brain are at their height from four to six in the morning. It's why both armies and assassins favor that time. Fear, anxiety, even paranoia are at their peaks."

"Are you saying I'm paranoid?"

"I'm in no position to judge. But I do know fear. I've smelled it many times in Sinai. Now sit still for another moment." He managed to hold the bandage squarely over the wound until the bleeding stopped. "There. All finished." He began to clean up. "Did you black out, for even a moment?"

"I don't think so, no."

"Headache?"

"No, but it burns like hell."

"Nothing the laceration wouldn't explain. Good. A concussion's unlikely then." He threw away the bloody cotton balls, returned the Betadine and the unused bandages to the kit. "We should keep an eye out, though, at least for the next couple of days."

"Okay, sure."

He sat down next to her. "Now. What are you afraid of, Angela?"

His mobile lit up again.

"Richard, I think Bella is trying to contact you."

"Avoiding the question won't make it go away."

I could say the same for you, she thought. And now she wanted to know more about Bella: Who was she? Was she anything like Angela had been when she was Bella's age and still Laurel? Was Richard a good father to her—what was their relationship like? She sensed trouble, but she didn't yet know what kind or how bad it might be. "It's not what I'm afraid of," she said. "It's who."

"Your ex-boss, I take it."

She was trying to decode him. He appeared to be genuinely concerned with her well-being. She found that she liked that. A lot. "Yup."

He lifted an eyebrow, making him look a bit impish. "His name wouldn't be Jordan Catalano, would it?"

She could see he was laughing, and she laughed too. "No, it isn't." Jordan was the name of Angela Chase's sometime boyfriend in *My So-Called Life*, the popular TV series from the nineties.

"I'm assuming you're a big Claire Danes fan." Claire Danes played Angela Chase.

"Huge."

"Me too." His eyebrow lifted again. "I suppose it's verboten to ask your real name."

Laurel Springfield. A chill went through her. No, no, no.

Recognizing the look on her face, he said, "Never mind. It doesn't matter." Smiling. "What's in a name anyway?" He regarded her levelly. "What are you going to do about this man who isn't Jordan Catalano?"

"I'm here." She stared down at her hands in her lap. "I've been running for four years."

"You can't stay an exile forever."

She nodded. "I know."

"No, I don't think you fully understand."

Her eyes rose to meet his, and she recognized a friend. She was only able to do this by trusting herself again, by letting go of the wariness that had dogged her, the dreadful legacy of her involvement with Dey. For the first time it dawned on her that this was another gift Richard had given her: to be able to recognize a friend.

"Exile is the twin of death. Exile is a living death." A small silence before he said, "I'll help you."

"What? How?"

That conspiratorial smile he'd shared with her their first day together. "I know people."

Richard's mobile lit up again. It was right beside her, and she saw a photo of a young girl, Bella; she could see something of him in her, especially around the eyes. But Bella's expression was so familiar—withdrawn, intelligent, isolated—that for a disorienting second Angela thought she was looking at a photo of herself a decade ago.

Scooping up the mobile, she held it out.

He looked from her to the mobile, ran a hand distractedly through his hair. "I always seem to make a mess of it with her. She's so distant after my being gone so much. I know she must resent me, which is why, I guess, I've never been able to reach her. She's like an alien creature who speaks a mysterious language of monosyllables and silence."

All at once, he had transformed into a different man, bewildered, unsure of himself, and she knew this was what was on his mind during his long silences at dinner. He was suddenly smaller than his surroundings, his golden glow shrunken, his charisma dimmed and flickering. It was shocking; she felt herself staggered and then closer to him than ever. She could not help thinking of how often she'd had difficulty talking to her own father. What kind of barrier had been raised between them? She had never been able to find out.

At that moment, Richard rose. He stared at the phone as if it had come alive. "Why don't you give it a try."

"What? I don't even know Bella."

"Pretend you're me. That will give you sufficient latitude to say whatever you please."

Was that a touch of bitterness in his voice to go with his crooked smile? "Richard—"

"You owe me. No, that's unfair."

"Yes, it is." She thrust the mobile at him, but she didn't really want him to take it. This was a way to help him. This was trust. Without trust there could be no joy.

His brow crinkled, and that silent pain returned, flickering across his face like heat lightning. This time it lasted under her gaze. He seemed vulnerable. "You're only nine years older than she is. Fix this. Please." He crossed to the tent flap, stepped outside.

Angela scrolled back to the beginning of the conversation.

Maggie's a hot mess, she read, noting the name, not Mom.

And Richard's reply: What else is new.

This time it's diff, Bella had written. She's going under.

Richard: She's never cared abt you. Why do you care abt her?

Bella: lol just relaying news.

Nothing from Richard, interrupted as he'd been by Angela. Then the second unanswered text from Bella: OK maybe not news 2 u. And this last: guess ur gone again. What else is new.

Angela glanced up from the screen. "Jesus, Richard," she whispered.

Shaking her head, she returned her attention to the screen, began typing with her thumbs. How bad is she?

just told u, Bella fired back.

Sorry, we've come upon a potentially huge find here. I've been distracted.

Yr ALWAYS distracted

I'm all yours now.

Wow!

I mean it.

ROFL

C'mon, Bella.

C'mon yrself.

It's v early here, no one's around. We have time. Talk to me.

Silence.

Bella, tell me how you're doing.

Silence.

OK, now yr frightening me.

Silence. And then: How does it feel?

And that was it. Bella refused all of Angela's efforts—masquerading as her father—to get her to respond further. But she had learned some crucial information concerning the difficulties between father and daughter. Someone not as attuned might have assumed that Bella was simply acting out an angry-teenager phase to a father who clearly was never home enough for her. But to Angela, whose own father hadn't been there enough for her when she needed him most, another thread had revealed itself. Richard had been right about her own fear, and now she could sense the same feeling in Bella. His daughter was afraid of something.

Stepping out of the tent, she found Richard staring at the eastern horizon, colors changing every moment. Seabirds rose and fell, crying, as they searched for breakfast. Far out, the silhouette of a fishing boat was visible, black against the pinkish sky.

"How did it go," he said.

"How do you think it went."

"Uh-huh." He sighed. "Anyway, it had to have been better than if I had continued."

"Remember what I said about females in a room full of men never being heard? The same can hold true for one man." When he said nothing, she tried to give him back his mobile. He didn't want it.

"I want you to keep trying, Angela. For Bella and me it might already be too late."

"You don't know that."

He turned to her, eyes dark and gleaming. "Oh, but I do know. All too well."

This was a side of him he hadn't revealed before. A private side. The carefully lacquered shell had cracked. He was no longer the star, the belle of the archaeological ball, so to speak. His facade was gone, and in its place was a man who had failed at being a father, a man who loved his daughter but had no idea how to show that love. The simple fact was that he trusted her to see him like this, to know that she wouldn't make fun of him, wouldn't be contemptuous and turn against him. She was astonished by his trust, bowled over by it, and inevitably began to wonder whether she deserved his trust. His cracking open was huge, monumental for what it portended for them both. What could she do to be deserving? She could listen to what he said, to hear what was going on beneath: *I need help. Will you help me?*

And the fact was she wanted to try. No one had tried to get through to Laurel—to her—or if they had, they had eventually betrayed her. Who would she be if there'd been someone who'd tried harder? She wanted to do this for Richard, for Bella. For herself.

SEVEN

It took Maggie over four months to find a nanny she could abide. Weeks on end neighborhood girls came and went, dismissed almost as soon as they sat down across from her at the kitchen table. Too much makeup, too inarticulate, too giggly, too stupid, too eager, too young, too venal, too dark, too light. The list of flaws was endless. All under her half-crazed eye deemed untrustworthy to be in her house, to take care of the baby who had invaded her life.

The Baby. That was how she thought of Bella in those days. It was easier, somehow. It lightened her burden, as if the Baby were some other person's child, a temporary glitch, a bump in the road. But then, each morning as she passed the full-length mirror, she realized that the Baby in the next room must be hers—because look what it had done to her.

Then Elin was sitting across the kitchen table from her. Elin, whom she recognized from the neighborhood, whose family lived two streets away. They were Muslim, sound citizens, kind, but to her, at least, enigmatic people. She had been brought up with the Bible, with Christ, with bedtime prayers, within the Episcopalian world. What was the meaning of the Qur'an, the hajj, halal meat, their aversion to alcohol? The collision of their world with hers confused her, made the chaos of the world more palpable, like a heart beating with a strange rhythm. Maggie had met Elin's parents, Lely and Hashim Shehadi, at a block party she had forced herself to go to the previous year. She liked them. They weren't friends, exactly, but still . . .

Elin was neither slim nor particularly heavy. But then who could tell under her modest dress? She had large dark liquid eyes, a wide forehead, and a decidedly Semitic nose, which did not bother Maggie in the least. Neither was her hijab a problem. It framed her olive face, might have hidden any otherwise exposed defects, like acne or moles. After twenty minutes of increasingly intense conversation, Maggie was convinced she had found the right person. Though Elin was young, she possessed a seriousness and an air of responsibility beyond her eleven years. Nothing seemed to faze her; her calm demeanor soothed Maggie's frazzled nerves. And Maggie's instincts proved correct. Bella took to Elin and Elin to her from the first moment they clapped eyes on each another. If Maggie had been a different sort of person, she might have felt a pang of jealousy. As it was, she felt nothing at all. Well, maybe relief, but that was short-lived. It wasn't long before Elin became a fixture in the household. She arrived promptly thirty minutes after school let out and stayed until after dinner. Eventually, at Maggie's request, she began staying later and later, until after the baby was asleep, subbing for Maggie for the first night feeding. Formula. Breast milk was out of the question. By that time, Maggie was already researching the ways to make her breasts perkier, not make them sag all the more.

There came a time when Elin's parents allowed her to stay over one or two nights a week, and Maggie was glad of it. For some reason she couldn't pinpoint, the house was creepy when Richard was away. Such was her mania, her guilt.

Elin proved to be the ideal companion: obedient, quiet, never getting underfoot, always, always respectful. Good upbringing, Maggie thought. And automatically thought even better of her mother and father. Elin was also instantly responsive on those rare occasions when Maggie was moved, either by extreme loneliness or by despair, to talk. Dimly, as she and Elin spoke, she realized how lost she was. Elin understood loneliness. She was the only female child in a family of four brothers, all apples of her father's eye. To him, she said, she was of another species, lower, less interesting, less important. Maggie understood completely. Often, after these talks, she would sit on the side of her bed, staring blindly at the blue-and-white vinyl wallpaper, silent as a ghost. Defeated. Defeated because she could never tell Elin the source of her despair, her inexplicable rage, her homicidal feelings. Indeed, when they arose like specters in the middle of the night, so real, so wrenching, they forced her out of bed and whipped her into the bathroom, where, on her knees, she vomited up everything in her stomach.

A week after Richard left again, when Elin had been with her for five years, she looked at herself in her bedroom's full-length mirror for the last time. When she smashed the mirror, everything changed. She had come to the end of her stay in the real world. It was as if the universe, having rejected her, had released her from its dreadful grip. A perfect egg-shaped shell that only she could see had formed around her, a shell that obliterated both past and future, that kept her in the eternal velvet now conjured up by Vicodin, oxycodone, and fentanyl. In this state of nothingness, detached from the gravity-bound body that was no longer hers, she floated in a sea of self-abnegation. She was nothing: from nothing she was born; to nothing she would go. In this state she did not have to remember the terror of having acquiesced to her husband, the horror of giving birth, the great serpent of animus that slithered within her belly, devouring everything in its path. In this state when she looked at her daughter, she saw nothing.

EIGHT

From: RB_Mathis@gmail.com
To: MBella2316@gmail.com

Hey, Rabbit,
We've had a tremendous breakthrough today. We've been trying to determine whether this is the site of a big Etruscan cemetery. We've had inklings, which is why I was sent for so urgently, but today . . . well, today we unearthed a tomb guardian—the first intact one in the world! I felt like Indiana Jones. But don't worry—there's no Temple of Doom here! LOL!

The guardian is a stone lion with wings. Marvelously carved. It stands over three feet tall (that's an estimate—it'll take days to unearth it entirely, but, wow, is it big!). I could describe it to you, but if you click on this link from Expedition, you'll see the partial on the website for the Penn museum.

Ours is in much better shape, and, even more astonishing the lion is clearly female. A lioness.

Maybe we've stumbled upon the tomb of an Etruscan empress. Wouldn't that be something? And you're hearing it first!

Needless to say we're all very excited—all except the site director. Poor fellow, he was hoping to find signs of the Minotaur—that half man, half bull from Cretan mythology (have you read about him? I think you'd love the myth, very mysterious, like our winged lioness).

BTW, I got an assistant when I arrived. Angela's funny and smart. Only nine years older than you. I've told her all about you. You'd like her. She's starting to think of herself as Lara Croft. My influence, I'm sure! She asked if she might write or text you sometime. That would be cool, right? I'll bet you guys have things in common.

I wish you were here, Rabbit, but you're too young. Safety first! Rules are rules, isn't that what I taught you? And then there's school. But maybe when you finish high school, you might want to take a year off and spend it digging into the past with me. Would you like that?

Anyway, I have to go. We're working thru the night to get our guardian lioness unearthed. But listen, Rabbit, I know I don't say it much, but I love you. And I miss you all the time. I have to go to Sinai for a bit when I'm finished here, but then I'll be home—I promise. And we'll go away for a long weekend, maybe to Washington to see the White House and the Capitol and all the monuments. You've never been, and I think we'd have a grand time. I have friends all over. We could have a private tour of the Smithsonian.

Write and tell me how you are. How's your mother? How are you getting along with Elin and the family now that things have gotten so rotten for Muslims?

Xoxoxo
FR (Father Rabbit)

~

"Did she respond?" Richard said when Angela returned from the soft night above the dig, where she had sent the email.

"No. I waited, which is why I was gone so long."

In front of them, vivid in the semicircle of LED lights, was the winged lioness, eyes widened, mouth open in a snarl, wings unfurled, great claws rampant. Its triangular ears were back, and the small tuft of mane on the top of its head was nonexistent, one of the clues to its gender. Deep ridges at the base of its wings spoke of their power; the delicacy at their chiseled tips revealed their grace. Its deep chest was bifurcated, another clue the talented sculptor had provided. Richard had told her these Etruscan beast gods had their origins in ancient Asian cultures, brought to Egypt and Anatolia, thence to Greece and Mycenae. By the Etruscans themselves? No one knew. In all, the lioness was, as she had written, a majestic and magnificent beast.

"So she didn't write back." Richard continued to flick dust and crumbled rock from the lioness's haunch with a sable brush. "Well, what would she have said anyway?"

"Richard—" She watched him working in his careful, concentrated way. "Maybe she'll write in the morning. You don't know."

"Yeah," he said, his voice betraying his exhaustion, "I do know."

"Whatever you think, whatever the case, I won't stop writing her."

He turned to eye her, his brush suspended. "You think it's that important, huh?"

"I wish my father had written me letters from work. I wouldn't have felt so alone, so isolated."

As he went back to work, he made a sound deep in his throat, as the guardian might make were she alive.

"You know," she went on, "writing this email was like talking to my younger self."

Brush-brush, brush-brush. "And how is that?"

"My own father used to call me Rabbit."

Richard paused, turned to her. "Really?" He smiled. "How extraordinary!"

She had his full attention now. She very badly wanted him to hear what she said next. Really hear it. She cleared her throat. "I signed the email 'FR.'"

"FR," he said, brow wrinkling. "What's that?"

"FR: Father Rabbit."

For a moment he stared at her in astonishment. Then a great smile spread across his face. "Father Rabbit," he repeated, as if testing the name. "That's quite brilliant. You see, I was right to have you write for me."

"A strange twist on *Cyrano de Bergerac*."

He laughed but could not keep the tightly held sorrow in check, and the laugh ended as a kind of sob.

"Richard—"

"Don't," he snapped. It was the first time she had heard him raise his voice. In his occasional altercations with Kieros he lowered his voice, deepened it. It took on an unmistakably steely edge that invariably caused the director to back off.

There was nothing for her to do but to return to their silent work, watching the great winged lioness awakening as they slowly freed it from its ages-old entombment. A tiny sliver of fear slid between her ribs to touch her heart. He was angry with her; would he stay angry? What would happen then? She couldn't bear the thought. The thing she must not do, she kept telling herself as she worked on the claws of a forepaw, was to mention Bella again, though Bella was who she most wanted to know more about. A kinship was forming, thin yet, like the first icing of a lake, but where the ice stretched itself, where it met the water, there surely was an inescapable bonding between the two. It was then she pledged herself to writing Bella every day—as Richard or, as she had suggested to Bella, herself.

Hour after hour spent itself, melting into the rock dust of the underworld in which they stood. At length, Angela became so tired that she was sure the lioness had moved. Richard had named the lioness Cul, after the Etruscan infernal goddess of gateways to the underworld. Unable to keep her eyes open, Angela dropped her brush and lay down, curled herself around Cul's powerful forepaw, and fell fast asleep.

She awoke, achy and stiff, to find Richard sitting beside her. He was staring into her face, almost as if he was deep in conversation with her. It took a few moments for Angela to realize that she had awoken with none of her anxieties. For the first time since she had run from Dey's employ, she was free of pounding heartbeats, cold sweats, the dread of the past catching up to her. Her gaze ran softly between Richard and the demonic Cul, who seemed more a friendly companion than a ferocious guardian to her, and she thought, *It's because of them.*

~

The next evening, they broke off work at more or less the normal time. Even Richard was feeling the effects of their long day's journey through the night. After dinner, after the briefing Richard gave to the group at large, Angela went back to her tent, dragged her bedding and few belongings over to Richard's tent, and set it all on the floor.

If he was surprised, he gave no sign of it. They had a couple of drinks, talked about Cul and what her presence meant—Richard was of a mind that they would soon enough find her companion, another winged lion, perhaps a male this time, perhaps not—they did their quick ablutions and got ready for bed. By the light of the oil lamp, Richard entered the day's events in his old-school logbook, while Angela typed her second message to Bella.

> Dear Rabbit,
>
> We have named our winged lioness Cul, the guardian of the gates to the underworld. She's really coming into focus now, really beginning to seem alive to us. There's something curiously comforting and loving about her, as if she's protecting us as well as her ancient mistress. Sometimes she appears to be very close, then other times impossibly far away. Like you.
>
> xoxoxo, FR.

Angela sent the email. Richard shut his logbook, placed it on a narrow shelf beside his bed. "It's funny how we tell ourselves stories and later wonder whether they were true. Thinking back to just before I came here, I can almost believe I actually was in Ephesus."

Angela turned on her side, her head propped up on one elbow. "What do you mean? Where were you?"

"Home. Dearborn, Michigan." He shook his head. "I don't know." He was quiet for some time, his mind turning over something important.

All around the tent the shadows stretched and yawned as the wind billowed the fabric of the tent. A conversation came to them briefly, too far away to make out the words. Then the burble faded into the night.

"Why did you tell everyone you'd come from Turkey?" Angela asked at length.

"My wife is very ill. She's hardly conscious."

"I'm sorry."

"Don't be," he said sharply.

What the hell does that mean? she wondered. "Do you mind me being here? I sleep better when I'm near you."

"I noticed. Last night in the dig you slept calmly as a baby. It was quite beautiful." He was staring at the ceiling. "And when you woke up, I didn't perceive a trace of fear or anxiety in you. Not a drop."

She wondered what he was actually seeing now.

"You know, I was relieved when you dragged your things in here. I was actually worried you'd want to sleep with Cul from now on."

She saw his grin, and she laughed. "It's you, Richard. I feel—I don't know. Protected. Maybe that's the right word. I can sleep without fear someone is coming for me."

Richard let out an audible breath. "That's the greatest compliment I've ever gotten."

Angela didn't know what to say to that, so she said nothing. But her heart beat a bit faster even though she felt as if he had just tucked her in.

"You do understand that people will start talking," he said. "They always do at digs; it's such a small, enclosed society. Are you prepared for that?"

"I don't care," Angela said. "But what about you?"

"What about me," he said dreamily. Almost like the refrain of a song.

And then she understood why he had told her the truth about where he had been before coming to Crete. Whatever the stories that came about her sleeping in his tent, his wife wouldn't hear them; she was beyond being hurt by either lies or the truth.

"Tell me more about your father," he said, and now she knew what he'd been seeing as he stared upward.

"He wasn't a big man, but he was strong—burly, like an old-fashioned hod carrier. He had huge hands, and they were—once when he took me to the Central Park Zoo, I was able to stroke the horn of a rhinoceros. His hands were like that."

"What was his line of work?"

"He had two jobs, but he never spoke about what they were."

"You never asked?"

"We didn't have that kind of relationship. Looking back, he might have been a glassblower, a bricklayer, or a night watchman. He might have done anything that didn't have an office title or business card attached to it." She took a breath, memories flooding through her. "I don't think he was proud of what he did. But maybe my not knowing is partly on me; maybe I wasn't interested enough. The important thing, I guess, is that I was never with him, except on Sundays." She laughed. "Like God." Feeling a crick in her neck, she changed positions, lying on her back like Richard, staring upward. She wished she could see what he was looking at. "In the mornings he'd make coffee in an old, battered percolator. He loved the strong coffee that came out of it. He'd stir up hot cereal—oatmeal, Wheatena, cream of wheat. He'd rotate them. I hated cream of wheat. I'd have Corn Flakes or Wheaties those days, even if it was freezing out."

Richard was silent. He'd folded his hands across his chest. He was staring into his own life.

"You loved him," he said at last. "Your father."

"Very much, yes."

"Despite the fact he was almost never home."

Angela supposed the conversation was always heading in this direction. "I never felt abandoned by him. Not until he died, and then I hated him even while I was crying for him and for myself."

"*Sorry* sounds so inadequate," Richard said. "And yet I am."

"He was a wonderful person, my dad. He just never knew how to talk to me."

"Did he ever tell you he loved you?"

"When I was little, before his heart was broken. Afterward he said it, but in a kind of rote way. But every time he called me Rabbit, I knew."

Richard was still as death. Angela felt that it would be an invasion of privacy to look at him. She could hear the breath soughing in and out of him, like wind in the willows. She remembered reading *The Wind in the Willows* and wishing herself into Toad Hall.

Without warning, Richard reached up, switched off the light. She imagined herself curled around Cul's forepaw and, in that safe place, passed into a deep and dreamless sleep.

NINE

When Elin first came into the household, her presence caused nary a ripple. Elin was exceptional in taking care of Bella and was nothing but solicitous with Maggie. Still, though Maggie appreciated Elin's help, the girl was an employee, and Maggie was scrupulous in keeping their exchanges to the bare minimum. Often, she wouldn't even see Elin, even though they were in the same room together. To Maggie, Elin was a piece of furniture, albeit one that moved and took care of the Baby. Only when she was at her worst would she talk to Elin, out of an intolerable desperation.

In her downward spiral, drinking took up more and more of Maggie's life, and so did the pills of varying flavors and efficacy she started ingesting when, years later, alcohol was no longer sufficient to send her under the rainbow. That she restrained herself, painstakingly abstaining from all of her necessities, as she privately referred to her drugs of choice, when Richard was home was another symptom of her unsupportable burden of rage and guilt. She had become clever in the specific ways of criminals and madmen.

By the time she was four, Bella had grown to love Elin; certainly she relied on her, felt safe with her, was comforted by her when she was ill. Elin provided all the empathetic responses that her mother was incapable of giving her. The core of her had imprinted itself on Elin in much the same way a dog will give its unconditional love to the human who feeds it, holds it, coos to it, loves it. At that age, God alone knew what she thought of her mother. Later, when she was older, perhaps seven or eight, when Elin had all but moved in, she knew Maggie was her mother, but her understanding of the word *mother* was vastly different than anyone else's her age. "Mother" was someone who occupied the house she and Elin lived in. She always called Maggie by name, never Mother. That sobriquet was reserved for Elin's mother, whom she lovingly called Umm, just as Elin did. As for her birth mother, she reacted to Maggie's antipathy by shrinking away from her, closer to Elin and to Umm.

Her daughter's disinterest in her was precisely what Maggie had been working toward. Elin, however, was not so easy to keep at a safe remove. Elin was unrelenting in her attempts to get closer to Maggie—to understand her? Good Christ, Maggie did not want that. Nevertheless, it was fortuitous that Elin was in the house when Maggie had her first full-blown panic attack. Elin had the presence of mind to leave Bella, who was eight at the time, in her room. The edge of hysteria in Maggie's voice fanned the fires of Elin's innate empathy. She found Maggie lying on her bed, curled on her right side, in a fetal position, knees drawn up to her chest. She was turned away from the door; all Elin saw was her back, curved like a turtle's shell.

"Mrs. Mathis," she said softly.

Maggie moaned. She seemed frozen in place.

"Mrs. Mathis, what is it?"

No answer, or rather nothing coherent. Now Elin did something unusual. Instead of walking around the foot of the bed to get a look at her employer, she climbed onto the bed, kneed her way to Maggie's side. Then she lay down beside her, waited. When she received no negative sign, she wrapped one arm around Maggie's waist. Waited for Maggie to shrug her away. When that did not happen, she drew her own body against Maggie's, began to gently rock her.

After what seemed an eternity, she became aware that Maggie's shoulders were shaking, that she was silently weeping. Then she felt Maggie's fingers find hers, interlacing.

"Shhh," Elin said softly. "It's going to be all right." As if she were the mother, Maggie her daughter. She recognized, perhaps instinctively, that something essential inside Maggie was broken, that she was spiraling down into a pit of despair, and she thanked Allah for placing her in Bella's path. In those days, in the aftermath of 9/11, she had already experienced enough despair to last her a lifetime. Unfortunately, the world had changed irrevocably; the calamity to befall American Islamics had just begun.

As it turned out, Orfeo was far from a great chess player. Within eight months, Laurel was regularly beating the pants off him, to his unconstrained delight. In fact, she often drew some of the old hands, who watched her play with the concentration of crows on a treetop. More often now, passersby would pause in their peregrinations, curious as to the proceedings. Then the crowds started to form, three and four deep. Laurel would ignore them all, concentrated wholly on the march of her plastic soldiers and royal family across the checkered terrain. Her strategies were mercurial, one day attacking as boldly and methodically as a Roman legion, the next hanging back, cagily pouncing when her opponent made a mistake. And if all else failed, if she saw that she was being outmaneuvered, there was always the Sicilian Defense to fall back on, reimagined, remade, remodeled.

Orfeo was far better at playing the guitar than he was at chess. Laurel found this out one evening when he invited her home for dinner. This was perhaps five months after they had met. It was November 1, the leaves on the plane trees sparser, letting more sunlight through than at the height of summer. It grew darker earlier. A smoky melancholy was in the air.

"But don't you need to ask your folks?" Orfeo asked when she accepted his invitation. "Don't you need to call 'em or something? Else they'll worry about you."

"As long as I take a couple of hours to get home and fix dinner," she said, "it'll be okay."

Orfeo's thick eyebrows scrunched up like a Muppet's. Then he shrugged. "We eat at seven."

"No problem," she said. "I'll see you at six thirty."

Orfeo lived in the far western precincts of Fourteenth Street, in one of the row tenements so old all the sharp edges had been worn off the corners of the brownstones. The last vestiges of the Western European immigrant waves had mostly departed decades ago—Irish, Spaniards, and Italians, barbers, window dressers, bartenders, housekeepers, masons, waiters, carpenters, shipping clerks, messengers, beef slingers at the nearby Meatpacking District, and the enterprising owners of a shoe-repair shop, a deli market. All gone now, giving way to a mixture of working-class Hispanics and a growing number of young, upwardly mobile Caucasian families.

"So," he said just after he had opened the front door with a key that looked like an antique, "now you must tell me about your parents, even if it's the bare minimum." As if this was the price of admission to his home and hearth.

She thought about how she would go about explaining the inexplicable. "Let's see," she said, stalling for time. "My mother's a ghost. She could be living in Paris or Istanbul or around the corner." She paused, summoning up a healthy serving of chutzpah, as her insightful English teacher, Mr. Solomon, a Jew of the old school, would say. "As for my father, he's always been a hardworking guy, holding down two jobs. That was before my mother left us. He wore himself out for her." She heard the bitterness in her voice. Judging by his expression, Orfeo had, too, but she didn't care.

~

The pressed-tin-ceilinged vestibule smelled of cooking grease, fried spices, and old leather. A narrow, recursive staircase graced with a volute newel post and beautifully turned balusters led steeply upward. The handrail, polished to a dull luster by time and calloused palms, was cool and silken under her hand.

As they approached the first landing, she saw an arched niche in the wall ahead. When she asked Orfeo about it, he said, "For bringing down the dead. Coffins are too long to make the turn otherwise."

This was her introduction to the matter-of-fact manner in which people with one foot in the Old World viewed the continuum of life and death. Deep inside her, she was wary of their sainted forebears.

Reaching the third floor, Orfeo led her down a hallway so narrow they were obliged to walk single file. The door was flung open even before he could put key to lock. A round-faced woman with flushed cheeks and wisps of damp hair coiled across her forehead smiled broadly, and when Orfeo introduced them, Sofia drew the girl to her prodigious bosom, sheltering her with her arms and showering her with kisses.

"For so long Orfeo has spoken about you and promised to bring you home." She had a voice like a trained soprano, high and clear and inherently musical. "Now, at last, you're here."

In this effusive way was Laurel welcomed into Orfeo's Italian home as a member of the family. An orphan coming in from the increasingly cold and dark city streets. Somewhere deep inside her she was wary, holding back much of her real self, hiding it from these people who opened their arms to her. This came as naturally to her as breathing.

The apartment was a bubbling warren, filled to the brim with Orfeo and Sofia's three children, a boy of eight and two girls, twelve and thirteen; an uncle and aunt, apparently feuding, from opposite sides of the family; and most notably Orfeo's mother, whom everyone called Nonna, rather than her Christian name, Rosa.

Laurel's first impression of Nonna was of an old, crooked Italian woman with voluminous white hair, tied severely back in a bun at the nape of her neck. Nonna's face was a cameo from another, gilded age. Her gaze was curious, keen as the blade of a knife. She wore a flowered housedress; old-fashioned lace-up shoes, blocky as a man's; and a sprightly yellow apron. Cradled in the crook of Nonna's arm was a bundle wrapped in layers of pure-white cloth that Laurel at first took for an infant. Nonna would not let it go, no matter what else she was doing.

Laurel made friends with the girls as if it was nothing at all. Their shared computer wasn't working correctly. She sat down in front of it and within three minutes had identified two viruses and three Trojans piggybacking on sketchy executable files the girls had downloaded. In those days viruses were few and far between, and those that did exist were rudimentary, as hackers were just starting to experiment with them. She got rid of them all, discovered a tricky rootkit virus, which took her fifteen minutes to clear out. Then she restarted the operating system, and all was as it had been before the infections. The girls were so grateful they listened intently as she tutored them on being more careful about what they downloaded.

As suppertime neared, Laurel was astonished to see that the bundle Nonna was cradling wasn't a baby at all but a huge ball of dough. Orfeo, laughing, explained that Nonna needed to keep the dough warm while it cured, so to speak. Nonna's hands might have crepey skin, but they were as strong as a man's, as capable as the finest craftsman's. Thirty-five minutes later they were all sitting down to a feast of fresh salad and the best pizza Laurel could ever remember tasting.

"Buono?" Nonna inquired of her from across the table.

And Laurel, ever the natural linguist, ever the bookworm, grown up at light speed, said, "Sì, sì, Nonna. E' delizioso. Mille grazie," which brought a big smile to Nonna's gorgeously creased face, a Renaissance portrait, a Madonna in comme il faut decline, while all around them raucous laughter radiated like a halo.

Afterward, Nonna gathered all the children, Laurel included, and bundled them off to the compact city church on Eighteenth Street for a late Mass, this being All Saints' Day, a Holy Day of Obligation on the Church calendar. Nonna made sure Laurel sat next to her. "Believe it or not," she said softly, intimately, "there are lessons to be learned in high places." By this, Laurel took her to mean holy places; even she, so far from God or faith of any kind, intuited that.

Nonna pointed out the acts and scenes of the Mass but fell silent when the sermon began.

"Today, we take example from the book of Job," the priest said. "We hear the word of God through Job's trials and lamentations. 'God has made my heart faint,' Job cries to the heavens. 'The Almighty has terrified me. If only I could vanish in darkness, and thick darkness would cover my face!' What does this mean? God has forsaken Job. He is nowhere to be found—not in the shingle of land on which Job stands; not in the depths of the sea, among gliding monsters; not even in the bird singing its sweet song on the hilltop behind Job. God has turned his face away from Job, who has, after all, been God's faithful servant in every way."

Laurel, thinking of chapter 9 in *Moby-Dick*, where Father Mapple delivered his terrifying sermon on Jonah and the whale, was both electrified and spellbound.

"'God,' Job asks in utter despair, 'what more doth thou require of me?'

"And the answer is this, my friends: God requires everything of you and nothing at all. God requires only faith. Faith to set aside all earthly treasures, for they are not treasures at all. Acquisitions of money, properties, power are fetters that bind you to the earth, that blind you to God's words, numb you to God's love.

"You who are as Job once was are alienated from your family, your community, your country. From yourself. You cannot hear God. Neither can you experience God's divine love. But, hark, you are here now, and here in God's house you will hear his words; you will feel his love. This is my promise to you. What you experience now is the beginning of faith. Because God is within each and every one of you. Each and every one of you has the power within him to return from the wilderness in which you've been lost. To be human is to change: this is one of the greatest gifts God had bestowed on us. You have the power to change. You have the power to redefine yourselves, to become better."

Afterward, Nonna did not insist that Laurel take Communion. Laurel watched her herding Orfeo's three children down the center aisle, there to take into their mouths the blood and body of Christ. Laurel, who had never before seen such a rite, though already she was well read enough not to be ignorant of it, found something of the barbaric in it, something atavistic, so primitive that it might even have preceded the Catholic Church itself. It was, in its own way, akin to the scene in a TV documentary she had seen of a crocodile, a survivor of a prehistoric age, eating a goat. The terror in the goat's devil eyes as it was being devoured was impossible to forget.

She mentioned none of this to Orfeo, who asked in his good-natured manner what she thought of a Catholic Mass when she trooped into the overly hot apartment, Nonna gasping at their heels. Instead, she gave a more measured answer: "The priest seemed to think that alienation is the flip side of faith."

"And how do you feel about that?"

"I think alienation has to do with feeling different."

"True. But it also has to do with depression. Seriously depressed people feel themselves isolated, misunderstood, or, worse, ignored. Could be this is how sociopathic behavior is born, tested, tolerated, and, finally, embraced."

"Are you talking about anyone we know?" she said with a sly smile.

~

They had cake Nonna had baked that afternoon. The adults had coffee, the children milk. While Sofia and Nonna cleared away the dishes,

Orfeo ducked into his small bedroom, returning with a guitar, and for the next hour and a half he played and sang plangent Italian folk songs, composed long ago in the verdant hills of Tuscany. His singing voice was revelatory, angelic. He ended the impromptu concert with "Maremma Amara," which told of the hardship of life in Tuscany during a time when Saracen pirates were sacking the cities and towns along the coast. In those days malaria had been rampant. The Etruscans had begun an extensive project to drain the marshlands in an attempt to create more arable land. As the Romans rose to power, they continued the complex blueprint laid out by their forebears. But the fall of their overextended and decadent empire returned the Maremma and its surrounds to their primeval and perilous state. Thousands of men seeking their fortunes died there, hence the song's title, "Bitter Maremma."

All this was described to Laurel and the other children by Orfeo in a voice effusive with drama. She had the impression the kids had heard the story many times before; all the same they seemed as rapt as she by this lovingly told slice of history.

When she announced her departure, Orfeo touched her arm. "Let me walk you home."

"Thank you, Orfeo, but I'd rather be alone." She shrugged. "I'm used to being alone."

"Were you alone this evening?"

She scrunched up her face. "Of course not."

"Piccola," he said, his level gaze on her, "everyone needs a home, especially those who think they can do without."

Out on the street in front of Orfeo's building, Laurel turned to head east on Fourteenth Street; then, almost immediately, she turned back. As she looked up at the warm, gentle light streaming from Orfeo's apartment, tears started to overflow her eyes. *There's a family up there,* she thought. *A real family. Generations. They have swept me off the street, out of the cold. They have taken me to their bosom.* In that moment, it was never more clear to her what she had been missing, what she never had, what she might never have, despite Orfeo's family's warmth and generosity of spirit. She had never met people like them. Perhaps she never would again.

But of course there was more to it than that, and the true poignancy of the latitude and longitude, as Melville would put it, of her situation threatened to drown her. A longing rose in her with such strength she nearly staggered. Family, people who loved you, a place to belong. Not even up there, in that warm, fragrant apartment.

She raised her hand to wipe the tears from her cheeks but checked herself in midmotion. Those tears were an unexpected explosion, like fireworks lighting up the night. They were a badge, proof that she was really and truly alive.

TEN

The resurrection of Cul took up all their daytime hours. The more they uncloaked her, the more amazing she became. There had never been a piece of Etruscan art unearthed in such a perfect state. "As if she had been in suspended animation," he said. "Partly that's due to Crete itself. The dryness of the climate and the nature of the rock here. Where I worked previously in southern Tuscany—especially around Vulci, Tarquinia, and Orvieto, for instance, where the majority of sites are found—the stone is tufa, very soft, porous, embedded with harder pebbles that fall off over time, leaving holes and gaps. Here, Cul is whole, complete. A miracle."

He pointed out the vertical indentation down the center of her forehead, the shape and position of the ears, the musculature and tendons of the legs. "All of which," he said, "are consistent with carvings from the last quarter of the sixth century BC." Brushing away a film of grit that had settled on her nose, he continued, "What I find personally fascinating is that even though Cul was carved to strike fear and dread in those coming upon it, she has the opposite effect on you."

"I think she's cute."

Richard stopped what he was doing. "Cute?"

"Well, maybe not cute, per se. But she speaks to me."

"One lost soul to another."

"Yes, but you see, after all these centuries, she's been found. By us." She pointed. "Look at that face, Richard. She loves us."

He laughed, shaking his head as he went back to work.

~

Five days later, Richard and Angela uncovered the left forepaw of Cul's consort. Angela, who had been reading up on the Etruscans in between writing her unanswered emails to Bella, immediately named him Culsans, the god of doors and doorways, the Etruscan precursor to the Roman two-faced god, Janus: one aspect watching the world of the living, the other observing the underworld. Her supposition of his gender was confirmed the instant they freed his head, which, unlike Cul's, sprouted a central mane that began just above his eyes and, as they discovered a day later, ran up and over his skull and down onto his muscular back.

Richard was obviously pleased and impressed by her research. But he was even more pleased that the two tomb guardians were four and a half feet apart. "Just the right width for the entrance to the tomb," he said. But they could not dare tackle drilling through what Richard confirmed was solid rock—perfectly set blocks, Egyptian-style: no mortar; Cretan granite, not Tuscan tufa—until both Cul and Culsans had been completely freed from their entombment. With the discovery of the second guardian, excitement ran like electricity through the already buzzing site. There developed a veritable scrum of professors and archaeologists who had abandoned their own finds to work at Richard's site. The area was too small to accommodate everyone who wanted to pitch in. To Angela's great surprise, Richard left it to her to choose the two or three people who would help them each day. From Kieros's point of view it was bad enough that Richard had hijacked his dig, but when the discovery drew members of his crew away from the Cretan areas that were near and dear to him, he almost had an embolism. But there was nothing he could do. The discovery was its own unstoppable force.

As for Angela, the archaeologists' respect for her work with Richard and their desire to stay in her good graces so they could work on the Etruscan find vied with their opprobrium over her affair with her mentor. Quite quickly, Angela realized that his decision to allow her to pick their assistants was deliberate; he was conferring part of his power to her, someone who, until he arrived, had been treated with disdain. Because Richard was unperturbed by rumors, she resolved to ignore them, looking each man in the eye as she picked him or passed him over each morning. As rumors will, the stories became wilder and wilder, until Kieros, driven to distraction, as Richard had rightfully foreseen, called a halt to all gossip. "Return to your work," he admonished his staff one evening at dinnertime, when they were all assembled. "Has it lost its importance?" He glared at each and every person as his gaze circled the room. "Have you forgotten why you're here? Have you forgotten who you are? Shall you force me to ask the museum to replace you?"

Later, outside the communal tent, he took Richard and Angela aside. "Look, you two, what you get up to on your own time is your business."

"Stay out of my personal life," Richard said.

"We're both wholly focused on Cul and Culsans and what they're guarding," Angela added.

Kieros looked hard at both of them. "Just be more discreet, will you, hmm?"

Angela realized that Richard had been right about this too. No matter what they said or did, no one would believe they weren't having a torrid affair à la Liz and Dick during the filming of *Cleopatra*. The die had been cast; it wouldn't matter if she moved back into her own tent now. Richard had seen this coming the first night she'd come to sleep in his tent, and yet he'd made no move to send her away. He knew what sleeping next to him meant to her. He knew what people would think and didn't care. She loved him more and more each day, in glittering moments like this, seeing in him the love and care she wished she'd had from her mother and father.

> Hey, Bella,
>
> This is Angela, your father's assistant. He told me it would be all right if I emailed you. He's told me so much about you I feel I already know you tho we haven't even met! There's so much happening here, and it's happening so fast it's made my head spin. We've discovered that Cul has a mate. He's fiercer looking than Cul, tho maybe that's just my imagination. Or it could be his male energy. Who knows? I think abt you, believe it or not. So many things abt both our childhoods that line up, like the moon & the earth during an eclipse.
>
> I spend nights wondering who's behind the wall to the tomb. I get shivery thinking about it—wouldn't you? We'll have to drill thru the rock face & that may take time. We've been working 18-hr days. Your father and I are both exhausted. I wish we could take a break, if only just for a day. Wouldn't that be nice?
>
> Maybe there's some news of your own you could send me. If not, that's OK too.
>
> Your friend,
> Angela

It was very late when Angela sent off this last email to Bella. She knew she was taking a chance, making it from her, but she was hoping

Bella wouldn't notice the stylistic similarities to the emails she'd sent as Richard. If Bella read the emails at all. There was, of course, no way to know. But, somehow, just writing and sending them made her feel better, closer to Bella and in a funny way to her younger self.

Beside and above her, Richard seemed to have fallen asleep with the light on, his open logbook lying across his chest. She listened to the familiar sound of his breath, even and comforting. Silently she rose. At the edge of his bed, she leaned over, switched off the light.

It wasn't until she was back on the mattress, settling the blanket over herself, that Richard said, very softly, "There are venomous forces in the world."

She lay unmoving, saying nothing, wondering where this was going. His voice was so light and low maybe he was talking in his sleep.

Then he said, "I exposed Bella to one of those venomous forces. My wife. And what did I do to protect her? Nothing. I knew I couldn't take her away from Maggie. I absented myself from an intolerable situation."

Tears slid down Angela's cheeks. Her heart broke for him. She felt crushed beneath the weight of his words and recalled the silent grief in his eyes while he had been trying to text with Bella. Was this how her inarticulate father had felt? A wracking shiver went through her. At last, she understood. It was like a chain, strands of DNA twining, spinning out across generations: her father hadn't been able to talk to her because she was a mystery to him. She was a mystery to him because he was a mystery to himself. She had told Richard that her father was a good man, but now she understood that he hadn't known that about himself. She saw all this replicated in Richard, clear and painfully sharp in the darkness of the tent.

She wanted to get up, put her arms around him. Was he crying too? She did nothing, however, sure that she would be crossing a tacit line in their relationship. He wouldn't want her to see him crying. Surely that was the reason he had waited until the light was off to confess. So what then? What could she do? She found herself in an internal debate. To speak or to keep quiet.

"It's not too late to begin again with her," she said in a quavery voice. *It's not too late to begin again with me*, she would have said to her father if she could go back in time, if she had known then what she knew now. But how could she have; she hadn't yet experienced enough of life to really know, to really see. To really act. Her education at school and at the library, vast as it had been, was inadequate in so many ways. You only learn by taking the journey, not reading about it.

Richard stirred. "Do you really think so?"

In truth, she didn't know. Still, she said, "I do," in her bravest voice, daring to hope that she, too, would be a part of their reconciliation, the precious thing she'd never had with her father.

In the charged silence, he remained silent and the darkness of his own private underworld closed around them both.

ELEVEN

When she was five years and three months old, Bella was afflicted with night terrors. Not so unusual for a child of her age, but yet another horror afflicting Maggie. In those days, along with her beloved pills, she was sucking down tequila and mescal like nobody's business, having developed a taste for the fermented fruit of the blue agave plant during her honeymoon in Tulum.

Bella, frightened out of her wits by monsters she could neither name nor remember, called for her father. But Richard was in the Tuscan hills or Troy or Sinai. In any case, very far away both in distance and spirit. Maggie, too, stayed as far away from Bella as she could, wrestling with her own nightmare, which, unlike Bella's, was all too real. And so, as always, it was left to Elin to soothe the child's frazzled nerves in the wee small hours of the night.

This was when Elin started recounting to Bella the curious and mesmerizing lives of jinn, supernatural beings from Arabic mythology, born of fire. Elin had learned all about jinn from her mother, who claimed, rather absurdly to all but her rapt children, to be descended from a female jinn—a jinni. But Elin's mother wasn't kidding, and Elin took her seriously. But then Elin was a serious teenager; she had popped out of her mother's womb with a fierce and serious stare no one but her mother could fathom in one whose tenure in the world was measured in minutes. Whatever the truth or falsity of the claim, Elin learned all about jinn at her mother's knee, and now, at the very tender age of sixteen, she had the opportunity to pass on that knowledge to a child in need of both attention and distraction. It was clear to Elin that Bella's night terrors were a direct consequence of an absent father and a mother addicted to her own depression. Who needed that? Certainly not a child of five years and three months. Furthermore, she reasoned with an adult's faculties, it was up to her to keep Bella from descending the same slippery slope that Bella's mother was swiftly sliding down.

"The thing about jinn, the really cool thing," Elin said while she held Bella in her arms, rocking her back and forth, "is that they're made of smoke and sand. And they can take all kinds of human shapes. I could be a jinn—but I'd be called a jinni because I'm a girl."

"Are you?" Bella asked, her eyes wide. A moment ago they had been magnified by tears. "A jinni, I mean."

"I could be," Elin said, thinking of her mother, of bloodlines, and of desert shape-shifters. "If you want me to be."

"I do!" Bella said. "Oh, I do!"

"Well, then, let me tell you more about ji—us." She smiled, kissed the top of Bella's damp head. "A long time ago in the Arabian Desert, a castle appeared."

"Where did it come from?"

"No one knew," Elin said. "And what's more, only a few people could actually see it."

"You mean it was invisible?"

Elin laughed. "Well, yes, in its own way it was invisible."

"Because it was made of smoke and sand, just like the jinn?"

Any minute now, Elin thought, *if I'm not careful, this girl is going to outflank me*. "Close," she said. "The jinn had spun the castle out of smoke and sand, fusing them together to make a kind of glass."

"Is that how you make glass? Really?"

"By making sand burning hot," Elin said. "Yes." She had just learned this in science class.

"I bet not everyone can see a jinn," Bella said, thinking it through.

"That is so true, *ukhti sghira*." Elin often called Bella "little sister," which Bella loved. "But *you* can."

"Why is that?"

"Because though jinn have very short tempers, they are also kind and generous. Best of all, they're loyal. And protective."

"Tell me."

"Well, in this desert castle the family of jinn I come from gather, riding out on their horses of smoke and light to do battle with nightmares and monsters. And you know what? They always win. Always."

"So as long as I have you, I'll be safe."

Elin smiled, thinking, *One day you'll become your own jinni*. She laid the girl down, pulled the bedcovers up to her chin. "Time to sleep. No more bad dreams."

Bella snuggled into the bed. *"Habibti?"* Elin had taught Bella to say *my beloved* in Syrian Arabic.

"Yes, *Ukhayyah*."

"Would you sleep with me? Please. Just for tonight."

Without waiting for an answer, Bella held the covers up for Elin to slide in beside her. With Elin's face next to hers, she closed her eyes. Moments later she was fast asleep. For a long while, Elin listened to the child's heartbeat, slowing. It calmed her, and then she, too, tumbled into a slumber without dreams or nightmares.

~

Laurel's mother, Kelli Springfield, left when Laurel was one month shy of her sixteenth birthday. It was raining that night—a prolonged heavy downpour. It was Halloween, the last weekend in October, and the rain was mixed with an early wet snow. Huge flakes, swirling past the streetlamps, tumbled toward Laurel's third floor bedroom window, vanishing like phantoms while the rain lashed the panes.

What woke her up, a thunderclap or the front door slamming? Either way, she bolted out of bed and, as if struck by a dreadful premonition, rushed to the window, which overlooked the narrow West Village street, familiar as her own face.

Except on this night the scene below her was different. There was a black sedan idling in front of their house, smoky exhaust whipping upward almost as soon as it escaped its tailpipe. She might have thought nothing of it if she hadn't seen her mother hurrying down the front stoop stairs, without either umbrella or hat in her haste to be gone. Laurel tore herself from the window, raced down the stairs in time to see past the curtains in the front living room. Her mother passing between the jack-o'-lanterns Laurel had carved, grinning gargoyle faces with teeth like wolves. Kelli Springfield turned sideways, slipped between the bumpers of parked cars. A figure emerged from the sedan's driver's-side door, flipped open an umbrella, hurried around her mother. The two came together like magnets, Laurel thought, but an amorous lovers' embrace didn't happen; neither did a kiss. Just the man opening the rear door for Kelli as she veritably lunged inside with the kind of frantic energy Laurel lately had gotten used to seeing in her mother. Tonight, though, it seemed far worse, a culmination, the eruption of a volcano that had been rumbling for months. It was as if Kelli could not bear to be on this street, in the West Village, New York City, one minute longer, as if even a steaming shower couldn't scrub off the stink of her family.

Laurel caught a glimpse of the man as he furled the umbrella, slid behind the steering wheel. Her mother in the back seat, a passenger. The man was not her lover but a driver.

Then the car was gone in a cloud of exhaust and with it, Kelli Springfield, sometime wife of Eddie Springfield, runaway mother to her daughter, Laurel.

Forehead against the cool glass, Laurel recalled a time when she had been very ill. She had been four, perhaps five—at this moment of abandonment, she couldn't recall exactly. She had had a fever. When it had spiked to 105 degrees, her mother had brought her into her bed, caressed her burning flesh with ice-dipped face cloths. Laurel could recall with absolute clarity the scrape of the icy terrycloth across her skin, drawn tight over her muscles and sinews. At one point, she had drifted off into a shallow sleep or else hallucinated.

"Mom," she had said in a small voice.

"Yes, honey."

"I dreamed you were dead."

Her mother had smiled. "But I'm right here, Laurel." Leaning over, she had pressed her lips against Laurel's forehead. "Oh, Lord, you're burning up."

"But you're not dead."

"Laurel, honey, do I look like I'm dead?" She had shaken her head, hair bouncing on either cheek. "I'm never going to leave you. Never."

Now that the car was gone, and her mother with it, Laurel tore herself away from gazing into the empty street as if it were a crystal ball. Racing back up the stairs, she hurled herself into her parents' bedroom. Her father was out working. As usual.

Laurel threw herself onto the bed, buried her face in her mother's pillow, inhaled her scent. She wished her father was home.

Laurel rose from the bed to stand in the hallway, midway between her parents' bedroom and her own. She stood as if paralyzed between two poles. But her paralysis came from another source. She felt inside her the blade of a knife. Her mother's leaving had pierced her to the core. Unbidden, tears flooded out of her, and, sobbing, she collapsed to her knees, rocking back and forth. *Mom, where did you go; why didn't you take me with you; why did you leave me here?*

Gone. Without a warning or a goodbye—certainly with no explanation, although, with the passage of time, Laurel came to realize that no explanation would have sufficed or made her feel the loss any less deeply. A knife had been plunged into her chest, the blade dragged across her heart, scarring it forever. There was no cure for being abandoned, then, later, ever. A mother's rejection was worse than her death. At least in death there was a body to mourn, an incomparable love lost, which later, in the fullness of time, was to be treasured. Abandonment was a darkened house, an empty room, a terrible certainty that if only she had done something different—anything—her mother would still be here, her presence felt, the song of her voice like the warmth of a summer sun. Now only winter, eternal winter.

TWELVE

"You want us to drill through this wall." Kieros rubbed his deeply ridged forehead. His fingertips came away salty wet with sweat. He looked nervously from Cul to Culsans, both of which were now completely free. "We'll have to take these things out of the way first."

Richard stepped closer, ran the flat of his hand over Cul's flank. "No drilling."

"What?"

"The granite blocks need to be taken out by hand, one by one."

"But . . . but that's impossible," Kieros spluttered. "Look! There's no mortar, no space between the blocks at all in which to gain purchase." He shook his head. "The only way is to drill."

"There's another way," Angela said. Kieros goggled at her as if she had grown another head. She could see the unspoken words in his expression: *Why are you even here?* But Richard was displaying that wicked, conspiratorial grin she had come to know and love. She and Richard had discussed the idea; it had been his desire that she tell Kieros. He thought it would be more fun, and, as usual, he was right. Kieros was apoplectic.

"The other way," Angela said, "is to drill out one block—just one. Once that's dealt with, you'll have the leverage you need, and the rest will be easy."

"We used a similar technique at the Tomb of the Silver Hands in Vulci," Richard said, "and were rewarded by a treasure trove of Etruscan royal life. And we never found anything intact like we did with these huge guardians. God alone knows what treasures we might find here."

Kieros made a conciliatory gesture. "Okay, I take your point." He clearly had no intention of getting in Richard's way; his fear of him was palpable. He tried to smile, but it came out as a grimace. "We're not used to Egyptian-style architecture here. Unlike the team at Vulci we don't have the specialized equipment to lever these blocks out without running the risk of ruining everything." Again he swiped at his profusely sweating forehead. "I'll have to send to Athens for the equipment. It'll take at least two days, maybe three, depending on those dolts at the museum—the hand implements are quite expensive. Anyway, it's for the best. You two have been working a full week with very little sleep. Take a couple of days off to recoup your strength and mental acuity."

"Thanks, but I'd rather stay on-site," Richard said. "There's more work to do on the guardians—"

"Richard, I'm very well versed in your reputation for getting up in everyone's face. You won't be able to stay on-site without constantly pestering everyone, especially me, about the timetable. I want you and Angela rested for when we break through into the tomb itself. Doesn't that make sense?" He seemed perfectly sincere. "Leave the procurement to me. I know the museum people; I can handle them."

Richard seemed to understand this, even if a bit belatedly. "Okay. You're right. Each to his own bit of expertise, eh?"

"That's it." Kieros, visibly relieved, became magnanimous. He waved a hand. "Fly to the mainland. Rent a boat. Relax. Take two days. As soon as the equipment arrives, I'll summon you back."

Perhaps that was a poor choice of words. Richard stiffened slightly. "I'll check in with you."

"I'll be down here most of the time, directing the drilling. I've got to organize the portable generator, the masks, all of that. I won't be able to—"

"In the evenings. Late," Richard said firmly and then almost cruelly added, "I'll wake you up."

He meant to say, *I'll* fucking *wake you up*. Angela could feel it. She sensed in his subtle stiffening that Kieros did too.

~

"I know what you're thinking," Angela said.

"Really." The hint of a smile on his face. "Go ahead. Amaze me."

They stood close together on the deck of a sailboat Richard had rented. A Saracen moon, the points of its crescent sharp as knife tips, hung above them in the velvet sky. The seabirds were in their rookeries, heads tucked, sleeping peacefully, while the nighttime insects ate their fill. Here amid the glittering night, the dull slap of the water against the wooden hull, the pinging of rigging against mast, they were virtually alone. Now and again a storm petrel fluttered by, as if attempting to eavesdrop on their conversation. As they dipped, they rid the air of insects. Angela felt a kinship with night birds; she had tried to carve them into her jack-o'-lanterns but never seemed to completely succeed. People mistook them for bats.

"You're reveling in the look we put on Kieros's face, your little triumph over him."

He laughed. "Well, I couldn't have done it without you."

Now that they were really and truly all alone, away from the hectic anthill of the dig, away from Crete itself, removed, in a way, from everything familiar, she took a chance. "When you see Bella again, say something that complimentary to her."

At once, his face darkened, like thunderclouds rising up from the horizon, and she was sure she had made a mistake.

"I'm going to tell you something I've never told anyone else before," he said in a strange voice, as if the words were being forced out of him through a narrowed passage. "My father was a physician—a thoracic surgeon. He was exceptionally good at his job. Renowned, I would say. But there were days . . ." Wind blew Richard's hair into his eyes, and he brushed it roughly back over the crown of his head. "Inevitably, there were times when he couldn't save a patient, despite every heroic effort. He shouldn't have taken it as hard as he did, but that was my father all over. Following each of his what he called 'failures,' he'd lock himself away in his workroom. He had squads of toy soldiers, battalions of 'em. They were made of some metal, bare, blind, lifeless as skeletons until he painted them. 'I hold the power of life and death over these men,' he told me once when I asked him why he was so fascinated by toy soldiers. 'Here, I am the ultimate power. I can control . . . here, no one ever dies. Here order is restored to the world. Here I regain my balance.'"

Richard lapsed back into silence, staring upward into the star-studded sky. Some sixth sense in her perceived that he wished he was up there among those stars, that he had had enough of whatever mistakes he had made in his private life—or he believed it was too late to make amends for those mistakes, to go back, as she longed to return to her father, to talk to him as the woman she had become.

"I've never caught my balance," he said, "not with Maggie, not with Bella. Things happen that are out of your control."

Angela thought of her flight from America, from Dey. "When I left the States, in those early years . . . I had been working for an evil man—a gangster. There's no way to sugarcoat it."

Richard's brow creased in surprise and concern. "That was a very bad mistake, Angela."

She ignored his remark, went on: "I imagined being shot in the back of the head, being suffocated with a pillow in my hotel room in Geneva, or being bound and gagged, dumped at night in the middle of Lake Geneva, being knifed in the side amid the crowds of an Istanbul maidan, or having my throat slit while I shopped at the Grand Bazaar. Those were days and nights of sheer terror. It became clear to me that everything is out of our control. Even the very concept of time, the calendar, they are man-made things, illusions created to keep us from seeing the chaos of the universe. To keep us sane. But my flight had torn that curtain, and I was now face-to-face with that chaos."

"That really is chilling," he said. "I wish I could have been there to stop you."

"Nothing would have stopped me," she said.

He nodded without understanding; how could he? It was an acknowledgment of his acceptance of her, even after this revelation. The wonderment of what he had just done brought tears to her eyes.

He misunderstood those tears, thinking they were creatures of the dreadful memory she had shared, and now, in response, he sought to normalize the conversation: "But illusions do keep some of us sane. For others, it's as if they never existed at all."

She recalled how he had described Maggie as venomous, how he had left Bella in the poisonous environment of that venom, and she felt an involuntary spasm of anger toward him. As she had toward her father. And that, of course, vaporized the anger immediately. She was quits with that kind of anger, the kind that ate at you, hollowed you out inside, made of you less than what you were, forced you to bow down before it.

"But I've been thinking about what you said the other night, about it not being too late." Richard pursed his lips, as if he were about to kiss her, but he faced her and sang a riff on the first verse of Edward Lear's poem "The Owl and the Pussy-Cat," rearranged to suit his purpose:

"The Owl and the Rabbit went to sea
In a beautiful pea-green boat,
They took some honey, and plenty of money,
Wrapped up in a five-pound note.

The Owl looked up to the stars above,
And sang to a small guitar,
'O lovely Rabbit! O Rabbit, my love,
What a beautiful Rabbit you are,
You are,
You are!
What a beautiful Rabbit you are!'

"Once, long ago, before I left, I would sing Bella to sleep with that." Richard took a breath, let it out slowly. "When I go home after the Sinai assignment, I'm going to do everything you laid out in the email you sent to her."

He looked at her, his eyes glimmering in the moonlight. "I want my rabbit back, Angela. I want my daughter back."

~

In the deepest sleep, at rock bottom, Angela dreamed of the teenager Laurel, of her father's heavy tread on the staircase in the hour before dawn. The cold rain had briefly turned to wet snow and back again, making her jack-o'-lanterns glisten like glass. The house, which had been in her father's family for generations, creaked and groaned as the heat dried out the wooden floorboards and beams.

"Dad!" Laurel leapt up from her position curled around the second floor newel post. "Daddy!"

He paused on the stairway, the big man looking somehow shrunken inside his enormous lumberjack coat, droplets standing out atop its surface like a coating of dew on a field of flowers. He looked up, his eyes darkened, his lips chapped from his walk through the icy night.

"What is it, Rabbit?" At the sight of her anguished face, rushing up the remainder of the flight. "Why are you up at this hour?" Taking her into his arms, the wetness of his coat, warming between their bodies; she felt as if she were being hugged by Nana, the Newfoundland sheepdog in *Peter Pan*, her favorite book until she read the first page of *Moby-Dick* and fell head over heels in love. "Are you all right?" Checking her forehead with the back of his hand, which he had first breathed on several times to rid it of its chill.

"Mom is gone," Laurel said, her voice full of fear, anger, and despair.

"Gone? What d'you mean 'gone'?" He took her by her shoulders, held her at arm's length. "Honey, you're not making sense."

"She's left us—both of us. Some man picked her up in a car outside and took her away."

Her father's face darkened. "What man? Took her where?"

She just shook her head, sobbing.

"C'mon, Rabbit." Putting his arm across her shoulders, he took her into the master bedroom. He left her side to look in the bathroom, then pawed through his wife's closet. He turned back to her, his voice almost accusatory. "There's nothing missing, Laurel." He only called her by her name when he was angry with her. "All her clothes, her toiletries, not one thing is missing. And no note." He took a step toward her. "Is her leaving a dream of yours?"

"No! I was awake! I saw what I saw!" She was near to shouting now, beside herself at not being believed. She lifted her arms, dropped them to her sides. "Where is she! Where has she gone?"

"I don't know." Her father sat heavily on the side of the bed, passed a hand across his face. "But she'll be back. I mean, how could she leave us?" He offered the shadow of a smile. "You'll see, Rabbit. She'll be back before noon. I promise."

But she wasn't, and it was at that point that the center ceased to hold, and things fell apart.

Dusk stretched cool and gray as a Siamese cat. Gunmetal clouds roiled the sky, seeming close enough to reach up and touch. To the north the horizon vanished in midnight-blue downpour. A moderate chop, the water ruffled like a sea eagle readying itself for flight.

They had been napping. She came awake a few moments before Richard, still enmeshed in her dream. Grabbing his mobile, she checked to see if there were any replies from Bella. There weren't. She debated for a moment, then quickly wrote:

> Out here @ sea, it's so peaceful & calm for as far as the eye can see. So different from being on land, even this island. Your father wishes u were here; he talks abt u so much it seems I already know u. You remind me of myself. Is that silly to say? I mean, we haven't even met. & yet I feel we have. I feel u.
>
> Angela

Coming up beside her, Richard looked out over the water and said, "Okay with you if we go back this evening?"

"You're the captain." She saw that he was looking over her left shoulder, northward. "The storm's some way off," she added. "Using the engine, we can make shore without a problem. Should we haul up the anchor?"

"Stay right where you are." He vanished belowdecks, returning moments later with a pair of binoculars. Pointed them due north, toward the darkness.

"If it's the storm you're worried about," she said, "we'd better get started."

"What did I say?" He almost barked it. "It's not the storm I'm worried about."

Frowning, she looked north. "What is it? What?"

He handed her the binoculars. "Aim at that white dot," he said, pointing.

Putting the binoculars to her eyes, she turned the center ring, refocused them. The white blob resolved itself into the bow wave of a motor launch. It was coming directly at them full speed. "What?" she repeated.

"Go below," he ordered. "Put on a pair of jeans. You're already wearing a windbreaker; zip it all the way up. You have a scarf?"

She nodded, bewildered.

"Wrap that around your head." He gestured with his chin. "Now go, go, go."

She did as he asked, no more questions. When she clambered topside, he handed her the binoculars. She refocused as the launch came on, frighteningly closer now in the short span of time she had been below. She saw the men, then. Six of them, the lower halves of their faces covered, black headbands streaming out behind them. And the semiautomatic weapons they held aloft.

"Jesus," she said under her breath. Now she knew why he had ordered her to cover herself, Muslim-style. "Jesus Christ."

Thrusting the binoculars back at him, she rose, heading for the anchor. Richard pulled her back down.

"What are you doing? We've got to get out of here."

"That's precisely what we won't do."

"But they're armed. Pirates. Terrorists, probably."

"I have no doubt. But you saw how fast their boat is. We can't outrun them."

"So what?" She searched his face for some reassurance. "We just wait here for them to board us?"

"Pretty much," Richard said.

She shook her head. "I don't understand. Richard, they'll kill us."

"Maybe they will, and maybe they won't," he said. "If we run, they will shoot us dead. This way we have a chance."

"My God, my God. What kind of a chance?"

"No one knows." He gripped her arms, held her close. "I'm asking you to trust me. Don't move; don't say a word, even if provoked. Nothing. You don't exist—hear me?"

She nodded, terrified. Her mind had already left her body, was hovering somewhere a hundred feet overhead. Safe. *In your dreams*, a voice laughed hysterically inside her head. *What kind of a world is this?* she asked herself. One minute you were happy as a lark, eating breakfast with your friend, the Mediterranean your oyster; the next you were under threat of death or possibly worse. Incarceration, deprivation, with no hope of escape. Then she laughed, a thin, sickly utterance that made Richard flinch.

"Don't lose your nerve now," he said, misinterpreting the sound.

No, the joke was on her. For the first time since she'd changed identities, fled the States, become lost, she had ceased to fear Dey's long arm. Dey was nothing, a mere speck in her eye, wiped away with a stray mascaraed lash. The advent of the speeding launch had thrust her into an entirely new universe, one where all her meticulous planning, her wildly expensive camouflage, her launch of a new identity meant absolutely zero. These people boarding the sailboat now didn't care whether she was Laurel Springfield or Angela Chase. Feeling the rise of hysteria inside her, she cautioned herself. *Don't lose your nerve now.*

Four men boarded; two stayed behind, the driver and an outrider, haunch on the starboard gunwale. The men were like something out of a documentary: thin, bearded, sunken eyed, the fever of extremist fervor igniting their entire beings like infernal auras. They were young, these four—one no more than a boy, and yet in many ways he seemed the fiercest, the most heavily indoctrinated, hate and rage absorbed, bitter mother's milk nurturing him.

The leader said something in what sounded to Angela like a rough and cracked version of Arabic. To her monumental surprise Richard answered him in the same language. The leader looked only slightly less stunned than she felt. There ensued a rapid-fire conversation. Not one of the extremists so much as glanced at her; all their attention was riveted on Richard. She had been reduced to a nonentity. She did as Richard had ordered; she did not move or say a word. In fact, she scarcely looked at anyone, recalling admonitions not to make eye contact with wild predators, an instinctual sign of aggression.

In real time, the conversation did not last long. For Angela, it was a lifetime, every second another beat ticked off toward the ending of her freedom, her life. There arose in her now an acute realization of, Dey or no Dey, how privileged her life had been as an American citizen living in the United States, even with the rise of homegrown terrorism; how far away all of her fellow citizens were from the violent reality of the world, day in, day out being reshaped by extremists of all stripes; how strong their rage was; how monocular their savage gaze; how desperately they needed something, anything, to strike back at, even if it meant the loss of their own lives. The veil had lifted. How precious was everything she had taken for granted, how fragile, how ephemeral. Life was a passage, the flutter of a bird's wing, and then it was gone.

People on the boat were in motion, and she tensed, feared now all was lost. But the leader and one of his men were ducking down into the small cabin. Searching for—what?—while the third man stood in front of Richard, studying him as if he were an insect pinned to a table. The fourth man—the kid—strode over to her. His outsized cockiness would have been amusing in anyone else his age. Not this boy. He stood in front of her, staring at the scarf she had wrapped around her head to cover her hair, ears, and the corners of her face, as if looking for a flaw in her makeshift hijab, looking to punish her for even the tiniest infraction. She could tell from the intensity of his gaze that no infraction would be insignificant. Then his gaze lowered, bit by bit, as if in a slow-motion film shot, to the swell of her breasts. His hand came up; the grubby fingernails bitten almost to the quick were ragged, feral looking. He started to reach out toward her, then, like a hyena sensing the presence of a larger predator, turned his head. Someone out of her field of vision must have been looking at him because his hand withdrew; his gaze moved on. She registered all this out of the periphery of her vision, staring as she was into the middle distance over his head, wishing nothing more than to lie down, close her eyes, count sheep. She bit her lip, forcing back the words she longed to speak to him, the sorrow of seeing so much hate in such a young face. She wanted to tell him that it didn't have to be like this, but with the reemergence of the extremists from belowdecks, she understood how wrong she was. It did have to be like this. Hate was the essence of these people: it had molded them into who they were. It made them tick.

The leader spoke briefly to Richard again in that rapid-fire way of his. They exchanged words, not as friends but, it appeared, not as enemies either. Then the four men were back on their launch; its motor revved up, and they were pulling away. Angela watched in a kind of rapt detachment as the launch described a semicircle, white foam rippling out, rocking the sailboat in what seemed to her like a last warning gesture. Then it headed back the way it had come. It took her some time to breathe normally again. The storm, blackening the horizon, had advanced no farther.

THIRTEEN

For a long time after that neither of them spoke. Angela could have taken off her scarf, but shock and fear ensured that she didn't. She stared out over the sea to the long smudge of land she knew to be the island of Crete, while Richard weighed anchor and got them underway. Crete had been a way station for her. Now it was not even that, merely a bleak and desolate pile of rocks. For her entire life she had had no direction home . . . now home was Richard. The only rock that meant anything to her was Richard. The danger they shared had shaken her. The bonding that resulted had altered her reality to its core. Perhaps she had been so long unmoored in the world that it had taken this long—or it had taken this terrifying incident—for her brain to catch up. And while it would take time for the fear to subside, for the first time in her life, she felt berthed in a harbor filled with sunlight and calm waters, everything shining, etched in sharp relief. The realization pierced her so deeply that tears sprang out in the corners of her eyes.

Misinterpreting her incipient tears, Richard finally broke their silence. The shoreline had become a firm brushstroke in the early evening moonlight rather than a pointillist blur. The wind was at their backs, so he could have used the sails. She didn't think either of them wanted that.

"I was in Sinai over 9/11," he said without preamble. "Two years to the day after the birth of my daughter. The dig was long and arduous, and then we got the message. We stopped working, sat stunned, not looking at one another. We should have come together, but we didn't. For some reason the news blew us apart. We all went to our separate corners, like wounded animals looking for a safe place to lie down. As it happened, there was no safe place.

"As is usual, our group was multinational: British, Italian, Jordanian, Palestinian. American, of course. There was even an Iranian, an incredibly beautiful woman who knew more about what we were finding than all the rest of us put together.

"Anyway, it was the next day, the twelfth of September, along about sunset. I was standing with one of my American compatriots, a jolly fellow. Ben, his name was. Benjamin. From Nebraska—or was it Illinois? I'm sure I've made myself forget. So we were standing at the eastern edge of the dig, discussing—what?—the Beatles versus the Rolling Stones—can you believe it? All at once, there was a colossal noise. The back of his head exploded. I was covered in blood and brains and bone chips."

"Jesus, Richard. I'm so sorry."

"It's all right," he said. "It's in the past."

"What happened to Ben?"

"Dead, of course. Shot to death by one of our porters. A Syrian with, as we found out later, ties to some obscure extremist group or other."

They were near enough to the shore now to pick out individual rocks and up on the cliffs the dusty trees, leaning as if into an eternal storm. The wind had died to nothing. The sea was following them home.

"That's when I became interested in these splinter groups—small, deadly, infinitely more fanatic than al-Qaeda or the Taliban. I spent longer in Sinai than I had expected. Most everyone at the dig wanted to go home, of course, especially the Americans. And there was Ben's body to consider, not to mention his family. But of course none of us could get back to the States for weeks. I stayed on after, learning everything I could."

"Wasn't that dangerous?"

"In a way, that was the point, wasn't it?" He slowed them, steered for their landing place, where the boat's owner waved in cheerful welcome. They paid no attention to him. "I mean Ben and I were side by side. He died, and I didn't." He shrugged. "Survivor's remorse all over again, right? Anyway, I learned a lot in those six weeks after 9/11, including how to speak with these people." He sighed. "Also, we were incredibly lucky today. They were looking for a sailboat filled with drugs. Nothing to do with us. Nothing at all."

~

Of course, she didn't believe him—not completely, anyway. But it wasn't until they were back on dry land, the sea and the launch with its bristling peril behind them, that she felt enough time had passed to ask, "What really went on between you and the pirate leader? Was he really looking for a sailboat full of drugs?"

"Absolutely."

They were climbing the steep, heavily striated slope from the shingle to the top of the headland. The moon was high in the night sky now, and its light threw the landscape into a chiaroscuro of black and white. She felt a cool breeze on her back and, shivering slightly, wound the scarf tighter at her throat. The scarf was a favorite of hers, a blue-and-purple Udhampur Indian print she had purchased in Diwali, a shop on the Ile Saint-Louis in Paris. Permanently imprinted by this morning's invasion, she would never look at it the same way again. The Udhampur was a symbol both of her terror and of her release from its grip.

"You're giving me the CliffsNotes version."

"And?"

"And cut it out." She gripped his elbow, turned him toward her. They smelled of sweat and the sea.

He smiled, but there was no mirth in it. For a moment he looked away, out to the sea, which was a shattered mirror reflecting moonlight in a multitude of tiny crescents. Not a sign of their encounter remained or would ever be found. It was lost in time, if not in memory. Nevertheless, all her emotions had been brought to the surface; she felt raw and for the first time in years terribly vulnerable.

"All right."

They walked on a bit in silence. Above them stretched the stars in profusion, the Milky Way a ghostly river, the sky both infinite and intimate. There was something primitive about the night; if they had been walking this strip two millennia ago, she had the sense it would look just the same. This notion soothed her somewhat.

Was he trying to order his thoughts, or was he debating how much to tell her? She fervently hoped it was the former. She felt she had earned the right to hear it all. She was shaken, and she wondered how he could be so cool and calm.

At length, Richard said, "The leader's name was Achmid."

"Arachnid is more like it." Make a joke, defeat the memory's power. "A big-ass spider."

Richard gave her a weak smile.

"He was, indeed, looking for drugs. He said they were his. Whatever. But I lied when I said he wasn't interested in us. He was. You, especially."

A cold hand clutched at Angela's belly. Her heart was in her throat; she found it difficult to swallow. "Go on," she said, though part of her mind was screaming, *Enough. You've heard enough.*

"He had taken a fancy to you. I told him that you were mine."

"You told him we were married?"

"No. Listen to me. What I told him was that I was bound to you through obligation."

"What sort of obligation?"

"Familial. That's what matters most. Family. There's an honor there that cuts through nationality, religion, ideology."

"It works," she said, "until it doesn't."

"Yes. ISIS, for example. But these people weren't ISIS."

"As you said, we were lucky. What did you tell him?"

"That I had promised your mother I'd take care of you or die trying."

"And he bought that?"

"Angela, it's not *what* you sell; it's *how* you sell it. I sold. He bought. End of story."

But it wasn't the end of the story, not for her and—miraculously—not for Bella either. Though Richard immediately fell asleep with his clothes on, she, wired and gritty, took a long shower, scrubbing her skin, as if she might wash away the day's fear. Not surprisingly, it didn't; her sleep was patchy and restless, invaded by nightmares that kept her near the surface of her conscious mind. As if hearing a noise she could not identify, she started awake. Richard was sound asleep. His phone was glowing, casting a bluish light into the darkness. She turned on her elbow and picked it up.

> Hey, from the other side. If there's a line to my father thru u I'll take it. Everything's so . . . nothing makes sense & it's worse bc of Maggie . . . I don't want to write abt her. Tell me abt u I want to know u shd I like u or b jealous?

Tears immediately sprang into Angela's eyes. The girl's emotions, even expressed electronically, reverberated through her like the tolling of a bell, echoing her own past so completely that she realized she would have done anything to have a lifeline to an older woman when she was Bella's age.

Heart and mind both racing, she began an answer to Bella, her thumbs blurred over the keypad.

OK if u feel both

After a pause:

lol

In this postmodern shorthand they conversed long into the night, near the end of which Bella wrote,

You don't know

This frightened her, and she immediately wrote back:

What don't I know? What's wrong?

Bella's last reply:

I wish I was like u. I wish I was u. I hate it here. I wish
I wish I wish

~

"I worked and worked, and what did she do? She bought and bought." Eddie Springfield sat hunched over at the kitchen table while his daughter served him the dinner she had made.

Ever since Kelli had left, Laurel had taught herself to cook and bake all of her father's favorites—steak frites, lamb ragout, fish and chips—as well as introducing him to dishes like lollipop chicken, pasta primavera, and chess pie, meant to cheer him up. He made them breakfast, as he almost always had, but he barely touched the food on his plate in the mornings.

He ate the dinners she prepared, though, grateful for her presence as well as her growing expertise. He was home by dinnertime now, and she made sure she was back at the brownstone to greet him. The one time she was late, she found him sitting on the stairs, in the same spot where she used to fall asleep waiting for him, his head in his hands, tears staining his face.

"Working two jobs, Rabbit," he continued now. "It was the only way to keep her happy, keep her in the clothes and finer things she craved." He looked up from the plate she'd placed in front of him, his eyes enlarged with tears. "But she wasn't happy, was she? It wasn't enough. It was never enough for her. She always wanted more, always berated me for being a failure. 'The only thing keeping me here,' she told me once, 'is this brownstone. I always dreamed of living in a townhouse in the West Village.' Can you believe that? 'What else can I do, Kelli?' I'd say, and she'd laugh and say, 'That's the problem, isn't it?'"

Laurel put her own plate down and went to him, put her arms around him, kissed his temples. "I love you, Daddy. I always have. I always will."

A sad smile broke out across his face. "I know, Rabbit. I love you too." And he kissed her in return. "What would I do without you?"

Some version of this conversation occurred at nearly every dinner, after which Eddie would disappear into the bowels of the house, God alone knew where. Laurel never followed him. She was too afraid of what she'd find. Sometimes, after she'd cleaned up in the kitchen, she'd find him in the living room, staring at the front door, as if by his will alone he could bring his wife back to him. Then she would sit beside him, quietly, feeling his sorrow flow into her in waves. When she couldn't stand it anymore, she read to him. He loved old-school detective stories—Sherlock Holmes and Hercule Poirot—but his favorite was Rex Stout's gentleman detective Nero Wolfe, perhaps because he lived in a Manhattan brownstone, and it was these books she read to him most often. His face would soften; his shoulders, up around his neck with an awful tension, would relax into their natural position; and he would sigh. "I love this guy," he would say every once in a while.

There was a rare Nero Wolfe he wanted Laurel to read to him. It took her two weeks of searching before she found a paperback copy of *Death of a Dude*, and when she started to read it to him, he turned and embraced her. “Rabbit, Rabbit,” he whispered. “Imagine Wolfe traveling halfway across the country to a dude ranch in Montana.” His voice wistful, almost eager, as if he, too, wanted to make the journey Nero Wolfe had undertaken. “I never thought I’d hear that case again.”

Later that night, watching him climbing the stairs to bed, Laurel couldn’t help but wonder what became of the brokenhearted.

The next day, after school, she went to a travel agent. Using money she had made winning chess games, she booked her father two weeks at the best dude ranch in Montana for the following spring. It was a Thursday, the day Orfeo asked her to dinner with his family. After preparing his meal, she left a note telling her father she’d be late, that dinner was waiting for him in the oven, the temperature already set. All he had to do was turn the oven on for twenty minutes.

She was jumpy with nervous excitement, anticipating the look on her father’s face when she presented him with what she was certain he’d call his Nero Wolfe Trip. Nevertheless, she was so beguiled by Orfeo’s family that she stayed far later than she had intended. She stayed too late.

Years later, she would come to the sad realization that for her parents it had always been too late.

~

The story of Richard versus the Terrorists was over, but the echoes would resound in the chambers of her heart for some time. But there was another story, in its way just as dramatic and far more public, about to be played out. It confronted Angela and Richard the next morning when they emerged from his tent to eat breakfast.

The entire camp was teeming with TV, film, and magazine cameramen; reporters; technicians; pyramids of electronic equipment from Hellenic Broadcasting, Rai, ARD, CNN, PBS, BBC, Reuters, AP, Archaeology Today, Stern, and, it seemed, countless indie internet outlets. Plus, the usual swarm of paparazzi abounded. The blogosphere was already alight.

Many in the crowd recognized Richard right away, came rushing at him, paparazzi in the forefront, as always, scurrying like cockroaches, peppering him with questions, both serious and inane, snapping endless streams of photos of the photogenic Richard—Angela hadn't fully appreciated just how handsome Richard was until this moment. And there she was at his side, too stunned by the entire force of the media assault to realize the danger to herself.

"God damn it," Richard raged, "Kieros has gone and created his own media storm."

"He must have broken through into the tomb without us," Angela said.

And then Richard's cell phone rang, and as he took the call, as he turned to stone, his face ashen, Angela repeated with more and more urgency, "What is it? What's happened?"

He sat down heavily in the spot where he had been standing. The media vultures, instantly sensing blood, crowded around, elbowing each other out of the way, clicking and shouting frantically. Angela, standing over him, hands gripping his shoulders, bared her teeth at them with such ferocity the ones facing her had no choice but to take a step back. Bickering, shouted epithets, and fights broke out as the vultures, flapping their wings, stumbled over one another.

So came the end, not in any way, shape, or form she ever could have envisioned. Their life here, sudden and transformational, had been shattered. In its place: sorrow, regret, responsibility, uncounted forks in the road.

THE RETURN

FOURTEEN

Jimmy Self sat behind his big oak desk, chewing on a wad of Juicy Fruit well past its sell-by date, but then Jimmy himself was well past his sell-by date. Dreaming of the cigars he used to smoke and wishing he were somewhere else—anywhere other than here. On the desktop: an ancient computer monitor, a stack of files covered in gray dust, a spiderweb glistening off one corner, a Police .38 Special. His rattletrap office, as much a relic of another time as Jimmy Self, stank of stale sweat, cigar smoke, and desperation. The office was lodged in a forgotten building in one of the last derelict streets of New York City. Layer upon layer—as if it were a tree, each ring silent witness to a life lived large, small, and all stages in between—the office, walls smudged the color of the grimy window, appeared nearly as exhausted as he was.

Once upon a time, he would put his feet up on his desk, blow blue Cuban cigar smoke at the ceiling, and call the shots for his well-heeled clients. Jimmy Self was one of those rare people blind to the distinction between good and evil, right and wrong. He had been given early retirement from the NYPD, a very generous one, indeed. This had been acrimoniously negotiated because Jimmy Self and his bosses were at a stalemate. To put it in its simplest terms, Jimmy Self was a dirty cop. Filthy as the gutters of the Bowery. If they had indicted him for all manner of sketchy dealings, it would have implicated colleagues both upstairs and in Internal Affairs. After a three-week vacation in Grand Cayman, he had returned to the city and advertised his PI business.

Immediately, his life had become all the sketchier, especially once he'd been hired by Byron Dey. Had he been born in an earlier era, Dey might very well have forged a bloody road for himself. But times had changed radically. The old ways were dead and buried. Dey had earned an MBA from Penn and, directly out of grad school, had used seed money from a close group of friends to found a business built on the ashes of carefully selected companies on the verge of bankruptcy. He'd fire all but a core group of employees, resuscitate the company, and then sell it for an enviable profit. He gave not a single thought to the thousands who lost their jobs and were thrown into poverty. His business grew exponentially, and yet he wasn't satisfied; he required a new world to conquer. He parted company with his group, buying them out at top dollar. Everyone was satisfied, especially Dey.

MBA and business acumen notwithstanding, Dey was plenty rough around the edges. He had a bad temper that could flare like Mount Etna at a moment's notice. He had already gone dark; now shed of his original backers, he went darker. With vicious cunning and strategic power grabs, he sealed worldwide alliances with the Albanians, the Mexicans, the Colombians, and the Russians—arms dealers and cocaine smugglers all. He thus realized the walloping gains inherent in outsourcing. Hence his hiring of Jimmy Self rather than using any of his own people.

That had been four years ago, four long ugly years since the morning Jimmy had first met Bryon Dey down by the Brooklyn docks.

Jimmy Self would never forget the image of Dey, in his stylish chalk-striped suit, glowering at Jimmy.

"I mean, come on, Self. I watched *The Godfather* and *The Sopranos* same as you. I know what button men were. I never in my life thought I'd need one. But now . . ." His shoulders lifted and fell. That damn suit fit him so perfectly it made Jimmy Self feel like a schlemiel. His cheeks were pink and newly shaved, his neatly parted hair as gray and stippled as the sky. Dey's steely eyes fixed on Jimmy Self's face. "Now I do."

Dey handed over a file and a ziplock bag of cash. The sky, piled high with clouds, seemed to lower itself onto Jimmy Self's shoulders.

"I want you to find a girl," Dey said.

"A girl?"

"Is that going to be a problem?"

Jimmy Self opened the file, stared down at a snapshot of a very pretty girl: oval face, large light eyes, sensual lips. "She's still got baby fat on her."

"Her tender age failed to stop her from stealing me blind."

A tugboat hooted as it passed a barge hauling a mountain of garbage, headed out of state. The waterfront had the melancholy air of a cemetery.

"In any event," Dey continued, "she's over the legal limit."

"Must be just," Jimmy Self opined. Then, beneath the gaze of those hawkish eyes, "Anyways, what happened?"

"It's all in there," Dey said, his voice now easy and light. "She worked for me. Frankly, and this pains me to admit it, she was the best business manager I ever had."

"At her age?"

"It happens, Self. Not often, but in this case . . . keep to the ratty shadows, the places you know. She's a goddamned prodigy. The truth is she made me a ton of money. I mean literally a ton. And she made sure the government knew nothing. Then she lit out with it. Took my IT people, such as they are, two weeks to break into her electronic books, and they're still unraveling the spaghetti she left behind. Her work's left them in the dust."

Across the river, dark waves lapped at eighteenth-century pilings, all that was left of the world-class piers. A Circle Line boat slid by, crammed with tourists, backs to the two men, snapping photos and selfies of the angular glass skyline of Lower Manhattan. Tourists neither knew nor cared about Brooklyn.

"So you want her, this Helene Messer."

"Head on a platter," Dey said. "Money too—every dollar."

"She might have spent—"

Dey sighed. "It pains me to say this, Self; believe me. But in that case take out of her hide every dollar you don't recover." Dey poked a well-manicured finger into Jimmy Self's chest. "She's a shadow; you're a shadow. Find her. Make this right."

Angela stayed on at the dig after Richard left, though within hours of his departure the armada of reporters, having squeezed every drop of news out of Kieros, passed on to newer stories on other continents. He had left when the sun was at its zenith, without a word, without shaking hands with anyone, without even a glance toward Kieros—who was, in any event, giving another in a seemingly endless string of interviews regarding the most current finds, not the least of which were the extraordinary Etruscan tomb guardians Richard had uncovered, explained to him, and indexed and catalogued for him.

Walking down to the shingle with Richard, she was aware of the buzz of the paparazzi, aware that the rumors of their alleged affair had escaped the hive and, like bees in search of pollen, were spiraling farther and farther afield. She found that she didn't care. Her sole objective had narrowed to Richard's shocked face. Still, they exchanged not one word nor even stood especially close. Just being in one another's vicinity was sufficient, as if they were planet and moon that had somehow lost any semblance of gravitational pull on each other. Drifting now, close, but not of the same system.

As she watched the seaplane take off, she thought of a bird returning to a nest that no longer held its beloved egg. She thought she caught a glimpse of his grim profile through the Perspex window as he was transported back to the mainland, on the first leg of his journey back to Dearborn, to his already-fragile wife, and to a house that no longer held Bella.

Bella was missing. She had told her mother she was going to study at the local library and walked out the door of the house, and that was the last anyone had heard or seen of her. Had she been kidnapped? Was she a victim of a hit-and-run, lying in a ditch by the side of a rural road? Or had she run away? She was desperately unhappy: that much Angela knew from her correspondence with Bella.

She did not enter the dig for the balance of the day; no one asked her to. In fact, no one approached her. She wandered the shingle, found the spot where she and Richard used to sit, gaze out at the changing colors of the water, and talk. She stared at it, not wanting to sit there ever again. The sun sank in a painfully slow retreat, and each moment of sunset reminded her of their time together. She ate dinner alone; she tasted nothing, left early. She could not bear to move back into her tent. Lying on her mattress in his tent, staring up at the canvas, she felt gripped by a terrible desolation, as if she had been evicted from her life.

Sitting up, she turned on the light, brought out her copy of *Moby-Dick*, and, turning randomly to a chapter, read for the umpteenth time and with great avidity how Mr. Stubb killed a whale. Melville's dense, precise prose brought to life a scene she could not on her own imagine, a braided strand of the past both courageous and harrowing. And through this alchemy her surroundings grew dim and hazed, the ache of Richard's absence receding. With Melville's numinous writing she was never alone; she was always close to what others might term God.

At length, her lids heavy and fluttering, she put aside the novel, turned off the light, and lay down again. Approaching the precipice of sleep, she willed herself to dream of Richard, of her father, of a meeting that would never take place in the real world but by her will would be summoned up inside her mind. She would dream of her mother, of a happy reunion. But dreams didn't work that way. They had their own logic—or illogic—formed and orchestrated by Morpheus, the Greek god of dreams. And so, deep in REM sleep, it was Bella she saw—Bella alive and afraid, backpack strapped on like a turtle's shell, winking in and out of shadows that crept and moaned like living things. Angela called out to her, but capricious Morpheus stole her voice away. Still, she screamed and screamed, Morpheus gripping her throat so that she was unable to warn Bella, unable to guide her home.

She awoke with that scream stuck like a chestnut burr in her aching throat. One arm swung off the side of the mattress, the back of her hand scraping the floor. In the dark, the feel of something hard against her fingertips: Richard's cell phone. Amid the dreadful frenzy of his departure, he had lost it. Grief-stricken, she had not thought of it until now.

She picked it up without conscious thought, without any feeling that she was violating his privacy, only grateful that he had left something behind, something she could look at and hold close. In her agitated state, with the dreadful feel of the dream with her and a bitter taste in her mouth, she pressed the messages icon to see if Bella had answered the last email she had sent. She had not. She plugged in the phone to recharge the battery and left it on, next to her, as if this connection could in some mysterious way become a ghostly channel between her and Bella.

When it had recovered half of its juice, she texted Bella.

Where r u? she wrote. Worried about u.

Nothing.

An hour later: Bella?

Bella, vanished, was silent.

~

The next morning, she headed back to her work—Richard's work, really—detailing Cul and Culsans. The doorway into the tomb was still closed. Kieros had not come near her, let alone spoken to her, since Richard's abrupt departure. She was the only one who knew of his betrayal of Richard, hijacking the media to cut Richard out, to take the credit for the stunning Etruscan find. As she approached the winged guardians, she was shunted to another part of the dig, where she was put to work labeling shards of Cretan urns. Of course she was angry, but in truth her mind was elsewhere, and she found that she lacked the energy to fight with these people or with Kieros. For the life of her she couldn't get Bella out of her head; she fretted all day over the sketchy details of her disappearance that Richard had hastily shared with her.

Every hour or so she returned topside, checking Richard's cell, hoping against hope that Bella had contacted her. Each time, she was greeted by nothing but silence. Anxiety, buried deep inside her since Richard's departure, began to grow, eating away at her, distracting her from her work. Was Bella still alive? Was she in danger? She had to trust that Richard would get to the bottom of those questions, that he would find Bella.

Just before noon, another archaeologist, a Brit named Nigel who had given her scarcely any attention in all the time she had been at the dig, stopped by and chatted in a friendly manner before offering to help her with the labeling. She was so floored she said nothing, simply nodded, gesturing her welcome with her upturned palm. In his company, the remainder of the day and evening passed bearably, almost pleasantly. She found Nigel engaging in that coolly detached way of the overclass Brits whose origins traced themselves back to the old stiff upper lip, fortitude in the face of adversity, self-restraint in all things, and all that rot, what? In fact, she found Nigel's gentlemanly companionship a kind of balm to Richard's abrupt absence.

To her surprise, he also had a wicked sense of humor.

"A handsome chap walking through Hyde Park at night hears a lady's voice in the bushes," he began as they made their way to breakfast on the second morning after Richard's departure. "'Fancy a good time, only five quid?' *Why not?* the chap thinks. He's just about to press himself against the lady when a policeman shines his torch into their faces. 'Oi! What's going on?' says the policeman. 'Do you mind?' replies the chap. 'I'm about to have sex with my wife.' 'Sorry, mate,' says the policeman. 'I didn't realize she was your wife.' 'Neither did I,' responds the red-faced husband, 'till you shone your bloody torch!'"

She was still laughing when Kieros hurried up to her, his face looking blanched, his expression pinched.

"Angela," he said, in a pained voice, "may I have a word?"

It was his solicitous tone that alarmed her. She and Nigel exchanged a glance before she nodded, following Kieros. He stopped beneath a pencil pine, opened his mouth, closed it again almost immediately. He seemed suddenly out of breath.

"Kieros, what is it?" she said coolly.

"It's about Richard," he said, mopping his brow with the back of his hand. "There's no easy way to say this, I'm afraid. Richard is dead."

FIFTEEN

Jimmy Self sat in his office, chewing on his wad of stale Juicy Fruit, mouth filled with the bitter taste of his life. Staring at the loaded .38. So much had happened in the four years since Dey had given him the Helene Messer job—just not to him. He was an asterisk in the criminal record books, an angry pimple on the butt of postmodern life. Times had passed him by, as they had Dey, God rest his soul.

No one came to see Jimmy Self now, which was sad but just as well, seeing as how his energy level was lower than ants' balls. A brain tumor would do that to you. Especially, maybe, the inoperable kind that pulsed inside his head, spewing its poison with every beat of his heart. The shit had hit the fan about nineteen months ago, when he had begun smelling smells that weren't there, having bouts of tunnel vision and massive headaches, and then galloped downhill fast from there like a spooked horse. The last surgeon he had seen had wished him well. Adios, amigo.

Time yet to reach for the .38, do what had to be done? His right hand twitched. As if it belonged to someone else, he watched it make its way toward the handgun, toward sweet oblivion.

He had four ex-harpies, two of them dead, thank Christ; the other two would happily dance on his grave, now they had sucked the fiscal life out of him. Well, they would get their wish soon enough. His first, the nastiest, had given him kids—a son and then, two years later, a daughter—whom he had rarely seen as children and never as adults. He had given them all the things money could buy: a decent roof over their heads, food on the table each night, then, later on, the best schools, ballet lessons, sports equipment, a never-ending parade of expenses, spent money he'd only ever see again in his dreams. Okay, so he was rarely home, and maybe he liked drinking a bit too much, a girl on the side or two or, one memorable time, three, but in his line of work that was par for the course. He was living in a pressure cooker, for Christ's sake. Even the strongest-willed man—which, admittedly, he was not—needed to work off steam every now and again. And with wifey unresponsive and the kids always around, no way was he getting his rocks off at home.

Speaking of which, every now and again he thought about putting the remnants of his talents for running lost people down to finding wifey. Never actually got up the will to do it. Or the nerve.

Well, but he had reason. Four years ago, right around the time he had accepted the commission from Dey, he had decided to go see his son. Adam worked at a high-tech startup. What he actually did Jimmy neither understood nor cared to. In any event, one late morning, understanding the time-shifted hours high-tech firms kept, he had taken himself to the Meatpacking loft, hard by the High Line, that was the East Coast headquarters of the company where Adam worked.

He stepped off the oversized freight elevator into a hive of worker bees. Exposed brick walls, polished concrete floor, high warehouse windows housed what seemed like endless rows of young men and women, staring into their workstation laptops—laptops so they could bring their work home with them, maybe. Backs bowed, eyes staring straight ahead, their fingers blurred over the keyboards. To Jimmy, the scene looked like something out of *1984*, a book he had read in college. At the time it had made him laugh; it seemed George Orwell had created an absurd future. But standing in front of the reception desk, from behind which a seeming teenager stared at him with wide-apart sloe eyes, as if he had gotten off on the wrong floor, he understood that Orwell's future had overrun his own.

He asked for Adam.

"Which one? Adam Howe or Adam Self?"

"Self," he spat out of his dry mouth. And when he gave his name, the receptionist said, "Oh wow. Are you and Adam related?"

Jimmy felt his tongue stick to the roof of his mouth. "Distantly," he managed to get out. She shrugged, not really listening, certainly not interested, and punched up Adam's extension.

Jimmy waited, feeling a numbness creep over him, the same numbness he'd experienced as a cop running down a dark alley in pursuit of an armed perp. Fear and excitement in equal measure.

At length, a tall young man in chinos and a polo shirt emblazoned with the company's logo appeared. Jimmy peered at him, trying to find traces of himself in the face. Instead, he saw his wife. Stronger genes, right?

"Yes," Adam said brightly. "How can I help you?"

"Adam," Jimmy said faintly, "I'm your father."

Clouds rolled in, dark and frosty as a winter night. "I don't have a father," Adam said.

"I'm not dead," Jimmy told him, voice stronger now, a soldier advancing through no-man's-land, unsure who he would be facing when he reached the other side. "Your mother might have told you that but—"

"What part of 'I don't have a father' didn't you understand," his son said coldly.

Before Jimmy could make the arguments he had rehearsed over and over or even open his mouth to reply, Adam had turned on his heel. Vanished back into the beehive of high-tech industry with an aggressive stride that was 100 percent his father's.

~

Now, watching a pigeon deposit its droppings on the sill of his single grime-coated window, Jimmy sighed. Was it any wonder he hadn't sought out his daughter? His right hand touched the cold blued steel. He felt the pressure mounting in his chest.

Still, he stared morosely into his smudgy computer screen. Habits died hardest. Every morning before he pulled up all the presorted news clippings, missing person reports, Amber Alerts, anomalous sightings, and mass transit surveillance footage available from every federal, state, and local law enforcement agency, he read the newspapers. He did this, frankly, not to keep up-to-date on world happenings, which he couldn't care less about, but to scan the New York City scene, trolling for new customers. Affairs, pols caught in sex webs spun out of their arrogance and entitlement, criminal indictments of shady men looking for any avenue of escape, no matter how grimy or obscene. His meat and potatoes, in other words. Now, at the end of the line, stuck in the terminal depot, it didn't matter. Like a dead frog jumping when an electrical pulse was put to it, he dutifully paged through the newspapers—the real ink-on-paper ones, not that electronic crap spewed out through the internet. He turned pages with a galvanic herky-jerky movement. On page 6, he paused. *Why bother*, he asked himself. He wasn't going to find work this way; he hadn't for nine months, three weeks, four days. He picked up the gun. The weight felt good in his hand, like coming home.

And that was when he saw Helene Messer. His heartbeat came out of its flatliner as the soles of his shoes beat a tattoo on the sticky linoleum floor. *Good Christ*, he thought, *could it really be?* But didn't Helene have light eyes?

With mounting excitement, he put aside the .38, reached over, unlocked a drawer. For a moment, he did nothing, stared as if mesmerized at the shadowed contents. Then, with a convulsive gesture, he drew out the file, much smudged, grease stained, and dog-eared, that Dey had handed him a lifetime ago on the Brooklyn docks. Opened to her photo. Yup, light eyes. But still . . . she could be wearing colored contacts, and the resemblance was just too close for him to ignore. He felt like he was witnessing the resurrection and the light. Spooky.

Helene Messer, the only case he'd never solved, the only lost person he'd never found. With his time running out, he could blow his brains out in his office turned waiting room, or he could get his ass in gear and solve one last case—find the only subject who had driven him to distraction even after Dey's untimely demise. The case was no longer his; it had officially gone dormant. The money had long ago ceased to come his way. But it wasn't dead. Inside his head, its heart smoldered; the subject lived and breathed. And mocked him.

Helene Messer. If this young woman who was, according to page 6, having a steamy affair with the handsome but very married archaeologist at her side was, in fact, Helene Messer.

Only one way to find out. He rose, his body and his chair groaning in unison; picked his way across the untidy space; hauled opened the protesting window. The alley outside smelled of stale Chinese food and urine. Moments later, holstering the police special, he left his relic of an office. He didn't bother locking the door. Let the pigeons claim it as their own.

SIXTEEN

Six weeks or so before Bella disappeared, Maggie actually made an effort to deal with the living nightmare—her own heart of darkness—that had held her captive ever since Bella had been born. Breaking ranks with the dealer she had years ago found by hook and by crook, she took herself to a meds psychiatrist; she had no desire to rehash the effects her mother and father had had on her childhood, mainly because she didn't understand childhood and so didn't believe in it. And she had no intention of telling a stranger what she could barely admit to herself. No, she wanted someone to dispense pills that would make her better, though by this time she had no clear idea what "better" would feel like or if, in fact, she would find it palatable.

In any event, she forced herself into a dress with a low, provocative neckline under the misguided idea that if the shrink was attracted to her, he would be more likely to give her what she wanted. Perhaps it worked, for precisely fifty minutes after she walked into his office, she emerged with a diagnosis of "alienated depression" for her medical insurance and, clutched tightly in her hand, prescriptions for a cocktail of Lexapro and Wellbutrin XL, which she was to try for three weeks before calling him. He said it would take that long for the compounds to reach full efficacy. She didn't feel like waiting for that long, but oh well.

The psychiatrist also strongly suggested that she get out of the house more, go to the movies, a museum, a civic event. Toward that end, he handed her a flyer for a lecture a week hence at the civic center, given by a world-renowned professor of sociology and comparative religions. It was called "How to Adjust to Our Changing World."

Against all her instincts she forced herself to go. She saw Elin's parents there, sitting by themselves, oddly enough, a square of conspicuously empty seats surrounding them like a waterless moat. She wanted to say hello, to thank Elin's mother—what was her name?—for allowing Elin to spend so much time at the Mathis's house. Not that Maggie wasn't paying Elin a damn nice wage for her services; nonetheless, it would have been the friendly thing to do, the neighborly thing. Trouble was she didn't feel particularly friendly or neighborly. Instead, she sat forward, hands obsessively fidgeting in her lap as if she were Lady Macbeth. She was antsy for the lecture to start; this was the first time she had been in an auditorium with so many people in well over a decade. Her periodic parent-teacher conferences were always one-on-one, set in an otherwise empty classroom. At the most recent one, Bella's teacher had told Maggie, to her vague astonishment, that Bella was a star pupil, excelling in everything she set her mind to, but that she could be a little standoffish, and some of the girls made fun of her because she never went trawling through the mall with them or gave them the satisfaction of rejecting her attempts to join their clannish cliques. Young girls had a pack mentality, which was perfectly normal, the teacher had explained. But Bella didn't. Did Mrs. Mathis think Bella had enough friends? the teacher had inquired, with a birdlike tilt of her head. Girlfriends were oh so important at this age, the teacher had babbled on—didn't Mrs. Mathis agree? Maggie had nodded, though she had no idea whether she agreed. What girlfriends had she had at Bella's age, or now for that matter? She could never make her way through that fog.

Sitting in the packed auditorium now, she was bound by terror, which was why she had doubled her dosage of Lexapro and Wellbutrin XL an hour ago. And before she had left the house, she had grabbed a handful of other pills. As soon as she had stepped out the door, her anxiety had risen like a fever, and now, as the world-renowned professor took the stage to polite applause, it commenced to skyrocket. She popped a pill, swallowed it dry.

"We live in an age of fear: it cannot be denied." Matthew Kirby was the evening's speaker, and his amplified voice penetrated into every corner of the auditorium. He was a tall, slender man, younger than she had imagined, though there were touches of silver, like wings, at his temples. He had an intensity that made her tremble and shake with anxiety, especially when she felt his gaze settle on her. Claws digging into her. "And what happens when we feel fear en masse? We retreat into tribalism. Why? Because tribalism defines the most primitive part of the human psyche: the reptile brain. Though we have evolved far beyond the reptile, yet that atavistic part remains. Why? Because the reptile brain sees tribalism as the self's last defense against danger. Its sole purpose is self-preservation."

The renowned professor paused to take a sip of water kindly provided by the staff of the organization sponsoring his lecture. In this interregnum he looked about the room, his gaze moving from row to row, alighting on first one face, then another. He smiled in what many in the audience took to be reassurance. Maggie, however, interpreted that smile as the consequence of a joke he had told himself at the audience's expense. She popped another couple of pills, rolled them around in her mouth like sucking candy or mints before swallowing them. She deserved the bitter aftertaste.

He cleared his throat and continued. "It is the great irony of the new age of fear in which we find ourselves that globalization has, in fact, spawned the return to tribalism. And what, precisely, is tribalism? It's the unshakable sense that I—and my people—are right, and everyone else is wrong, is out to attack me, lay me low.

"The rapid rise of Muslim extremism following 9/11, if we can force ourselves to pull back to an objective distance, is an action. So.

There must be, according to the laws of the universe, an equal reaction. And that, my friends, is the rapid rise of the extremist Christian right wing. Their rage has for years been directed almost solely at Muslim jihadi. But in the way of tribalism, their rage now has spread to include Americans who they consider enemies of the Christian State. These people would have you believe that their way of life is being threatened by the federal government, Muslims living here, Latinos living here. They want a clean sweep. They want a Christian nation, a theocracy, if you will, that ignores the fundamental separation of church and state."

There was more—surely there was—but Maggie ceased to hear it. Her anxiety spiked to an unmanageable level, which, in concert with the unholy cocktail she had ingested, caused her to lose consciousness.

When she awoke, she was in a hospital room, hooked up to IVs, monitors beeping in a rhythm that set her teeth on edge. Oddly, the first face that swam into view was that of Elin's mother.

"Mrs. Mathis. Maggie," Elin's mother said. "You're in the hospital. How are you feeling?"

Maggie opened her mouth but couldn't speak. Intuiting her problem, Elin's mother reached into a plastic cup, offered her a chip of ice. Maggie's mouth opened like a child's, and the ice slid onto her tongue. She sucked on this for a moment, unsure exactly what it was. Her head was swimming, her thoughts wriggling away from her like a school of frightened fish.

The ice melted; she swallowed and felt well enough to ask, "What happened?"

"They had to pump your stomach."

"What?"

"You were convulsing when they brought you in."

"How did I get here?"

"I called 911. I also looked in your cell phone and called your husband. He's on his way back from Ephesus, I think it is. He'll be here tomorrow."

Maggie didn't know how to answer. At the moment she had no idea what an archaeologist was. She couldn't even remember this woman's name.

"I'm Elin's mother, Lely."

She had a welcoming smile. Reassuring, which was more than you could say for the world-renowned professor. "That damn lecture," Maggie muttered, the recent past rushing back at her like a wall of water. "It was so frightening." She must have spoken out loud because Lely answered her.

"Yes, it was. Particularly for me and my family."

"That's why I fainted!"

Lely smiled gently, sadly. "That's not why they had to pump your stomach, Maggie. You were full of drugs."

"Prescribed by my shrink!" And then because her thinking was slow on the uptake: "Why for you particularly?"

Lely's smile turned sadder. "Surely you must know."

"Know what?"

Lely sighed. "I almost couldn't get up here, even though my husband and I were the ones who brought you in."

Maggie blinked, looked at her blankly. Then: "Oh, I see—because you're not family."

"No," Lely said slowly and distinctly, as if speaking to a small child. "Because we're Muslims."

Maggie's brows knit together. "What has that to do with anything?"

"Everything, Maggie. But let's not talk about this now. America and Americans are better than that. Freedom and liberty for all, yes?"

Lely paused as a nurse, bustling in, gave a cheerful greeting to her patient; checked the electronic readouts for heart rate, blood pressure, and oxygen flowing to her extremities; changed the glucose bag; made some notes; and bustled out again, all without saying a word or making eye contact with her.

"So how did you get in here?" Still focusing on herself.

"Elin talked us in; she's a jinni at these things."

"Jinni?"

Lely smiled. "Jinni are a kind of fairy. Very powerful."

Maggie frowned. Her thoughts were muzzy. "But they don't really exist, do they?"

Lely patted her leg. "Never mind. Just rest now, okay?"

"Richard. My husband . . ."

"I called him. I told you, remember?"

Maggie shook her head; her expression darkened. "Oh, I don't want him to see me like this. Not like this."

~

On the flight back to New York, Angela at last came to her senses. Thirty thousand feet above the curve of the earth, she realized the extent of the danger her relationship with Richard Mathis had put her in. Of course, on a purely visceral level she had been aware of the peril when she had made the decision to abandon the dig, reverse her disappearance, and make her return to the country and dangerous situation she had fled four years ago. Once Kieros informed her that Richard had been run down in the street forty-eight hours after Bella's disappearance, there was no question of her remaining on Crete. She was sorry to leave Cul and Culsans, the guardians she had come to love, and doubly sorry to have been kept away from them the moment Richard had left by the men who had never really had any respect for her. Now, in the terrible aftermath, they saw her as nothing more than Richard's whore. All except Nigel, who for some reason felt inclined to treat her with a modicum of kindness. Unsurprisingly, she could not bear to stay at the dig, on Crete, away from America one day longer. That suited the entire team just fine. Besides, by rights it was Richard who should have been the first person in the tomb, not Kieros and his crew; Richard who should have made the assessment; Richard who should have received the glory. Now that was all gone as if it had never existed. For herself, she was quits with being chthonic, buried underground, in fearful hiding.

As was often the case in the flawed perception of human beings, she hadn't really understood the depth or breadth of her feelings for Richard until after he was dead. To have him erased from Crete, from Dearborn, from the world of the Etruscans, from life itself was for the moment unbearable. But repeating in her mind like a mantra was his last wish to have his daughter back, to do all the things Angela had enumerated in her first email to Bella. He couldn't do that now. But she could.

I hate it here. I wish I wish I wish.

Did that mean that Bella had run away? But if so, where to? Surely not a friend's house; that would be the first place the police would look. And if she had run away, how often did that lead to very bad things happening: a hitchhiking pickup with the wrong person, a hit-and-run, falling in with the wrong people, a life of God alone knew what? And speaking of the police, she couldn't go to them with the messages on Richard's phone without putting herself in grave danger—they'd ask too many questions about her.

You don't know.

What didn't she know? Bella had never written, and this was what terrified Angela the most: the not knowing. Something had been terribly wrong in Bella's life. Despite their closeness, Richard had never given her so much as a hint of what it might be.

So much had gone wrong in her own life. The parallels between her and Bella were so stark, so obvious to her that she knew she couldn't let Bella's disappearance go.

You don't know.

Once again, she read the accounts in the copies of the *New York Times* and *USA Today* she had purchased at the Athens airport—threadbare though they were—of Richard's death. He had been struck two hundred yards from his front door by a hit-and-run SUV, a black late-model Chevrolet or Lincoln Navigator with blacked-out windows, according to the sole witness, a pensioner who lived across the street. He couldn't recall the license plate number; he hadn't been able to see inside the vehicle. It had struck Richard at speed, flung him ten feet away. He hit the back of his head on the curb, instantly breaking his neck and shattering his skull. His body was found sprawled in the gutter. That was the sum and substance of Richard Mathis's death. An accompanying article detailed how deeply he was being mourned by the entire worldwide archaeology community. The usual quotes of shock from Kieros, past colleagues, museum curators, university presidents, especially after the disappearance of his daughter. "All in total shock . . ." "senseless tragedy . . ." "irreplaceable loss . . ." "Everyone who knew him loved and respected him." "Our hearts and thoughts are with his family." It was astonishing how boilerplate and insincere impromptu expressions of condolence could seem. And then there was this: "Richard Mathis's alleged inamorata, Angela Chase"—how she winced at that name now—"abruptly left Dr. Kieros's team on Crete, vanishing into thin air." The same photo of her at Richard's side that had appeared on page 6 two days before, her face blown up, blurry, accompanied the sidebar. "Where is she? Who is she?" She was overcome by the magnitude of her mistake. Oh, God. Oh, Christ. Four years in the wilderness, meticulous in her disappearance, mindful of Dey's long arm every hour of every day. Only to be undone by her relationship with Richard. Of Bella, there was even less news; she was, in fact, a footnote. Angela had to comb the papers to find any mention of her: "mysterious disappearance," "ongoing investigation," "no suspects, no substantial leads, according to local police officials." Boring; no news there, nothing that passed as what journalists these days would call sexy. Jesus, what was anyone doing to find her? Clearly, news sources were not going to be of help. Boots on the ground.

There was actually more ink on Margaret Mathis, widow of the recently deceased Dr. Richard Mathis. Unwell for some time, Mrs. Mathis had suffered a complete psychological break following the twin shocks of her daughter's disappearance and her husband's death, had taken a fatal overdose of Vicodin and fentanyl. Angela thought again of Richard leaving Bella in the wake of Maggie's venomous force and wondered if Bella had been snatched up by a new one.

At least Kieros had kept his promise not to tell anyone when she left the dig; the delay in the media finding out had given her a head start. She did not tell him—or anyone—where she was headed. She was taking a very roundabout route back to New York. Still she knew it would be only a matter of time before some snoop scouring the airline manifests would trace her. By that time, she prayed she'd have disappeared from New York.

In the toilet at the rear of the plane, she wept for herself as well as for Richard, for Bella, whom she knew: "I hate it here. I wish I wish I wish"—and yet didn't know well enough: the enigmatic and frightening "You don't know." To fight the fucking chaos of life that shredded happiness, contentment, and security between its cruel teeth, Angela needed to find her, to save her, and perhaps, in the process, to save herself.

The plane bucked and jerked as it hit turbulence. The pilot came on, asking the flight crew to suspend drinks service, passengers to return to their seats and buckle up. Angela, ignoring the announcement, gripped the stainless steel sink with both hands. Stared at herself in the mirror: the coffee-colored eyes that, up close, didn't look quite right; her thick hair cut short, blonde as Monroe's. She tried to see what Richard saw when he looked at her but failed. We never saw ourselves as others saw us, she thought. Mirrors reversed our slightly asymmetrical faces, changing our appearance. She staggered as the plane dipped and righted. *Who am I?* she asked herself. *Am I Angela Chase, am I Helene Messer, am I Laurel Springfield, or am I someone else entirely?* Someone Richard Mathis had befriended, mentored, confided in. Trusted. She didn't recognize herself because she was no longer who she had been in Dey's world, no longer who she had been when she had disappeared, no longer who she had been on Crete. Who had Richard met there? Who had he trusted? She had no idea.

SEVENTEEN

When Richard pushed open the hospital room door the next day, he only had eyes for Lely, who had taken time out from her family to check in on Maggie. When she told him Maggie had collapsed at a lecture, what had ensued, he thanked her for being the first one to Maggie's side when Maggie had fainted, for calling 911, for asking her husband to follow the ambulance to the hospital so Maggie would see a familiar face when she woke up. None of this was easy for him. In his mind rose the specter of the jihadi who had shot Ben while they stood together in friendly argument as to who was better, the Beatles or the Rolling Stones.

"We can kill you," a spokesman for one of the extremist groups he had contacted had told him. "We will kill you if we so choose. Or torture you, bend you to our will. If we so choose." And they had said, "Your life is in our hands." And he had understood what it meant to have your life taken away from you. Armed with that knowledge, he had not shown fear, had not blinked under their fierce scrutiny.

"You are a disease, American," they had said. "You vomit your naked entertainment, your low morals, your money, weapons, drones here where we live, killing our women, our children, our hope for a righteous life. And because of you, all we have left is hate. That is our one weapon against you, American. It is why you will never defeat us. Never."

And he had said, "I understand all that. I am an American, and I understand."

They had laughed, and he had laughed with them. It had preserved his life.

Now it was Lely standing before him, but in his mind, he was once again speaking with the Muslim extremists at great personal peril, as vulnerable as if his life were an unmoored tent in a sandstorm. It was Sinai's bitter sand he felt in the back of his throat, Sinai's blinding sun in his eyes. He shivered in the hospital's prophylactic chill. As if he had never left Sinai. As if he had become an Arab.

"I'm so glad you're here," he said with a throttled voice. Warring emotions ran through him, stretching his professionalism near the breaking point.

"Perhaps I had better step out," Lely was saying now. "So you and Maggie can have some private time."

"Thank you, but that won't be necessary." He hadn't said a word to Maggie. He'd scarcely glanced at her, had no desire to do so. In fact, he found it painful to see her now. He thought about Bella, but that just brought more pain, another tide of unendurable emotions. Drowning. Drowning. Almost.

"Your wife is very ill, Dr. Mathis," Lely said. "She overdosed. She's been self-medicating."

"It was my doctor's fault. I was only taking the medication he prescribed," Maggie piped up in a weak attempt to exonerate herself.

Lely took Richard aside. "She had swallowed so much they had to pump her stomach."

He regarded her levelly, kept his own counsel, which seemed to vex her.

"Perhaps you should talk with your wife," she said at length.

Richard shook his head. "I'd prefer to speak with one of the doctors in the ER who worked on her."

Lely looked at him oddly, but he had no more time for her. The room was almost filled with water. If he stayed another second, he'd be swept completely under.

∾

He stood against the pale-green wall outside the ER, struggling to regain his equilibrium. Gurneys came and went, guided by harried nurses. Across from him an elderly man lay on a gurney, waiting to be seen by one of the overworked, overstressed doctors. Richard had tried to ask the doctor who had pumped Maggie's stomach to take a look at the elderly man, but the doctor, having answered Richard's questions in his terse, no-nonsense manner, had already turned on his heel, returning to the tumult of the ER. Richard crossed the hallway, dodging incoming gurneys traveling, it seemed to him, at terminal speed. He stood by the stationary gurney. The elderly man's face was white, wrinkled, skin parchment thin. Age had robbed his eyes of color and depth. They looked like currants in an unbaked hot cross bun.

"Are you all right?" Richard asked.

"What d'you think?" There was something defiant in his demeanor.

"Where is your family?" Richard asked.

"Where is yours?"

Unbidden, a chill snaked down Richard's spine, like cold sweat. "I wish I could help you."

A tightness about the man's liver-colored lips. "That's all right," he said. "You'll be here one day."

Richard returned to his place by the wall. Uncomfortable as it was, he vastly preferred it to returning to Maggie's room, to what awaited him there. Questions to which, if he were to be honest with himself, he did not want the answers. Unbidden, Lely's words rose into his mind: "collapse," "self-medicating," "stomach pumped." All true. According to the ER doctor, his wife was in a bad way mentally and emotionally.

"Fragile as glass" had been his exact words. Richard did not want to hear that. He could not spare the time from his work to tend to a sick spouse.

And what of Bella? He would see her in time, must see her before he returned to Turkey, although he was quite certain they would end up at each other's throats; that was their pattern, and it was difficult, if not impossible, to break.

What he wanted most was to get out of Dearborn as fast as he could; he wanted to return to the dig in Ephesus. Although—how could he know?—he would never get back to his beloved Ephesus but would be summoned to Kieros's dig on Crete. He stared over at the elderly man; as yet, no one was attending to him. He turned, strode into the ER, and looked around. Finding a doctor who was stripping off his latex gloves, having just finished with a patient, he guided him gently but firmly out into the hallway and over to where the elderly man was lying.

"Please," he said. "My father has been lying here for hours, waiting."

The doctor eyed the elderly man, took his wrist, taking his pulse. "What seems to be the problem?" he asked.

Richard was already too far away to hear the elderly man's reply. Outside the hospital, away from the busy entrance, he called Lely. He would not, could not return to Maggie's room. When she answered, he said, "You were right." He repeated the phrase the ER doctor had used: "She's in a fragile state. Fragile as glass. I don't know what to do."

"You could stay home," Lely suggested. "Spend time with her and Bella."

"I would if I could," he lied. He was aces at that, having quickly learned what the jihadi wanted to hear and selling it back to them in a package swathed in sincerity. "Unfortunately, my job doesn't allow it."

"Your bosses never heard of compassionate leave?"

This reminded him that he wasn't dealing with a simpleton, like the museum curators who took every word he said as gospel. "Of course, of course," he responded, "but it's, well, complicated."

When this politician's explanation was met with silence, Richard knew it was time to eat a slice of humble pie. Well, if that was what was needed to get what he wanted, so be it. He sighed, not too theatrically, which surely would have tainted what was coming next. "The truth is, Lely"—using her name for intimacy's sake—"the truth is I'm no good at this kind of thing. I never was. If I stay home, I'll only gum up the works."

"More than they already are?"

"Sadly, yes."

A small pause before she ventured, "You have a solution, I take it."

"I do," he said. "And it involves you."

"Me?"

"I'd very much like your help."

"Why not hire a nurse if you're too busy to be around for her?"

"It comes back to Maggie's fragile emotional state. She trusts your daughter. She trusts you. Plus I'm willing to pay—"

"I don't want your money, Dr. Mathis."

"This isn't charity, if that's what you're thinking."

"I want something far more valuable."

He recognized the poisoned-honey note of contempt he'd heard many times wherever he'd traveled in the Middle East and knew he had taken one step too far. He also knew there was only one way to apologize. "What can I do for you, Lely?"

"You are a professor at Michigan, a prestigious university."

"I am," he said, wondering where this was going.

"You yourself are prestigious. You're well regarded all around the world."

"I suppose you could say that."

"You have power."

"I don't know about that."

"A power I don't have and never will."

There was a small silence between them.

"I have done my best, but I'm not in any position . . . my husband has been questioned—taken away in front of the family and detained. Because he is an importer, because he does business in the Middle East. Because we are Muslim."

"I'm sorry."

"I don't need your sorrow, Richard. My husband is entirely innocent. We are good people, loyal Americans. But no one from the government is listening. They have turned a deaf ear. And now he has high blood pressure. Last week a case of angina sent him to the ER. There was never anything wrong with his heart. He is a strong, vital man, but now I am worried about his health, Richard, and I shouldn't be."

"I don't understand."

"Then find out," Lely said and severed the connection.

~

Because of Lely's request—at least that was how Richard preferred to term it—he stayed on for several days after Maggie came home. Whether Lely was telling the truth about believing it was his high academic standing that might give him the power to help her, or whether somehow she had found out about him, he left to others to sweat out of her. Another thing he did not want to know; he knew too much already, and it was slowly killing him. There were calls to be made, hasty meetings convened, contentious negotiations to hammer out, a gauntlet of hoops to jump through to get Lely's husband off the government's list of those suspected of aiding terrorist organizations. This tack made him no friends, but perhaps that would change. They had gotten nowhere with her husband, who seemed to be precisely what he claimed to be: a middle-management executive of an import-export firm that, to date at least, was on no one's watch list. Combing through his financials revealed him to be of no more than middle-class means, although these days the middle class seemed to have evaporated, leaving an ever-widening gap between the 1 percent and everyone else.

Whatever conscience hadn't been extinguished in Sinai made it impossible for Richard to leave when he would have liked to. "No one from the government is listening," Lely had told him. "They have turned a deaf ear." Wasn't that what Maggie had accused him of doing to her?

But those long, excruciating hours spent at home were a living nightmare. He was a stranger in his own house; it was no longer his home. He recognized none of the rooms, especially the bedroom he had once shared with his wife, though this fact seemed inconceivable to him now. Where was the full-length mirror he had installed for her? Photos of his wife and his younger self were unrecognizable, and the ones with a child might as well have been of an alien. Mementos—hand-thrown plates from Tourrettes-sur-Loup, Carlo Moretti glassware from Venice, vintage coffee cups from the Portobello Road flea market—must belong to someone else's past. No sign of the carpet he had brought back from Istanbul, the *zillij* tiles from Marrakech, a wooden cross from Sinai. Photos he had taken himself of artifacts from his various digs, blown up, framed, and hung were his only solace, and he clung to them like a man drowning in someone else's sea.

Once he had loved his wife; he was certain of that. But in the shower the second morning, he began to wonder whether his memories of that time when they were newlyweds were at all reliable. Memories were infinitely fungible, changing like chimeras. *I don't recall, Mr. Smith; not to my knowledge, Your Honor; not as far as I know, Officer.* Had he, in fact, ever loved Maggie? Water poured down his face as he contemplated this memory question without finding a satisfactory answer.

He thought of Bella, wrapped in her unfathomable thoughts, doing whatever it was teenagers did in their rooms these days. Elin had dropped her off and then left without so much as a word to him. For her part, Bella had scarcely looked at him. She'd had no reaction, so far as he could tell, to her mother's collapse, and she had flatly refused to visit the hospital. "Frankly," she'd told him, "I don't even know why I'm here."

"You live here," he'd retorted, his blood rising at her hostile attitude.

"I don't," she'd spat at him. "Not anymore. You'd know that if you were ever here. I'd rather be at the Shehadis. Hashim has been taken out of his house like a common criminal. They need me more than you do."

As a sickly infant she had never stopped crying; as a young child she had been a holy terror. Once, he had asked Elin why she couldn't control Bella better. "I'm sorry, sir," she'd said, "but she's only like this when you're home." And now, with a teenager's witchy skill, she knew how to press all his buttons. He didn't even know who she was anymore. Now, as he wandered aimlessly from empty room to empty room, he wondered whether he ever had.

The last night of his stay, Richard and Bella had dinner alone. Bella talked to him then, chattering incessantly of jinn, the mythical desert fairies spun of smoke and sand, an unreality no doubt promoted by Elin. But it was Richard himself who had met the real desert beings, and they were nothing like jinn. They were spun of hatred and metal. Their goal was death, for themselves as well as for their enemies. They were the human equivalent of antimatter.

"You talk about these jinn as if they were real," he said, unable to suppress his irritation at her naiveté. "There are no jinn. They're part of Arabic fairy tales." He shook his head. "Bella, these are childish fancies. You're no longer a child; it's time you grew up." A man of pragmatism, he took no notice of her reaction. His world was built on reason. He saw no romance in unearthing ancient cultures. He was drawn to historical foundations, to understanding the practicalities and perhaps, with luck, the wisdom of their lives. He found no difficulty in penetrating to the core of societies; it was individuals that bewildered him.

"And I think you're spending too much time in your room," he blundered on. "What do you do up there anyway?"

Bella's eyes glazed over. "Nothing."

The tines of Richard's fork scraped the edge of his plate. "This is how you always are when I come home." No reaction. He plowed on, even knowing this was all wrong, that it could not end well. He did not know how else to speak to her. He didn't like what he saw. "Sullen and distant."

"I don't want to talk about this," Bella said, eyes on her plate.

She was an enigma to him, as, he supposed, he was to her. But come on: What could he tell her about himself that wouldn't jeopardize her, that wouldn't make her see him in a different light? They might fight, it was true, but at least she didn't hate him.

They ate in silence. It might have been delicious; Richard had no appetite. He sighed and tried to start over. "Look at you. You're pale. You have rings around your eyes. You need to get out in the sun, have some fun, play with your friends."

"I don't have any friends."

"And that's another thing."

Bella jumped up. "There was a time when I thought this was all my fault, that if I acted differently—if I did this, didn't do that—then everything would right itself. But now I see the truth." In the doorway, she turned back to him. "It's you, Dad. Not me." Tears sprang to her eyes.

He stood up, suddenly appalled. He had no idea how this conversation had spiraled so out of control. He knew that with her he slewed like a skidding car between affection and tyranny. He knew he wasn't a good father, was baffled by fatherhood. The only area of his life where he was in any way incompetent. Their relationship was fraught with all this. But it was freighted with something else entirely, something too immense to face. A silent room, and in it . . . "Bella—"

"No!" She raised her hands defensively. "Stay away from me. That's better for both of us, isn't it? I mean, you hate it here; your home is Turkey or Sinai or Tuscany. Under the earth, not on it." Her eyes overlarge and liquid, as if dipped in oil. She shook her head, and tears flung at him as if they were weapons. "And you know what? Between us nothing will ever be right. How sad is that?"

~

The night he returned from the dig on Crete and from Angela, he lay again on the sofa in the den. The house was unnaturally silent. Bella was gone, who knew where, and Maggie was in a facility. He had just come back from the police station, but the detectives there had been of no help whatsoever. They had no idea whether Bella had gone off on her own or been abducted. On his way out, he overheard one of them say to the other, "What's the use? With abductions you only wind up chasing your own tail. I'd rather be chasing tail down in the Meatpacking District." He stopped in his tracks, even turned around, steeling himself to attack the detective who had said that while he could still hear it. But then his better nature slowed everything down, allowed him the time to think of the consequences. He couldn't help Bella if he was in jail. Instead, he resolved to call the people in DC he more or less worked for and get them involved in the search for his daughter. It was the least they could do for him.

He returned directly home, bypassing the facility in which Maggie lay. Merely coming near her felt repellent, as if by a reverse magnetic force. They no longer had use for one another. He had long ago ceased to feel sorry for her, ceased to feel anything about her, about anyone, really. Except Bella. And he was no good with her. It *was* sad. Damn sad.

Between us nothing will ever be right.

How right she was, though she must never fathom why. As he stood amid walls hung with his framed honorary doctorates from universities in Munich, Athens, Cairo, and Casablanca, staring up at a ceiling lit by an antique Moorish brass lamp, the one gift his wife had not put away, he turned his mind away from his only child—the phrase made him writhe as if in agony. She wasn't his only child, and yet she was. That thought wouldn't do; it wouldn't do at all. It was so inadequate to the situation. But this was the prison he found himself in, one for which there was no key.

Instead, he contemplated the elderly man on the gurney outside the hospital ER he had encountered on his last unhappy trip home. Replaying, as if on a tape loop, their conversation:

Where is your family?

Where is yours?

I wish I could help you.

That's all right. You'll be here one day.

The power and concision of haiku. Not so very far from the song that had been his touchstone since adolescence, the Who's "My Generation." He shuddered, sweating. Wishing he were anywhere but here. Wishing it were morning and he could leave. Wishing there were a jinn in the brass lamp who owed him a favor in exchange for his release. *I want to die before I get that old and infirm*, he'd tell his jinn.

It was at that moment that the phone rang, and his heart turned over, as if he already knew bad news was on its way. For a moment, he considered letting the call go, as if that denial might serve the larger denial, whose truth had already taken root inside him.

"Yes?" His voice thick, barely recognizable.

"Mr. Mathis?"

"This is he."

"Sir, I regret to inform you that your presence is required back in DC."

For a moment Richard was bewildered by the message, so crass, so emotionless, as if the facility had directed a robot to call him.

"Do you have any idea what's going on here?" Richard shouted into his phone.

His voice was greeted by silence. Which finally provoked him to explain: "My wife is in the hospital. She collapsed. The situation is not hopeful."

More silence. And then: "Nevertheless." That single word, the voice of death announcing itself in the most banal fashion, as if death were nothing more than a functionary in an immense bureaucracy.

And that was it. The call ended, Richard's lifeline to another human being, or what passed for human these days, severed. He sat for a moment, motionless save for the pulse of his blood. Bella gone, his wife gravely ill, and he ordered away. It was all too much. The phone was in his hand. Useless thing—he threw it across the room.

Rage and sorrow swirled inside him like a wizard's brew. And there was something else, something shameful buried deeply inside him: an unequivocal sense of relief, an insupportable burden lifted. With an animal cry, he buried his face in his hands, and despite all that had happened, despite the width and depth of the chasm that had opened up between him and Maggie, he wept bitter tears for everything that might have been and never would be.

EIGHTEEN

Wheezing and groaning, Jimmy Self hauled his body across town, using the subway, which he hated on account of the damn stairs, to a gleaming glass-and-chrome office building with a red-granite lobby three stories high, as bustling as the flyblown lobby of his own building was dead. Except for Stinking Man, who slept on stained newspaper in the far corner nearest the stairs to the boiler room. Every morning, on his way into the office, Jimmy Self bought a Venti for himself at Starbucks and two sandwiches—ham and cheese, tuna salad, or roast beef—and a carton of orange juice at the deli next door, setting the sandwiches and juice down in front of Stinking Man, who preferred to remain nameless. "Once you're lost," he told Jimmy Self one time in a noxious cloud of garlic breath, "it's best to stay lost."

Jimmy Self felt himself lost amid all the postmodern grandeur. This was not his world; it would never be his world. He'd never understand or feel comfortable in it. Take the elevator situation. There wasn't one; there were two banks of eight each! He took one, but it didn't go to the floor he needed. Faced with walking up more stairs, he took it back down to the lobby, searched for an elevator that did go high enough. Then, when he reached the right floor, the corridors were so confusing he got disoriented. Finally, he threw himself on the mercy of a denizen of this monstrous labyrinth to guide him through the hallways and turnings to the right door. The worst part was that he'd been here before, numerous times.

Feeling defeated, he lumbered through the glass doors, was given a dubious glance by the twentysomething-year-old behind a semicircular facade. She was dressed in black, wore black nail polish, and was made up like a street waif strung out on smack. She was reading a much-scribbled-on paperback of Jack Kerouac's *On the Road*. *Perfect*, Jimmy Self thought. He introduced himself as Dean Moriarty. She blinked at him, apparently not getting the joke, because she said into the mic strapped around her head, "Mr. Goodwood, there's a Dean . . ." She looked expectantly at Jimmy Self, and when he mouthed the name, she went on, "Moriarty here to see you . . . yes, sir." Again, she glanced up at Jimmy Self. "Are you from San Francisco, Mr. Moriarty?" When Jimmy Self, smiling wickedly, nodded, she said into her mic, "Yes, sir, he is." She gestured. "Go right in, Mr. Moriarty. Third office on your left."

Sal Goodwood sat behind a desk littered with photographs. Hardly surprising, since photographs were his stock in trade. Though these days most of the photos resided on his server, Goodwood was old-school enough to enjoy best poring through the actual print photos.

Goodwood worked for one of those skyrocketing upstarts rivaling Reuters and AP that documented the world's news large and small through photographs.

"Fucking cell phones're killing us," Goodwood said without preamble. He threw up his hands. He was a blocky man of Jimmy Self's vintage, with a bulbous nose and an inveterate drinker's burst capillaries decorating his cheeks like tribal scars. His office, a jumble of file cases, favorite photos, art books, and an old light box for looking at negatives, more or less reflected its occupant. "Look at this! Professional photographers who've done beautiful work for decades, Pulitzer Prize–winning stuff, for Chrissakes, out on their asses, replaced by snaps from the putz on the street whose favorite piece of equipment is a selfie stick. Positively disgraceful."

Jimmy Self, staring out at the vertigo-inducing grid-work office building across Lexington, let Goodwood blow off steam. They were drinking buddies rather than friends. The two were not synonymous, not by a long shot. Calling for a drinking buddy was like making a booty call—there was an immediate itch that required scratching. Beyond that, not much else. The exchange of favors was the commodity that made their relationship work.

When the verbal shit storm inevitably ran its course, Jimmy Self unfolded the page 6 chronicling the alleged affair between Richard Mathis and one Angela Chase, a.k.a. Helene Messer. Maybe. He hoped. Why he was here.

"What's this?" Goodwood said, taking the page, smoothing it out with the professional's practiced gesture.

"Girl with the glamor boy. I need to see the original of that shot."

"Why?" Goodwood looked up, one eyebrow raised. "She giving you a hard-on or something?" His gaze returned to the photo. "She would me. I like a woman with some meat on her bones."

"It's business, Goodwood."

"Really?" That eyebrow again. "And here I was under the impression that your business was pushing up the daisies."

"Resuscitated." Jimmy Self poked a finger at the photo. "If you can't, if you're not up to the task—"

"Don't be ridiculous." Goodwood went to his computer keyboard. "By the way, how's our good friend Sal Paradise?"

"Still on the road, so I hear."

Goodwood chuckled. "Odds are Stephanie out front didn't have a clue."

"You'd be surprised."

"Really?" Goodwood shook his head mournfully. "Seems millennials have no interest in history. Too busy taking selfies and posting 'em online." He shrugged. "Okay, got the roll. Come on around here, and take a look." Goodwood stood back to make room for Jimmy Self. "There she is in all her glory."

Goodwood wasn't kidding. As Jimmy Self zoomed in on the face, he could look beyond the short, blonde hair; the brown lenses over blue eyes. He knew he wasn't looking at Angela Chase. Angela Chase didn't exist. But Helene Messer did, and she was looking right back at him.

~

Laurel's reentry into the United States went unremarked, which came as a vast relief to her. She remained ahead of the curve. However, she knew she had to act fast to remain in that anonymous position.

To that end, she took herself to Gael's as fast as the brutal New York traffic would allow. She recalled the first time she had met Gael Luzon. The introductions had been made by Orfeo via cell phone, both as an atonement and as a going-away gift. He knew he would never see her again. She had fallen in love with Gael the moment they had met in the hushed atmosphere of a cavernous Chelsea art gallery. Surrounded by paintings of attenuated people in distress, he had looked like he'd stepped out of a color-saturated Mexican film; he had burned with a curious copper light. And strangely enough, he had known how she felt about him, had sensed it the moment they had first met. She had felt safe being near him.

"You need to get away," he had said.

"Yes."

"Today. Now. This very minute."

"Yes."

"From whom?" And when she had hesitated: "I need to know. It will shape the how and the where of your disappearance."

He had a very beautiful voice. It had pierced her in a pleasurable way, and again she had felt safe.

"Dey," was all she had said, all she had needed to say.

Now, her taxi sped by the immense cemeteries that yawned off the sides of the highway into the city from JFK, vivid reminders of *ars longa, vita brevis*, the Latin translation of an aphorism of the Greek physician Hippocrates. In plain English: time limits our accomplishments. Beyond, massive steel billboards rose, blank as the faces of the buried. The traffic built up on the approach to the Midtown Tunnel. Cops in flak jackets were everywhere, eyeing the slowly passing vehicles, sipping coffee out of Styrofoam cups, occasionally pulling a truck or a van over for a spot check.

Manhattan itself seemed much as she had left it, until her cab started to inch crosstown and she saw the unbelievable amount of new construction. Streets reduced to single lanes, cement trucks grinding away, and cranes rising everywhere. Everything had accelerated. Her four years away seemed like a lifetime. Everyone was on their cell phones, whether they were hurrying along the sidewalks, jaywalking, in intersections, sitting in restaurants, alone or with companions. Person-to-person conversations seemed so yesterday. Everyone speaking at disembodied voices from across town, across the country, on the other side of the world. The interconnectedness of life that had shrunk the world to one square block had also severed people from those around them, alienated them from themselves. She felt as if she had never lived here. The machine-gun chatter of jackhammers, the toothache throb of massive diesel engines, the soaring skeletal desolation of construction site after construction site. Was this her New York? Had she landed somewhere else when she had stepped off her journey's last segment? At a red light, a gleaming white SUV pulled up beside her taxi. The tinted windows were down, and the guy sitting in the shotgun seat, covered with tats, turned, gave her a toothy grin. Hip-hop bass and backbeat emanated from the interior, sounding like a living thing, a boxer being beaten into unconsciousness. The light changed, and she was rushing away in the Mach 1 manner of cabs. Life in an NYC that no longer seemed hers. Staring out the window at a sea of blurred faces, she took a deep breath, trying to settle herself. But she could not help asking herself where she fit in.

From Midtown, on her way north, she could see Central Park South, now known as Billionaires' Row, the fingerlike towers reaching skyward.

Gael Luzon had told her he'd moved into one of these supertowers when she had called him from the transfer lounge in Istanbul.

"What took you so long?" he said when he opened the door. He was a slim, athletic man with broad shoulders and narrow hips, fawn-colored eyes, and a nose like a Catalonian aristocrat. In his midthirties and he had not an ounce of fat on him. "Didn't you miss me too much?"

"You wish," Laurel said with a snort. "Anyway, I told you everything on the phone."

"Hardly everything. You must tell me more."

Young people darted about, glued to their cell phones or their tablets, sometimes both. Everyone spoke in sibilant whispers; everyone wore black; everyone was tattooed. It was like standing in long grass surrounded by the buzz of inscrutable insects.

"It's complicated," Laurel said, sidestepping a very thin young man with the manic look endemic to people who existed in this new constantly interconnected world. "Right now . . ."

He nodded gravely. "Of course."

The next forty minutes were spent immersed in the blissful luxury of one of Gael's marble-clad bathrooms. She used a TOTO toilet that did everything for her, including drying off her ass with jets of warm air; then, in a shower as large as most bathrooms, she scrubbed off the stink of canned air, sorrow, and almost constant anxiety. On the way toward human again, she pulled on the soft clothes Gael had set out for her. He kept a spare wardrobe for all his clients.

Once she was dressed, they sat on a sweeping plum-colored sofa in a living room as vast as a country club, part of Gael's palatial full-floor apartment overlooking Central Park from ninety-one stories up.

"Thirty-five million," he said. "That's over seven thousand a square foot." The view was endless, like being in an airplane.

"Why are you living here?" she said, disoriented by the sheer dimension of opulence.

"I like it." He grinned disarmingly. "Also, my father designed it." Shrugging. "It's like the real estate people say, thin equals exclusive. One residence to a floor; it's not an apartment. It's an urban home. Ubersecure. Plus, I don't have to wrangle with a bunch of geriatrics on a condo board who distrust Latinos like me."

Reaching over to a drinks trolley, he poured two glasses of aged mescal. "At last we're together to celebrate." Clinked the rim of his glass against hers: "¡Salud y plata!" Good health and money!

Her brow furrowed. "What are we celebrating?"

"What? Really? Dey the madman is dead."

Sirens sounded. She felt a tsunami of emotion engulf her.

He pursed his lips. "My God, you didn't know?"

"I cut myself off from everything. I had to in order to put the past behind me." She set down her drink. "When?"

"Three and a half years ago."

Crashing against her, making her tremble so badly, Gael reaching out as if to steady her.

"Laurel . . ."

"I'm okay." Even though she wasn't, not by a long shot. Dey dead, his long arm reaching out for her gone in a puff of smoke. "What happened?"

Gael laughed. "You happened," he said in what seemed too casual a fashion. "After you plundered the bulk of his money, he struggled on while he hired people to find you, find his money. He had small accounts here and there, which I'm sure you knew."

"Too small for me to bother with."

"Right. Which Dey found out too late. He had enough to fund his enterprise for maybe three months, but because you anonymously informed his enemies, they began to circle like vultures. They shorted him on payments or didn't pay at all. They know what happens when you knock out three legs of a stool. Dey tried to negotiate, but that only cemented his weakened state. Then one fine night the Russians, or maybe it was the Mexicans, blew his brains all over Jersey City."

"Jersey City isn't Juárez."

"Not yet it isn't. But in the future, who can say? Medellín, Cali, Mexico City, Juárez." He grinned, showing off his perfect white teeth. "The Mexicans are already here. More to come." Just as quickly his huge smile vanished. "It's the innocents who get caught in the crossfire. The innocents always pay for the sinners' transgressions; the sinners see to that."

Her heart fluttering, she gave him a hard look. "Gael, I really had no idea my . . ."

"Revenge. That's the word you're looking for."

She nodded. "I didn't imagine it would be so complete."

His gaze was steady, unblinking. Hard as granite. "None of us is innocent. The human condition sees to that." He eyed her. "Just out of curiosity, what did you do with all that money?"

"When I left here, my first stop was Geneva. I anonymously donated half of it to several foundations for helping homeless children worldwide."

"Christ, Laurel, you could have been the richest heiress in—"

"It's blood money, Gael. I'm an alchemist. Blood into gold. Now half of it's being used to help the kids who need it the most."

"And here, ladies and gentlemen, we have an entirely new definition of money laundering." He laughed, lifted his glass. "You are a woman of rare and bewildering talents." Clinked the rim against hers. "As they say in Mexico, *plata o plomo*." Money or lead, as in bullets. "But come on—after what he did, I'm betting you'd have liked to have seen Dey's head in the street."

Laurel thought of Richard's flung body in the gutter in front of his house and trembled. "I just want to get to Dearborn."

"Okay." He brought out a thick packet in a manila envelope. "Everything you need."

She reached out a hand. "Give it here."

"Will you tell me what the hell you think you're doing?"

Her fingers wriggled emphatically.

"Of course." Sighing, he spun the envelope across the table. "Headstrong bitch that you are." Only Gael could say that without her taking offense.

Even though Dey was dead, she couldn't take the risk that the file on him was still open, that someone in law enforcement wasn't looking for her, even after all this time. "Who am I this time?" she asked, opening the clasp.

"Jennifer DeAngeles." Gael hunched over as she went through the new docs he had made for her. She had dumped everything identifying her as Angela Chase, including her brown contact lenses, the moment she was through immigration and customs at JFK. She still had blonde hair though; that would have to change. "You're a stringer for *Shut Up!*, an online investigative webzine."

She glanced up at him. "If someone checks?"

"All squared away." Gael frowned. "Again I must tell you I don't understand. Why come back here when you could have gone anywhere in the world, remained Angela Chase forever?"

"Angela Chase was outed on Crete, my photo splashed all over the internet as Richard's other woman."

Gael's bafflement increased. "You could have disappeared again, lost yourself in Istanbul or Hong Kong. Anywhere but here."

"I couldn't."

"You came back for Richard." His expression grew serious. "You loved him."

She nodded. "Not in the way you mean."

"Does it matter?"

"It matters very much to me."

"Okay, okay, don't bite my head off!" He shook his head. "You're a very clever girl. Smart, too, this I know. But what you do now seems foolish. Richard is dead. Think of your past." He sighed deeply, genuinely, sorrowfully. "Love is tragedy: this is a truism. Why involve yourself? Leave it be."

"I didn't come back for that, Gael. I came back to find Bella, his daughter. She's missing."

"But why? What's she to you?"

She shook her head. "It's complicated."

Gael pursed his lips. "Yo, Laurel, this is me you're talking to."

"She and I . . . I don't know. We share something at the very core of us. She's as lost as—"

"You told me. She's been missing a few days, right?"

"Yes, but—" Laurel shook her head. "That's not what I mean. We're both lost in the same way. We have no life—we don't even understand what life is. We go from day to day, just . . . I don't know . . . just surviving. I've been thinking . . . I think we need each other."

Gael cocked his head. "Why d'you say that?"

"We might be the only ones who can understand each other." When Gael said nothing, merely kept looking at her in that gimlet-eyed way of his that must unnerve so many people, she went on. She didn't believe now she had any other choice. "Gael, please understand that she and I have nothing."

"Come on, Laurel. You have wealth, your independence; you can go anywhere, do anything. You have everything."

"Wealth? And yet I have nothing of real value." She met his gimlet stare with her own. "But to be honest and with all due respect, I don't know whether you can understand that."

He held her gaze for a moment; then his eyes slid away, along the fabulously expensive carpet, over the fabulously expensive sofa, to the even more fabulously expensive view out over Central Park.

"One minute everything, then nothing," he murmured as much to himself as to her.

"Listen, Gael, I found a very special person on Crete, and then he was gone, as fast as blowing out a candle. And on the way back here I realized that I'd had my father's love back, at least for a time. Bella has nothing. She was never loved, at least not the way a child should be loved, by her parents. Who, then, will speak for her? Who will save her from whatever has happened to her? Who will save her from herself?"

"What if she's dead, Laurel? Have you thought of that? You'd be putting yourself in danger for nothing."

"She's not dead," Laurel responded with such utter conviction that Gael would not gainsay her.

Laurel closed her eyes, summoned up her dream, saw Bella, backpack strapped on, walking between the shadows, vanishing into them. *Where are you?* she whispered to herself. *I'm coming. Wherever you are, I'll find you. I'll find us.*

"Gael," she said aloud, "time is against me."

He nodded briskly, as if emerging from a semitrance. "I've arranged for your transportation to Dearborn. The most secure, okay. You don't leave for some hours yet. Which gives us time for a makeover."

She nodded. "I'm ready."

He hesitated. "Understand that even though Dey is gone, remnants of his will may remain. People he hired may still be looking for you."

Laurel touched his cheek, rough as untanned leather. "*Ándale, brujo*," she said, rising. "Work your magic on me."

NINETEEN

Maggie's overdose and hospitalization came as an unexpected blow to Bella. She felt strange, as if she herself had had some doing in her mother's collapse, as if she had willed it, as if she had asked her jinn to cast a spell to remove her mother from her life once and for all. Now that it had happened, she felt at once elated and remorseful, as if her private jinn had taken her at her word, had gone one step too far. On the other hand, she felt an unconditional freedom that dazzled her. No restraints! No more excuses, lame though they might be, no more voices raised in anger, no more doors slammed in rage.

She had been with Elin, of course, when Maggie had forced herself to go to the lecture recommended by her doctor. And she had been with Elin when her mom hadn't come home. When Elin had received a call from Umm, Bella had been on her headphones, perhaps listening for the last time to the music of Britney Spears, Miley Cyrus, and Demi Lovato and couldn't hear Elin's side of the conversation. Elin had a way of arranging her expression—respectful, astute, and loving—that made it clear who she was talking with. This particular night, however, Elin wasn't doing much talking, which was odd. Elin's twice-daily phone conversations with her mother were always on a two-way street. Lots of give and take. Not this night, however. Plus Bella could see that her expression went from sober to grim in about a nanosecond. Bella popped out her earbuds. "What's up?" she mouthed. To which, also odd, Elin turned away, kept listening to whatever her mother was telling her.

As soon as Elin finished the call, she turned back to Bella. "Your mother has collapsed. She's in the hospital. Put on your jacket. We'll go there right away."

There was silence for some time. Bella made no move.

"I don't want to go," Bella said at length. "Really, I don't. Please don't make me."

Elin watched her for flickers of reaction. Was she in shock? Should she heed her charge's wishes? What would be best for her? She knew the dreadful relationship between daughter and mother better than anyone, possibly even Bella herself. "All right," she said. "We'll go to my house."

"Is Umm okay?" Bella's concern was for Elin's family. She loved them with all her heart. She felt dispossessed in her own house, far more comfortable at Elin's, where lately she had been spending a good deal of her time, to Maggie's relief as she sank further and further from reality into a land of shadows and malevolent phantoms.

"Umm is fine." Elin put her arm around Bella's shoulders. "Now, let's go. She's made a tray of *halawat el jibn*." Phyllo pastry rolled with cheese and a custard like heavy cream, *halawat el jibn* was a favorite of Elin's Lebanese father, lately more and more nostalgic for his mother's cooking. It had become Bella's favorite dessert as well.

"Oh, good," Bella said. "Can I have it with rosewater?"

"Of course," Elin said, laughing. "You can help me chop the pistachios for the topping." They stepped outside, Elin closing and locking the door behind them. "But first we have to stop at Ali's All-Night for a bag of them."

The night was calm and gentle. Little traffic passed by. In the distance, an ambulance siren seemed to put Elin on edge. She herded Bella along at an accelerated pace, sheltering arm across her shoulders. Bella didn't mind. In fact, she leaned into her "big sister's" side, feeling safe and content in the arms of one of Allah's children. Until recently, she had only a rudimentary knowledge of Allah and his teachings, but she was learning more every day. The peacefulness of Elin's household drew her like a magnet. It was hardly surprising that she wished the same for her own home, sure in the knowledge of its impossibility.

Three blocks to Ali's All-Night, the corner ablaze with light and hand-painted signs touting the new shipment of black and green cardamom pods, Aleppo pepper, sumac, orange flower water, pomegranate molasses, and *urfa biber*. Inside, below the rows of dusty, buzzing fluorescents, the shelves, bins, and open barrels were crammed with exotic foodstuffs and spices that created their own dizzying atmosphere appropriate for jinn. Or so Bella imagined.

Ali, a stick of a man of Egyptian descent, stood behind the counter in the rear. His skin, dark and glistening as polished amber, hid his cuts and bruises until they approached him with the big jute sack of Antep Turkish pistachios: **Small in Size, Big in Flavor!**

"Ali!" Elin cried. "What happened to you?"

"I ran into a flurry of fists." Ali, a gentle man with the kindest heart who always gave Bella a sweet or two when she came in with Elin or with Elin and her mother, smiled sadly. "It was only a matter of time, love. It's nothing. I'll heal."

"Did you call the police?"

"Yes," Ali said, straight-faced, "that would have made everything better." He accepted the money for the pistachios. "I go on with my life." He smiled again. "What else is there to do?"

But for the first time in Bella's memory, he forgot to give her a sweet.

~

The agents of the federal government with whom Richard had occasional contact were not of his world, not of his ken. As smart and as clever as he was in his own sphere, these people from DC inhabited an alien universe, one in which a lie was substituted for the truth in everything they said and did. They saw themselves as a breed apart; there was Them, and there were Civilians, and though they had recruited Richard, he was and always would be a Civilian. In other words, those high above Richard had lied to him; their belief in their mandate was stronger than his conviction. He was important to them, in his way, and so they accommodated him when and if they could—or at least they allowed him to think as much. They let Hashim go, called off the tails. All was normal again until three days after Richard left the country, when he was no longer in a position to stick his nose into their business, and they went about the business they had always had in mind.

~

Flashing lights—alternating red and blue—drew them like fireflies to Elin's house. Three police cruisers were parked willy-nilly, blocking the driveway. The front door was wide open, light spilling out onto the front steps. A black SUV rode partway up the lawn. A crowd of neighboring Muslims had gathered, chattering among themselves, shuffling, nervous, tense. Their anger was palpable, ripping through the starless night.

Elin's four siblings crowded the doorway but parted slowly, grudgingly, for two men in dark suits. Held between them was Elin's father, Hashim. He looked pale and shaken in the illumination of the revolving lights, the lenses of his glasses made opaque.

"Papa!" Elin, breaking away from Bella, charged through the perimeter the police had set up. But as she rushed toward her father, being led down the front steps toward the waiting SUV, she was caught around the waist by one of the uniforms, swung up into the air, legs pumping futilely.

Hashim began to struggle. "Take your hands off my daughter!" he yelled.

For this outburst, as well as for the crime of being Muslim, one of his escorts struck him on the back of the head so hard his glasses flew off and his knees buckled.

"Papa!" Elin screamed. Restrained, she watched her father being roughly bundled into the back seat of the SUV. When he tried to resist, he was struck again, in the small of his back.

Bella was close enough to hear him groan, to hear one of the cops mutter, "Fuckin' raghead."

Elin must have heard, too, because she shouted, "He's Lebanese, not Pakistani, *bala'a il a'air*!"

The cop holding her swung her around. "What did you say, raghead?"

"Nothing," Bella said, running up to them. "It's her father; she's upset. Leave her alone."

"And who are you?"

"Her sister."

The cop looked skeptical. "Funny, you don't look—"

"What's going on?" Bella interrupted. "Why are you taking him?"

"Matter of national security." He leered at her. "Know what that means, girlie? The raghead's a terrorist—that's what."

"What?" Elin cried. "That's insane. You have the wrong man."

"Right." He jerked his chin at Bella. "Now clear out."

"Okay, he's in," the leading uniform shouted. "Let's roll."

The cop holding Elin set her down. Before he let go, he said to Bella, "Keep her under control. I don't wanna have to come back—hear me?"

Bella grabbed Elin's hand the instant he let her go, drew her away. Tears were streaming down Elin's face. "Papa! Papa!" she cried, as, one by one, military-style, the three cruisers backed out, turned, and, in the wake of the SUV, drove away in single file, lights revolving. The stunned crowd seemed to come alive, pouring into the street.

Elin's eldest brother, Gabriel, threw a bottle after the cruisers. "You hate us, we will hate you," he shouted. "You wrong us, we will make you pay." Then others in the crowd joined in, shouting and gesticulating wildly. An aggrieved ululation rose up, sweeping through the neighborhood like a whirlwind in the desert.

Caught up in the shocked anger, Bella, weeping herself now, hurled the sack of pistachios into the hail of bottles. The jute split open, pale shells spilling across the glittering, starry street, joining the helpless protest. Holding on to Elin with the tenderness Elin once held her, she wished she were a jinni. She wished she could do more.

Moments later, Lely arrived, having driven like a maniac from the hospital the moment she had gotten the hysterical call from one of her sons. Opening her arms wide, she consoled her children, Bella included. Once inside, she got on her cell phone, desperately trying to find out what had happened to her husband and why. Bella could hear the stone wall rising with each frustrating call Lely made. At length Lely consulted Google, started dialing the best local lawyers. She left messages with their services, having little faith that any would get back to her.

"Of course they won't call you back!" Gabriel cried. "We're Muslim. Papa is right. What are we doing here? We don't belong here—they don't want us."

"Calm down, Gabriel," Lely said, sitting in the center of their kitchen, her children clustered around. "Being a hothead won't get us anywhere."

"It's the *only* thing that will get us anywhere!"

In an almost lazy gesture, Lely reached out, slapped him hard across the face. "I don't ever want to hear you talk like that again. Violence is against the teachings of Allah. Here, in this house, we respect every aspect of Allah's holy teachings."

Gabriel dared not touch the hot spot on his cheek. "Violence against infidels is part of Allah's teachings, Umm."

Lely stood, and her children took a step back almost in concert, leaving Bella nearest her. She gave her eldest son a hard look. "Who have you been listening to, Gabriel? Those boys hanging around Ali's All-Night? Haven't I told you—" She stopped abruptly, suddenly aware of Bella's presence. Moving closer to her, she put her arm around Bella. "How can you even think of talking this way, Gabriel? Go up to your room."

"But, Umm—"

"At once!"

Gritting his teeth, Gabriel turned on his heel, stomped away. They could hear him muttering to himself as he went up the stairs. Lely returned to her cell phone, and this time the call seemed to bear fruit. She spoke in Arabic, so Bella could judge only by the tone of Lely's voice and the subtle changes in her expression. By the time she ended the conversation, she seemed slightly less tense and worried. Bella felt that perhaps she had found a way out of their dilemma and felt a surge of relief. She loved this family. She didn't know what she would do if anything happened to them.

For the next half hour Lely reassured her progeny that everything would be all right, that their father's arrest was a simple mistake, a case of mistaken identity. That he could be home in a day or so.

At length, they all trooped upstairs. Bella could feel the edge of terror in each of the siblings. She wanted to put her arms around them and, one by one, reassure them as Lely had, but of course she did nothing. She slept in Elin's bed, lying curled beside her while Elin read from the Qur'an. The language surrounded her like beautiful rain, warm and deep, filled with graceful filigrees, embroidered arabesques.

Bella was in the borderlands of sleep when something crashed through the window, shattering glass, slammed into the wall over their heads. Bella grabbed Elin, pulled her prone as two more shots thundered through the room, covering them with glittering glass shards, islands of wallboard, lozenges of painted wall.

Screaming. Running feet. Bella, trembling, holding on to Elin for dear life. Tremors running through Elin. A ringing in their ears. No sirens, no flashing lights, no cops. Just a dreadful, hollow silence. Out of which Lely's voice, rising, calling her children to her. That resonant voice, made wondrous, even divine, by disaster.

TWENTY

"I won't wear a wig made of human hair," Laurel said flatly. "I'll only have nightmares about who the hair was taken from."

Gael grunted. "Then you won't wear one at all." He waved a hand. "Anyway, they all look fake after a while, even the best ones." He ushered her into another of his residence's many bathrooms. "Fine for the movies, but in real life, uh-uh." A window overlooked a vertiginous view of high-rises to the east, pigeons perched on ledges, and startlingly, a peregrine falcon in its nest, head swiveling this way and that.

"My roots are starting to show."

"I noticed," Gael said, lining up a number of small dark-brown glass bottles. "Not a problem. None at all."

For the first time, Laurel recognized a strange lilt to Gael's accent. She'd never been calm enough in his presence before to even think about it, but now she could hear it clearly. Maybe it had to do with his German mother. When she asked him, just before he put her head in the sink to take the red dye, he said, "My father met her in Berlin. He was there for six months supervising the building of the TV and UHF Tower. My father designed a ton of the new buildings in Mexico City, Berlin, Dubai, Chicago, and here in New York, this one and some downtown along the High Line." His strong fingers ran through her hair, working the dye in with a professional thoroughness. "My father is an architect of the old-school, you could say. He designs for the vertical.

I, having learned everything I could from him, am an architect of the horizontal—a postarchitectural graduate, you might say. I dreamt up a network of ace Germans, Russians, Chinese, Israelis, and—don't tell anyone this—Iranians, young women in Switzerland. Geneva, to be exact—working at CERN."

"Physicists?" Laurel said through the water pouring down. "What do you need with them?"

"The unique structure of the network, everyone connected by ones and zeros, the ultimate in secure compartmentalization. The Iranians took my idea, built the bones of the network; the Israelis refined it; the Chinese made it impregnable."

Wrapping her hair in a thick towel, he raised her head out of the sink, sat her down on the closed toilet lid, opposite a large mirror. "I consult with the top six or seven private security firms. I provide them with, well, whatever it is they need."

"Like fake IDs," she said. "Or private transportation."

He nodded. "Like the hair dye I've used on you. But whatever it is, you can bet it's arcane and proprietary. In short, I've elevated the shadow world into a high art. I traffic in fearful asymmetry, to update William Blake."

She laughed. "You're updating everything."

"Out of self-defense. If I don't, I'm going to get run over by an innovator who's younger, faster, stronger."

Rubbing the towel for the last time over her hair, he swept it away and, like a prestidigitator in the spotlight, revealed his newest illusion.

"Wow!" Laurel said.

Gael grinned at her reflection. "Wow is right."

~

There was a kind of exhaustion that came from imminent death sitting on your shoulder like a vulture waiting to pick at your bones. When the rot set in, Jimmy Self thought as he made his slow way back across town during Manhattan's long red afternoon, it took all your energy just to put one foot in front of the other. He meant to go back to the office, but he was too tired. Halfway home he gave up walking and hailed a taxi, his splurge of the day.

Dumped in front of his beaten-down tenement, he unlocked the front door and slogged up the three flights of stairs that had lately seemed like thirty, reminding him of his ascent up the Statue of Liberty when he was a kid, when his whole life was ahead of him and he'd been too stupid to realize it.

His apartment smelled of Lionel, his cat who had died two weeks ago. He knew he should air out the rooms, but Lionel's smell was all that was left of him. Hard to say goodbye these days. The cat had been his companion for four years. It had been a present from Dey—a kind of joke, he had latterly realized: one ratcatcher joining another.

Collapsing into his easy chair, cracked and duct taped, he pressed the remote, set the fifty-five-inch flat-screen to Netflix. Poured himself three fingers of Jim Beam while scrolling through potential candidates, the only multitasking he was up to these days. Sipped his whiskey, settled on *No Country for Old Men*, which made him laugh and cry at the same time. Anton Chigurh's toilet-bowl haircut, always good for a laugh, but the looming end of the line for Ed Tom Bell was pure anguish. The question Jimmy Self always asked himself was this: Was Ed Tom Bell's refusal to stand up to Chigurh fear or pragmatism? After all, if you know you can't win, why jeopardize your life? Frankly, Jimmy Self thought as he mouthed the dialogue along with the actors, in his current condition he wouldn't want to go up against Chigurh. Fuck him. Let him trigger his captive bolt pistol on someone else's forehead.

And what, he thought now, if his own Anton Chigurh was Byron Dey? Should he have faced up to him? Should he have taken the assignment to run Helene Messer to ground? Part of him had always been pleased that she had robbed the robber. The irony wasn't lost on him, though Dey had never wanted any part of irony. Wasn't in his bloodthirsty DNA. And yet, Jimmy Self thought, I took his money, willingly, greedily, without a thought as to what it meant.

Setting his glass of Jim Beam aside, he opened the manila folder on his lap, slid out the photo of Helene Messer that Goodwood had printed out for him from his digital files. Four long years he had looked for this girl, four long years of failure, of obsession while his business cracked, fractured, and fell to ruins around him. He hadn't cared. And now that he'd found her, what? Fly to Crete? Confront her? Get Dey's pound of flesh off her? Even if he did, who would he give the money to? Dey's heirs were either dead or in jail. Their successors were the Chinese, Russians, Vietnamese, whose history of violence and brutality Jimmy Self wanted nothing to do with.

While Chigurh was forcing his victims to flip a coin in order to stay alive, Jimmy Self stared at the photo of Helene Messer, not a girl anymore, but young, so very young. He fell asleep in that position, in that framc of mind, and had a similar dream to the one Ed Tom Bell related to his wife: Jimmy Self was in Chinatown with his father, who went ahead to hold a table for them. Then all the power failed, plunging Jimmy Self into absolute darkness.

~

The next morning, Jimmy Self, stirring in his chair, slowly revived. *No Country for Old Men* was long gone, and so was his dream of darkness, death. Nevertheless, he had the impression that his father was waiting for him somewhere ahead.

He rose with a groan and shambled into the kitchenette, but he was all out of coffee, and there was nothing in the refrigerator but a smell, as of a body decomposing. In the bathroom, he splashed cold water on his face, ran a comb through his thinning hair. He avoided looking at himself in the mirror. He was already frightened enough.

Downstairs, the gray morning struck him a blow that almost brought him to his cranky knees. Fumbling on a pair of sunglasses, he made his way the three blocks to his local Starbucks, where he ordered his usual Venti. When the salesperson asked him what brew, he ordered the Reserve Sumatra Longberry. He might be dying, but he hadn't lost his taste for good coffee.

While waiting for the coffee to be made in the Clover, he watched the girls come and go, admiring their legs and butts in the vague sort of way museum goers looked at sculpture they liked but didn't quite understand. He took his Venti and sat at the counter that overlooked the street. The very early crowd had gone, leaving behind the detritus of low tide.

Taking possession of a leftover copy of today's paper, he thumbed through it idly while the aromatic coffee stimulated his taste buds and his mind. His brain, sadly, was beyond help even from the Longberry.

The pages were filled with a double homicide in Brooklyn, a major fender bender on the Cross Bronx Expressway, the indictment of a local pol paying hush money to keep photos of him and a young man out of the press, another mosque burning in Michigan. Dearborn, was it? And speaking of Dearborn, a hit-and-run death, which would never be picked up in a New York paper except for the fact that the victim was Richard Mathis, renowned archaeologist, lecturer, and professor. Jimmy Self's heart skipped a beat, and for a moment, he was overcome by dizziness. When his vision cleared, he saw the photo of Mathis, and sure enough, it was one of the series that had been taken some days ago on Crete, standing side by side with Angela Chase, better known to Jimmy Self as Helene Messer. The paper had zoomed in on Mathis's face, but Jimmy Self could see just a bit of Helene's shoulder at the right-hand margin of the shot.

Mathis had left Crete, returned home, and was struck dead by a hit-and-run? He smelled a three-day-old mackerel. Slamming the top on his Venti, Jimmy Self exited the Starbucks, newspaper under his arm. Twenty minutes later, having delivered a pair of tuna sandwiches and a container of orange juice to Stinking Man down in the lobby, he was settling in behind his desk. He switched on his computer.

While he waited for the old machine to awaken, he gulped his Longberry and made some calls to very long lost friends, who nevertheless owed him big-time for a troublesome this and a let's-not-get-into-it that. Troublesome for them, not him. He was the one who had dragged their tits out of the fire. Now it was payback time.

While he waited for the info he'd requested to arrive via his cell, he thought again about Helene Messer. If Mathis had returned to the States, where was she? Should she stay, or should she go? His mind now in gear, he considered: if he were her, knowing that her photo was being plastered all over the newspapers and undoubtedly the internet, he'd get the hell out of Dodge on the first plane. But where would she go? That was the billion-dollar question.

Boot up complete, he sent out the first tentacle. Dearborn, Michigan, it turned out, had a large Muslim population, which had come under close scrutiny over the last nine months—imams questioned, suspected terrorists pulled in, mosques burned, blah, blah, yadda, yadda, yadda. Jimmy Self had no interest in Islamics of any sort. He didn't know any, didn't want to know any. He didn't get what they were about; he'd had a hard enough time figuring out what made the Italian Catholics tick.

The one story from Dearborn that held any interest for him was the description, brief though it was, of Mathis's death. It seemed he had been hit outside his home by an SUV with blacked-out windows going at an insane speed in a residential area. That was it. Only one witness, a pensioner who lived across the street. Looking out his window into the eternal gloaming of the alley, Jimmy Self, detective through and through, found the lack of other details curious in and of itself. He kept going but could find no investigation, no follow-up in any of the local papers. Also curious. He was hopeful the information he had asked for from those people who remained in power due to his burying their dirt would provide some answers.

Backing out of Dearborn, he turned his attention to the daily sites to which he subscribed, database updates on missing persons, surveillance tapes of airport departures and arrivals. After an hour, having finished off his Venti, he opened a drawer, popped a couple of stims. He couldn't afford to nod off. Eighty minutes later he stopped the streaming tape on the face of Helene Messer, entering the United States at JFK airport.

For long moments, Jimmy Self stared at that photo, a snapshot of a life in motion. Helene Messer was back in New York a day after her inamorato had been killed in a hit-and-run in Dearborn, Michigan. *Why would she risk coming back to the States?* Jimmy Self asked himself. But he already knew the answer. Once he had been a first-rate detective, once he was possessed of impeccable instincts. Now that same man, so long buried in the muck and mire of a life unlived, did not want the end of his life to be as meaningless as what had gone before. His instincts, now hauled out of mothballs by the scent of Helene Messer, told him that she had come to find out how and why Richard Mathis had died. After all, if he were in her shoes, he'd want to know. Hell, he'd *need* to know.

So. He knew where she was going.

TWENTY-ONE

Hashim was returned home in one of three official-looking cars. Thirty-six hours had passed since he had been taken forcibly from his home. He was let out of the middle vehicle without a word of explanation, let alone an apology. No one seemed in the mood for an apology. They turned him out as they would a street mongrel suffering from mange. It was clear he disgusted them.

The household rightly rejoiced. Hashim was overjoyed to see his family again, but he spoke frankly to Lely in the bathroom where she had guided him and was now ministering to his cuts, scrapes, and bruises.

"Where is that girl who has been living here?" he asked of Lely. "You already burdened me with one daughter. What need have I for another?"

Clucking her tongue, Lely crossed to the door, closed it to give them some privacy. "Husband, you make me ashamed—"

"A proper response, I assure you. Her people dragged me out of my home." He pointed to his forehead. "This is from them, a reminder of who they are and what we are to them. I don't know what's happening in this country; thanks to the actions of a tiny minority of Islamic fanatics, we good citizens—loyal Americans—are all seen as criminals and traitors."

"Well, it was Bella's father—one of those hounds—who was instrumental in freeing you."

Hashim stared at her, blinking slowly. "How on earth did he do that?"

Lely threw up her hands. "How should I know, Hashim? I made a deal with him."

"You made a deal?" Hashim stared at her wide-eyed. "With Bella's father?"

She nodded. "He needed my help. He was willing to pay me. I asked for your release instead."

"You begged him, you mean. Like a rank servant." He shook his head, rising to his feet. "Lely, my wife, you have made a terrible mistake. You have made a deal with the devil himself."

And perhaps she had. The next day, the same three black SUVs with blacked-out windows arrived outside the family's house. This time it was Lely who was removed while the family and the neighbors watched, helpless.

When Elin called her to tell her, Bella felt as if the rage inside her would burst through the walls of her chest. Umm being taken away. What had she ever done to deserve this kind of treatment? Lely was an Islamic; Islamics were now enemies of the state. Bella had been warned. She had been told not to be here, to distance herself from the Shehadis. She hadn't, and now this.

~

A decade before that night, Richard had flown back to the States from his third stint in Sinai, not directly to Dearborn but to Washington, DC. There, he had met first with a high-ranking executive at the State Department who, unlike his brethren toiling away in the Harry S. Truman Building, worked out of an anonymous office in the Eisenhower Executive Office Building across the street from the West Wing of the White House. He was a thoroughly unprepossessing human being with a steel-gray buzz cut; deep-set eyes, pouched and wounded looking; a nose that had clearly been broken more than once. Perhaps this man didn't work for State at all but rather the DOD, the Pentagon, the CIA. These were some of Richard's guesses, though he never did find out the executive's official affiliation. He introduced himself as Perry White, which Richard, conversant with *Superman* comics, took to be a joke. Except that Perry White did not strike him as one to make jokes. After five minutes with him, he was convinced that when Perry White had been born, the doctor had slapped all sense of humor out of him.

Richard had been romanced for sixteen months. It was Janet Margolies, his old comparative religions professor from Georgetown, who had done the romancing. She, heavy of beam and jaw, was an unlikely suitor, which, in retrospect, made her the perfect recruiter. She judged Richard an excellent candidate. His work took him to all the right places; he was so well respected in his field as to be above suspicion. He also, Perry White said in his bland midwestern accent as he paged through what could only be a government dossier on Richard, had had conversations with extremist elements in Sinai on three separate occasions.

Perry White, looking up from the dossier that Richard had no doubt contained every detail of his life, said, "That terrorist act in Sinai a day after 9/11 must've unnerved you."

Richard sat nervously, hands in his lap. When he became aware of Perry White staring at his fidgeting fingers, he clasped his hands together.

Perry White read through several more pages of the dossier, reduced to ones and zeros, then processed for his reading pleasure. The silence was unnerving, as, Richard realized later, it was meant to be. Pale-gray eyes flicked up. "That moment changed you. That's what you told Ms. Margolies in your last interview with her. You became radicalized, is what you told her. What were your exact words? 'As I was—'"

"Baptized in Ben's blood," Richard said, taking back control of his own words, wanting—needing—to have some stake in what he now perceived to be an interrogation.

"What precisely did you mean by *radicalized*?"

"Before . . . before Ben's murder I'd had no real stake in the war on terror. Afterward . . ." He seemed not to want to go on.

"Survivor's remorse?"

Richard cleared his throat. "What?"

Perry White contemplated him for a moment, turned over a page in the dossier. "Did you feel survivor's remorse?"

"I wished I had been the one to kill the terrorist."

Perry White nodded, his expression blank as a prison facade. "Are you aligned in any way with the extremists you met with on—" And here he named the three dates of the meetings.

The question was so absurd that Richard could not help but laugh, even though part of him was certain that Perry White found nothing funny in the question. He was correct.

"Why did you meet with them?" Perry White asked, following his
"Of course not."

"To understand them."

"Why would you want to understand them?"

"So that the next time I met them, I would know how to act and react."

After another forty minutes of questioning, which to Richard seemed all sound and fury signifying nothing, he was escorted down to a waiting car, which sped him through DC, across the Potomac, and into Virginia.

Forty-eight hours after being the guest of persons unknown who questioned him incessantly somewhere in the bowels of Langley, asking the same questions in slightly different forms over and over, he was deemed "sanitized," in the language of these people in the clandestine services.

Perry White came to see him off. The following five weeks were spent in a vast complex of anonymous-looking buildings set among the rolling hills of Virginia's horse country. At the Farm, as it was known colloquially, he was taught the fundamentals of field tradecraft. He learned signals, dead drops, code words—decidedly low-tech stuff he thought long out-of-date in the high-tech world of cyberwarfare and ubiquitous NSA surveillance.

"Not in your world. Not in the countries you work in. Not with the people you're rubbing shoulders with," his bruising instructor said, in answer to his query. "Besides, with all the firewall breaches, we're safer being neo-Luddites. No electronic data trail whatsoever."

Perry White was in the Navigator that transported him to Dulles International Airport. "Easier to control surveillance at Reagan," he said in a vaguely accusatory manner, as if it was Richard's fault they were going to Dulles. "But, hell in a freezer, we can cover anyone, anywhere."

Even in Sinai? Richard wondered, realizing with a minor shock that he was already thinking like one of "us." *That didn't take long*, he thought with a whole fistful of mixed emotions. *How easy it is to have one's view of the world changed.*

He rested for a while—or tried to. Sitting close to Perry White made his skin itch. He preferred to think of his control as his private nanny. It gave him a sense of freedom, however illusory. "How'd I do?"

"To specs," Perry White said. "Until this moment."

The rebuke shut Richard up for the rest of the journey. As the staircase of descending planes came into view, Perry White turned to him. "What we do, you and I, is a form of religion. This is something they don't tell you on the Farm. They teach tactics there. I'm all about strategy. Why? Because the enemy is all about strategy."

"Fight fire with fire," Richard said.

Perry White was unblinking. Also unnerving. "The enemy needs to be fought strategically. This is how you must think."

"I get it," Richard said, because slowly but surely that way of thinking was becoming second nature to him.

"No," Perry White said. "You don't." He shifted from one narrow midwestern buttock to another. "We have entered the Age of Destruction," he said. "An era where warfare has again come to the fore. Mankind's most primitive nature is now in play. The extremists on both ends of the spectrum are gaining ground with every day that passes. Every action spawns a reaction: it's a fact of life, of nature. Contempt breeds contempt. Hate breeds hate. Death breeds death. The unknowing, as I'm inclined to think of chaos, runs rampant."

He ran fingers through the bristles on his scalp and sighed. "That's why I got into this game—when it was a game—to do some good." He shook his head. "But it doesn't work like that. I feel like a salmon trying to swim upstream."

"It must be exhausting," Richard offered.

"Exhausting, yes. I expected that; how could it be otherwise? I had a friend who said to me, 'What are you doing? Beware working for the feds. They run around the world like headless chickens.' All right, I accepted that. What I came up against is the impossibility of the task. The people who run this country have no strategy. They had none in Vietnam, so any intelligent person would expect them to have learned from that debacle. But no, they steadfastly refuse to learn from history. Bull-rushed into Afghanistan, ignoring the long, drawn-out Russian defeat there. As is their avowed tactic, they armed the insurgents, who then, as the Taliban, used those weapons against them. Went into Iraq with absolutely no idea of what would happen when they won. Chaos ensued, creating the perfect breeding ground for extremists where before there were none.

"And now Syria, the ultimate catastrophe. Against my advice, the administration shelled out half a billion dollars to train five Syrians. That dumb bastard who got drummed out of the company suggests we arm Syrian insurgents, just as if that tactic isn't a clusterfuck disaster that always comes back to bite us in the ass. And now Russia piles in, which is a whole other level of fuck-me-in-the-ass." He shook his head. "Administration says no, but what we have in Syria now is war by proxy. Age of Destruction, brother. Age of Destruction."

Perry White stared hard out the blacked-out window; the passing lights dimmed, as if about to be shut down permanently.

"My predecessor committed suicide. He couldn't take it," Perry White went on. "'They're like a dozen clowns piling out of a VW,' he'd say to me. Until he couldn't say anything more, not with the barrel of his pistol in his mouth."

"Then why do you continue doing this?" Richard asked.

"Why?" Perry White turned his head back to stare at Richard. "Because someone with brains has to. Because I can't let the clowns win. And because we're between Scylla and Charybdis. ISIS wants us to respond, wants us mired deeper and deeper in its caliphate. And if we back off—if we, God forbid, withdraw from the region entirely? Their caliphate grows and grows until it has encompassed Egypt, Iran, Saudi, and even Turkey. Then the sewer we're in will be too deep to climb out of." He grunted, as if suddenly becoming aware of what had just taken place. "As previously outlined, your job is to ID the elements overseas who are in contact with the radicalized sleeper agents right here in America so we can take 'em out. You in the hunt?"

"More than ever." Richard realized that he meant it. There was respect now where before there had been only a blank slate, a tabula rasa.

"And by the way," Perry White said, "don't worry about your wife."

A slight quiver in the pit of his stomach. "What d'you mean?"

"The vetting process, of course." Perry White tried a smile that did not quite fit. "We know what happened. We're leaving her alone."

At the terminal, while they remained in the SUV, still under federal sovereignty, Perry White handed him a packet of instructions. "You have two hours before your flight to Detroit. Lock yourself into a cubicle in the men's toilet. Read up on your first assignment. Memorize it. Then tear each sheet into tiny pieces and piss on them. Flush at least three times. No floaters to be left."

Richard nodded. As he opened the door to step out to the curb where the driver had lined up his luggage, Perry White said, "Good luck, Clark."

What do you know—he had a sense of humor after all.

TWENTY-TWO

Jimmy Self suspected Helene Messer wouldn't leave the city until she had undergone another physical transformation, just as he knew he couldn't look for her on any transportation manifests as Angela Chase. Angela Chase was dead and buried; he had no doubt of that. Clean slate, odometer regressed to zero. He also suspected that Helene Messer had had help in disappearing. She couldn't have managed it so neatly and completely on her own.

All of this informed him that he had some time, while she changed identities once again. His focus was on discovering how she would leave New York for Dearborn. The airports were a no-go. Even with new papers there were the CCTV cameras to think about. She might take a bus, but he didn't think so. The Port Authority Bus Terminal was a cesspool of junkies and streetwalkers. As such, it was crawling with cops; the less she saw of them, the better. Also, more security cameras than you could count. Rental cars required too much ID, left too definite a trail. What remained was the train.

Consulting Amtrak, he discovered the most direct route to Dearborn. The 49 Lake Shore Limited, departing Penn Station at 3:40 p.m., arrived in Chicago tomorrow at 9:45 a.m. After a couple hours' layover, the 352 Wolverine got them into Dearborn at 6:16 p.m. There were other options, but they all required two trains followed by a bus ride of several hours. The 49 Lake Shore Limited it was.

He had learned never to leave anything to chance. As such, even though he considered the bus a long shot, he roused Stinking Man, took him for lunch, bought him a cheap burner phone, shoved photos of Helene Messer and Angela Chase into his fist.

"She's gonna look different," he said. "But underneath the same."

"Different but the same," Stinking Man said. "Gotcha, Chief."

"Don't call me Chief."

Jimmy Self sent him over to Port Authority. It was a far from ideal solution, but at his end-of-days career, it was all he could scrape up. He tried not to think about what that meant for him as he headed to Penn Station. Stopping at a deli, he bought a pastrami on rye, a double order of sour pickles, and a pair of Cokes from Mexico in bottles. No high-fructose corn syrup in Mexico, only good old sugar. And about the glass bottles: people didn't realize that the Coke recipe had to be rejiggered to compensate for the aluminum cans and the thin plastic bottles.

Descending into the bowels of Penn Station, he bought a ticket all the way through to Dearborn. Then he settled in to wait for 3:15 p.m. or so, the time he expected her to show. If he was right. *I can't afford not to be right*, he thought as he sat himself on a wooden bench worn smooth by a hundred thousand pairs of buttocks. He pulled his trench coat closer around him.

Penn Station, at any hour of the day, was not a place to hang. Now, after the morning crush had flushed out its tsunami of humanity, the place was positively ghastly. Worse than the lobby of his office building. A seemingly endless line of automated ticket sellers, dead sentinels. The Acela waiting room dark and deserted, its small detail of redcaps reading the papers or chatting among themselves. These hollow echoes of the morning gave the sense of being in a dark place where time was the only accepted currency. The leftover stench of humans on the run added to the atmosphere of a close and stifling underworld. The denizens of the station were thin and humpbacked, fat and greasy, shapeless in their layers of filth. Shifty characters who no longer felt comfortable on the streets of Manhattan—and that was saying something. They were human rats, scuttling around, hugging shadows to avoid the smattering of bored cops staring threateningly at everyone in sight, just for a giggle. When they could, the rats cadged a Snickers or a PayDay from a newsstand, picked a pocket here or there. Once he saw a band of them working in concert, but that was rare. For the most part, these creatures were loners like Stinking Man: homeless, nameless, forgotten by a society that never had use for them in the first place. Every so often one of the bolder ones would eye Jimmy Self. He'd pull his lips back from his teeth and clack them together, and they'd cringe away. One time, though, an Artful Dodger, thinking himself cleverer than the rest of his ilk, approached him from behind. Catching the movement out of the corner of his eye even before the vile smell hit him, Jimmy half turned, right hand around the grips of his suddenly revealed .38. That was the last time any of them tried to come near him.

And so he sat, certain that Stinking Man wouldn't call him, as the minutes and hours ticked by. Why had he put any faith at all in Stinking Man? Was it simply out of necessity? Stinking Man did not carry the air of the professional homeless. Surely he had been someone once, someone with a name, a job, a home, perhaps a wife, maybe even kids. Someone who wasn't lost. What had happened? Who knew? Jimmy Self scarcely knew what had happened to him, to be cast up on this bleak and desolate shore. But there seemed little doubt that he felt some strange kinship with Stinking Man. It was why he kept him in food and juice. Looked after him. Jimmy Self suspected that in keeping Stinking Man alive, he was also keeping himself from slipping all the way down. Eating his police special.

Jimmy Self stretched. He'd been on plenty of stakeouts back in the day, but he was older now and sick. His feet hurt, his arches fallen further than a hooker; his back ached, forcing him to get up once every ten minutes or so and travel in a small circle like a rotating watering head, with about the same amount of consciousness.

At three o'clock he got himself some black coffee. To his refined coffee palate it tasted like battery acid, but it was full of caffeine, which, at this stage of the stakeout, was all that mattered. At three ten, he bought two candy bars and stuffed them in his maw. Sugar. More caffeine. If he drank another cup of coffee, his bladder would be full when he needed to move.

Three fifteen passed. He was standing in sight of the gate to the Lake Shore Limited. His cell buzzed. He checked the number and exhaled; it wasn't Stinking Man. At last the favors he had called in were bearing fruit. He read the attachments while keeping one eye out for Helene. The news was bad. In fact, very bad. Worse than he had suspected.

Pocketed his cell and looked up. Three twenty, three twenty-five. The gathering of strangers had begun: a suit steering a young woman in stilettos, her ripe thighs sprouting from a short skirt; a pair of clearly drunk businessmen, laughing like loons; a tattooed, Rasta-haired teenager carrying a guitar case, nascent career on his back; a mother, sleeping baby in her arms, trailed by her husband, awkwardly lugging their suitcases; an old woman with a cane, her back as erect as a soldier's. A sorority of girls, giggling over their night in the big city, passed him by, vanished down the narrow stairwell. Their bell-like laughter floated up like comic book sound-effect balloons. How girls that age loved and loathed themselves, Jimmy Self thought. Everything at the extreme of emotions.

Still no sign of her. He tried to murder the thought that he had been wrong. What if she had taken a bus, and Stinking Man had missed her? Had fallen asleep or been rousted by the cops? He had been an idiot to enlist Stinking Man. Or maybe he had misjudged the time it would take for her to be made over; she had already taken another train, one that left before he arrived. Or maybe she had had someone rent the car for her, and right about now she was hurtling down the New Jersey Turnpike, whatever highway she needed to take to get to Dearborn. But for any number of reasons—mostly that no one he knew would set out on such a long car trip after an overseas flight—that didn't make much sense.

The worst thing a detective could do was to undermine himself. Being assailed by doubts was just about the best way to lose his quarry—or, worse, not to find them at all. All this he knew, and yet he bit his nails, tearing off slivers, spitting them out like cracked sunflower seeds. His stomach roiled.

Three forty. Where the fuck was she?

His cell buzzed, and so did his heart rate. It was Stinking Man.

"She there?" Not taking his eyes off the track entrance a flight down, but ready to move if—

"No-show, Chief. Should I—"

"Go home. Get some sleep," Jimmy Self said. "And don't call me Chief."

Shitshitshit. The evil scent of being wrong started to come off him like BO. Dim the lights; the party's over.

And then, and then at three thirty-one . . . *Holy mother of Jesus*, he thought. *There is a God.*

A moth fluttering in the pit of Laurel's stomach gave birth to an entire host, a soft bomb, as she headed toward the stairs down to the track where the 49 Lake Shore Limited was waiting to take her to Chicago. Along with giving her a vinyl airline bag of food and drink, Gael had outfitted her in a long granny dress—oxblood with tiny yellow, blue, and white flowers and a collar of white lace enclosing her neck—Dr. Martens two-tone Nightosphere's Looking at You boots, a black knitted jacket that looked as if it had come from a thrift shop.

"Why are you dressing me this way?" she had asked Gael. "I look like a molting peacock."

"The more people gawk at your clothes, the less they'll pay attention to your face," he'd told her. A face that, when she had regarded herself in the mirror just before she'd left Gael, looked at least a decade older than her real age. Gael's expertise with theatrical makeup and prosthetics was legendary among the discreet group of his clients.

"Don't you think these buck teeth are a little over-the-top?" she had asked.

"Over-the-top is what we're shooting for," he'd told her.

Then there was her hair, which was now a lustrous deep red, the cut, sweeping down over one eye, entirely European. "I look like someone imitating a Parisian street waif," she'd cried.

"Bingo!" Gael had kissed her on each cheek, in the European style. "Go with God," he had said as if he were a priest.

Carrying the airline bag and a battered suitcase with brass snaps and hinges that had gone out of style in the fifties, she kept her vision focused on the stairs down to the track. "Walk at a normal pace," Gael had said. "Not too fast but not too slow either. And keep your eyes on your goal. Don't go looking around for trouble, the way they do in the films—it's a dead giveaway."

Which was precisely what she did. She passed Jimmy Self without registering his presence, but then the terrified part of her was on the lookout for reporters, paparazzi, stringers, bloggers. She had no eyes for a detective, and even if she had, she never would have recognized him as one.

Down in the depths the train sniffled and sighed as if shaking off a cold. Amid a cloud of like-minded passengers, she found her car, boarded the train, and looked for a seat. Though she would have had no trouble doing it herself, a heavyset man in a well-traveled trench coat helped place her suitcase on the chrome rack above her seat. He smiled when she thanked him. It was a kind smile, an easy expression that seemed to her guileless. He took a seat more or less on the opposite side of the aisle and was immediately lost to view behind the *New York Times* he unfolded like gull's wings.

With a lurch, the train began to roll out of the station. Laurel sat back, deep breathing her pulse back to a semblance of normal. She was home free now; the gauntlet had been successfully traversed. But even so her mouth was dry, her breathing more rapid than she would like.

Go to a happy place, she ordered herself. Which would it be? Orfeo's apartment? Crete? The pathetically short list caused a sinking feeling in her stomach.

Unbidden, her thoughts settled on her father. Like a ghost, her father haunted her, sliding through her memories, slippery as an eel. While her mother had still been with them, how many nights had Laurel sat at her window, willing him to turn the corner onto their street, falling asleep without ever catching sight of him? But more often than not, there he was, sitting at the kitchen table when she came down to breakfast in the morning. He'd look up from his paper, grinning like a Toon. "Hey-ya, Rabbit," he'd say.

"Hi, Dad."

Putting the paper aside. "How 'bout it?" Holding out his arms.

She'd skip around the table before burying her nose in the hollow of his shoulder as he squeezed her tight. "How's my Rabbit. How's my Rabbit," he'd say in her ear, his blue stubble scratching the side of her forehead.

Why are you always working? she'd wanted to ask him while inhaling the smell of him, forever after her paradigm of a man's scent.

"Sit down now, Laurel," her mother would say from her station at the stovetop. "Time to eat. You don't want to be late for school."

Her father was always late. Sometimes that was all he was; she never actually saw him come home. Once, she had taken her pillow and curled up on the stairs to make sure she wouldn't miss him, only to wake up in her own bed, the morning light streaming in through her window. Unsurprising, then, that she was reluctant to let go of him, until he'd say in his best imitation of a movie cowboy, "Git along, lil Rabbit. Eat the grub ya momma fixed fer ya."

Laurel's mother would turn from the stovetop, spatula in hand. "Eddie, why d'you insist on talking to her like that?"

"Because she likes it." Eddie would grin. "Dontcha, Rabbit?"

She woke with a start, unsure for a moment where she was or what was happening. The train car rocked gently back and forth; the muffled clickety-clack of the rolling wheels brought her the information she needed. She was on the 49 Lake Shore Limited to Chicago, where she'd change for the train to Dearborn. She glanced across the aisle. The heavyset man who had helped her was still behind his gull wings of print. She sighed, turned back to stare out the window at the passage of nighttime buildings, local stations, black clumps of those trees hardy enough to subsist on a steady diet of diesel particulates. The stations were dark and deserted, but here and there like pockmarks, the buildings' windows were lit by the blue light of TVs or computers. Night owls or insomniacs hard at work passing the endless hours before sunlight flooded in again.

These lonely people made her think of Richard's dead wife, Maggie. What kind of a marriage could he have had with her? She had to assume that they had been in love when they had married. What had happened between them to sour that love, to turn it to indifference—no, more than indifference. A kind of silent warfare. Was that what had finally led Maggie to kill herself? She recalled her talk with Richard on the boat about how illusions kept us sane, and his response: *For others, it's as if they never existed at all.*

Richard, who was so closed off to Bella and, she surmised, to Maggie. And yet he hadn't been hard to read, not for her, at least. No, she decided, whatever the problem between them, it wasn't all Richard's doing. He wasn't into destruction; of that she was certain. Her brief time with him on the boat, the experience they'd had there, had revealed more of who he really was than the entire six previous weeks. She saw him as he really was and, as a daughter loves her father, loved him all the more for what his actions revealed.

But then Bella had gone missing, her mother had committed suicide, and forty-eight hours later Richard had been killed in a hit-and-run. In scanning the news on the new iPhone Gael had gifted her with, she'd found nothing to indicate Bella had been found or that the authorities had made any progress at all in finding her. Laurel didn't have to have seen a bunch of TV shows to know that the first twenty-four hours following an abduction were the most critical. After that, the chances of the abductee being found alive plummeted like a lemming off a cliff. Had the incident even been classified as an abduction? The Dearborn press was silent on that point as well. And yet she clung to her dream, clung to the belief that Bella was still alive. The most likely explanation, then, for Bella's disappearance was that she had run away from an awful homelife. She wouldn't be the first, and she surely wouldn't be the last.

Laurel fell back into a restless sleep, into a shadowland of her own design. She was heading down a winding road, like Dorothy in Oz. Rising at intervals on either side of the road were totems of her mother, her father, Orfeo, Richard, Dey—dead, and yet somehow, in the peculiar symbology of dreams, alive again—and at the far end, toward which she was heading, Bella. Not a totem, a flesh-and-blood person. As was the nature of dreams, she knew it was Bella, though it looked nothing like the real Bella she'd seen on Richard's cell phone. And as darkness began to gather at her back, she broke into a run, flying at Bella, who, no matter how fast Laurel sprinted, never seemed to come any closer.

She woke to the smell of a pastrami sandwich and sour pickles.

"Are you all right?"

She turned to see the heavyset man looking at her. His tray table was down, and he had a pastrami sandwich and several pickles set out on deli paper.

"Your hands were twitching."

"What?"

"Just before you woke up," the heavyset man said. "Your hands were twitching."

"I'm a restless sleeper."

"Uh-huh." He took a bite of his sandwich, half of which he held in his left hand.

"I haven't smelled pastrami or sour pickles in a long time," she said.

"Here." He lifted the other half of his sandwich in its paper.

"Thanks, but I couldn't."

He frowned. "Vegan?"

She laughed. "No, just—"

"Then come on." Reaching across the aisle, he held it out, smiling. "I hate eating alone."

She ducked her head, returned his smile. "Thanks." She took the sandwich, which felt as heavy as an Etruscan idol. "I appreciate it."

"Don't I know it. The food on this train sucks."

"You ride it a lot?"

"Shuttle back and forth three times a week, believe it or not. In that same vein, I'm a Fuller Brush salesman."

"Really?" Laurel was salivating even before she took the first taste. But as she ran her tongue around the prosthetic giving her a false overbite, she wondered whether chewing would dislodge it. "I thought they were extinct."

He laughed. "Everyone does." He chomped on a pickle. "But look at me: one foot's already in the tar pits."

She laughed too.

"My name's Jimmy," he said. "I'd shake hands, but, you know, the grease."

"S'okay. I'm Jennifer. Jenn."

"Right, Jennifer-Jenn. Take a bite of your pastrami on rye. You look famished."

She laughed again. "You have a good sense of humor for a salesman."

His eyebrows lifted. "I don't know whether to be pleased or pissed."

"Oh, pleased, I hope."

He nodded. "Pleased it is, then. Can't say no to a pretty girl." He frowned. "Or is that sexual harassment or something? I can never tell these days."

Laurel giggled. "I'll let it go this time."

"Much obliged, ma'am," he said in a mock cowboy accent that made her stomach lurch, the little girl in her crying out silently.

She lapsed into silence, and Jimmy followed her lead. She chewed slowly and carefully, savoring the flavors, but all the while she could not dislodge the image of Bella—a lost little girl, just like she herself had been—from her mind. There'd been no one to help *her* when she'd been Bella's age, unless you counted Orfeo, and she didn't. Couldn't forget. Couldn't forgive. Who did Bella have? Both her father and mother dead. Who would stand for Bella Mathis?

She declined Jimmy's offer of a pickle. "You don't know what you're missing," he said genially. They finished their food. Laurel thought that she had never had anything as good in her life.

Within the hour, they pulled into Chicago's Union Station, where she was to change to the Dearborn train. Jimmy helped her down with her suitcase.

"Well, I'm off to Dearborn," he said cheerfully. "Is this you here?"

"No, I'm going to Dearborn myself."

"Look at that," he said. "What are the odds." And laughed.

Together, they stepped out onto the platform with the other transferring passengers. They spent the next few hours at a restaurant that had passable food. A half hour later, she couldn't have told you what she'd eaten. The 352 Wolverine to Dearborn was late, not due to arrive for another six minutes. The passengers milled around, sat on benches or on their hard-shelled suitcases. Somewhere music was playing, possibly from a radio, John Coltrane, playing "Naima," adding to a sense of quiet desolation at this lunch hour when everyone should have been brown-bagging at their desk or sitting down at a restaurant, but some instead were traveling across the country, heading home or to a new place to play music, find a job, settle down. The long cross-country journey was very much in force.

A disturbance caused heads to turn: a high-pitched scream, followed by the sound of running feet as a twiggy teenager, gripping a woman's snatched handbag as a receiver clutches a football, burst through the ragged ranks of people who were half-asleep and too dazed to react. But Jimmy did. He whirled in the kid's direction and, at the last possible instant, stiff-armed him. The kid slammed to the platform, and Jimmy trod on his belly, knocking all the wind out of him. As delicately as a surgeon reaching into a newly opened cavity, he relieved the kid of the purse and handed it back to the winded woman, who thanked him profusely.

Applause all around as the passengers finally realized what had happened. At that moment, the train to Dearborn pulled into the station, and everyone gathered their belongings. No one paid any attention to either the woman or the kid, flat on his back. The show was over; time to get a move on.

The train rolled to a stop, the doors sighed open, and the passengers climbed aboard. Jimmy took a step toward the open door before he realized Helene Messer hadn't moved, hadn't even picked up her suitcase. He bent, did it for her, said, "Come on. You don't want to miss your train."

Laurel snatched her suitcase out of his hand. "I think I do," she said.

He regarded her quizzically, then followed the direction of her gaze. As he'd spun to stop the young thief, the right flap of his trench coat had caught on the butt of his holstered .38.

"Ah," he said.

Laurel moved away, but with lightning speed he grabbed her wrist, drew her back to him. "We're going to Dearborn together."

"You're not a Fuller Brush salesman."

"That would be self-evident."

"Who are you?" Starting to shake. What would Richard do in this situation?

Jimmy Self sighed. "Unlike you, Helene, I didn't lie about my name."

She started; dear God, her worst nightmare had come to life. She stood, paralyzed, staring at him.

The whistle blew, and he pulled her onto the train. He was not only quicker than he looked—he was stronger. "My name is Jimmy. Jimmy Self." The doors closed behind them. "Whoever you used did a bang-up job." They remained alone in the entrance well as the train rolled, began to pick up speed. "But I know pretty much all the tricks of the trade." He laughed. "How'd you like chewing with that thing in your mouth?" Abashed, Laurel removed the prosthesis. "That's better." He nodded. They braced themselves in a wide-legged stance. "Four years ago Byron Dey hired me to find you."

"Oh, God."

"And now, finally, I have."

Her worst nightmare made real. Laurel closed her eyes, her lower lip trembling. *Here it is*, she thought. *The end come so soon.*

Then she vomited all over Jimmy Self's shoes.

TWENTY-THREE

Richard, returning from overseas, used his layover in New York to buy Maggie a diamond necklace from Tiffany's. Today was two days from her due date. Armed with the long pale-blue box with its blue satin ribbon, he boarded his flight and, four hours later, was pulling up outside his house. Twilight had settled over the city. The streetlights shone, small beacons among the indigo. Far away to the west thunder rumbled, sounding like a giant clearing his throat.

As he was lifting his bags out of the back seat, he spied Elin heading his way. It was two years to the day before 9/11. Elin was eleven years old, and she looked very pretty in her jeans, long-sleeve shirt, and neat hijab. She was carrying a rectangular Pyrex dish covered with aluminum foil.

"Hi, Dr. Mathis!" she called cheerfully.

"Hello, Elin." He swung his bags onto the sidewalk. "How are you?"

"Very well, thank you." Always so polite, always smiling, always friendly, just like the rest of her family.

"How are the boys?"

"Growing."

"Aren't we all?" he said with a grimace. "Except I'm growing older."

She laughed, accompanied him up the steps to the front door. He noticed the lawn needed weeding. "What have you got there?" he asked, happy to set his bag down at home base. He'd been away a long time. He had the dust of history under his fingernails and in every crevice of his body. It would take three or four good scrubbings to come fully clean.

Balancing the dish on one spread-fingered hand, Elin peeled back a corner of the foil. "Baklava, Dr. Mathis. Umm made it especially for Mrs. Mathis."

"Wasn't that thoughtful of her," Richard said. "Please thank her for both of us." He took possession of the baklava and eyed her. "And you know, Elin, you're always welcome in this house."

Elin's cheeks went pink. "Thank you, Dr. Mathis."

"I wish you'd call me Richard."

"Oh, no. I don't think Umm would like that."

He bent over and, with a conspiratorial wink, said, "It'll be our little secret then." He smiled, saw that Elin was eyeing the baklava. "Go on. Take a piece." He winked again. "If Maggie asks, I'll tell her I couldn't resist a square on my way in."

Elin reached out—clearly wanting a piece, it seemed to him—but then something changed her mind, and her hand retreated. "No," she said. "It's yours, not mine." Then without another word, she whirled. "Wish Mrs. Mathis an easy birth from me, from the whole family."

"I will. Bye."

"Bye." She went down the steps, turned, and headed home.

Richard slipped his key into the lock. He had seen Maggie's car outside, so he knew she was home. Stowing his luggage in the hallway, he called out as he went through the ground floor. He expected her to be in the kitchen, sipping a cup of her favorite chamomile tea, but it was deserted. All the ground floor rooms stood silent and empty.

Setting the baklava on the kitchen counter, he went back into the hallway, called her name again as he climbed the stairs to the second floor, clutching the Tiffany box. Upon reaching the landing, he heard a muffled rhythmic sound and wondered if one of his neighbors were using an air compressor.

In the bedroom, the sound was louder, sharper, and he grew alarmed.

"Maggie?"

He found her in the bathroom, sitting on the porcelain lip of the tub. She was hitting her head against the wall.

He rushed to her. "My God!" Pulled her into his arms. "What are you doing?"

"I can't take it!" she cried, so thoroughly distraught she didn't in any way acknowledge his presence. "Twins, Richard. It's too much!" The last word was a kind of cry that pierced to the core of him. She looked up at him, her eyes enlarged by tears.

"Maggie, this was the greatest news! I thought you agreed."

She gave him a look so venomous he recoiled.

"You didn't?"

Maggie shook her head; bitter tears flung from her eyes. "Richard, you bastard, you talked me into this. I didn't want to have one child, let alone two!"

"But that's a good thing—a great thing." Stroking her damp, matted hair. "I don't understand."

"Of course you don't understand." She was near hysteria now. "You aren't listening to me—you never have. Why? Are you deaf when it comes to me? I didn't want one—now I'm going to have two!"

Richard smiled encouragingly. She was right. Caught up in the excitement of imminent immortality, he hadn't heard her, and now he reacted to her hysteria as if she were a child afraid of the dark. "It's going to be all right, Maggie. Better than all right—it's going to be fantastic! A whole new chapter of your life is about to unfold."

He kept stroking her hair, keeping it away from the egg-shaped bruise in the middle of her forehead, like a closed third eye. "It's a new adventure, one we've been looking forward to for nine months!"

She stared at him as if she had never seen him before. "How can you say that?"

"Because, my darling, it's the truth. You'll see it soon enough."

Maggie threw her head back and began to howl. And at that precise moment, her water broke.

~

"You have a healthy baby girl," the doctor said, straight out of the wide doors that led to the surgical wing.

"Then why did you have to take my wife into surgery?" Richard had been pacing back and forth the last seventy minutes, since a pair of nurses had rushed Maggie past him on a gurney. "Is she okay?"

"Maggie's fine," the doctor assured him. He was an older man, an Indian, with very dark skin and a lilt to his English, as if he were singing rather than speaking. "She's sedated at the moment. She—and we—had some difficult moments. She lost a lot of blood. But not to worry."

"Wait. You said a healthy baby girl. We're having twins." A coating of frost was forming in his lower belly, contracting everything around it, as if trying to protect him. "What about the second baby?"

"Ah, that is where the difficulties arose." The doctor gestured. "Why don't we sit down?"

"I don't want to sit down." Richard's nerves had been frayed far enough. His heart beat like a trip-hammer; there was a reddish pulsing behind his eyes. He could scarcely draw breath. "What's happened? Please tell me, Doctor."

"It's like this. There were two fetuses, as the ultrasound showed." Richard had been away for that; Maggie hadn't told him then. "The child that was born, she was turned so that her elbow pressed against her twin's chest. We tried to save the twin. Her heart beat for perhaps ninety seconds or so. Then she expired. We did everything we could." The doctor's eyes were dark and liquefied. "I'm so sorry for your loss,

Dr. Mathis." He waited a beat. "Some parents feel . . ." He cleared his throat. "Would you care to see the body?"

~

There she lay, in an antiseptic room, wrapped in a bloody towel, tiny, bluish white, nameless. Blameless. A life lived in not quite ninety seconds. Had she even taken a single breath while her damaged heart fell off the cliff? He had forgotten to ask the doctor, and now, for some strange reason, it seemed important to know. He desperately wanted this child—his daughter—to have taken at least one breath, to have come fully into his world before she had been snatched away. Delivered into the hands of God, some would say. Richard didn't believe that. No God could be so cruel as to end an innocent baby's life in ninety seconds. It was unthinkable.

And yet here she lay. Nameless. Dead. Forever beyond his reach. He felt as if he had been struck by a train, thrown onto the tracks, crumpled, dying, while his heart broke. "She was turned so that her elbow pressed against her twin's chest," the doctor had said. Arbitrary, unjust, inexplicable. The world slid away, failing to make sense, as if gravity itself had ceased to exist, as if he were choking on the air he breathed. He saw nothing but chaos ahead.

With trembling hands he took her up, held her to his chest, close to his heart, as if with proximity and force of will he could transfer some of the beats of his heart to hers. She did not stir. She was cold and waxen. And yet he could not have loved her more.

Nameless. He could not abide her going to her grave without a name, and so he named her Alice, after his mother. Alice Mathis.

"Hello, Alice," he whispered into her ear. "I love you." His vision grew blurred, and his voice broke on the last word. "Goodbye."

TWENTY-FOUR

When she was seventeen and a half, Orfeo taught her how to play "Malagueña" on the guitar. Three weeks later he took her to the famed shop on Bleecker Street where all the great musicians bought their instruments. Gibson or Martin: that was the question. Laurel quailed at the prices. "Both are too expensive," she said. "I can't afford either."

"Nevertheless," Orfeo said, "pick the one you like best."

She let him buy it for her and wasn't sorry when she brought it back to Orfeo's apartment, and they spent the next hour playing duets to the delight of the family. Applause all around. And then a feast of a dinner from Nonna. She felt as if she were on top of the world, as if the atmosphere she was breathing was heady with brilliant possibilities.

The following week, Orfeo embarked on his grand project with her: Joaquín Rodrigo's *Concierto de Aranjuez*. At Orfeo's she had heard Miles Davis's truncated version and had fallen instantly in love. Now Orfeo was teaching her to play the entire concerto with him, bouncing the melody between them, working the trills and the complicated Moorish arabesques of the composition. Six months later, they were ready. Nonna arranged for them to give the concert at their church. The entire neighborhood came out, filling the pews to capacity and beyond: standing room only.

Orfeo and Laurel played as if they were twin suns, their strumming and picking on fire, flawless, glittering with the Spanish proclivity for conjoining bravado and wistful melancholy. Afterward, during cake, cookies, and coffee, Orfeo, beaming like a kid, worked the room, introducing Laurel to his friends and neighbors, all seemingly dazzled by the performance, congratulating them both. One of them was a handsome, saturnine man, dressed in a bespoke silk suit that showed off his broad shoulders and narrow waist.

"So, Orfeo," he said with a leathery smile, "this is Helene Messer, the girl you've told me so much about." He held out his hand, and for the first time but surely not the last, Laurel shook hands with Byron Dey.

~

"Wretched things had worn out their welcome, anyway," Jimmy Self said, staring mournfully down at his ruined shoes. "I was beginning to feel the pavement through the soles." He dumped them in the toilet trash bin, then in his stockinged feet led Laurel through to the next car. She felt as if they were trailing her stink with them. When they found two seats together, he handed her what was left of his Coke. "Get the taste out of your mouth."

She took the bottle, swallowed gratefully, set it down at her feet.

"Now what?" Tried to calm her wavering voice. "Dey's dead. What d'you want from me? Money?"

"Byron wanted the money you stole from him," Jimmy Self said. "He hired me to find you and get his money back."

"Well, it's gone."

"In that case, I'm supposed to take it outta your hide."

She stared at him. "And yet you worked for him."

His meaty shoulders lifted, fell. "Hey, a guy's gotta make a living."

She gave a derisive laugh.

"Joke. I hated Byron Dey."

"You were happy to take his money."

Jimmy Self nodded. "That I was. No question."

She slid him a sideways glance. "You don't seem the better off for it, if you don't mind my saying."

"I don't." Jimmy Self laughed. "I couldn't've said it better myself."

Laurel waited a beat, reluctant to ask the question that needed to be asked. "So now that you've found me . . ." Her voice trailed off. The end of that sentence resided in the unknown future.

Jimmy Self grunted, put his steepled fingers to his temple. "You smell oil smoke?"

"What? No. Why?"

He winced. "Just clarifying my situation."

"What situation?"

He took a deep breath, let it go. He seemed suddenly pale. Beads of sweat stood out on his forehead before he swiped them away with a forearm. "You ever hear of a bucket list," he said in a voice made watery.

She frowned. "Sure. Things to do before you die."

"My bucket list is short. Only one item on it. Finding you." His voice seemed to steady. "You were my last important assignment, more or less. The only person I couldn't find." He put his head back. "Now that I've found you, I can set fire to that list."

"I don't understand."

Outside the grimy windows, the night raced by, black and affectless. They could have been traveling anywhere to get somewhere else. The terrain remained the same.

"I'm dying," Jimmy Self said. "Inoperable brain tumor. That's the long and the short of it."

"I'm sorry, Jimmy."

He turned to her, smiled wanly. "I can't tell you how long it's been since a woman called me Jimmy in that tone of voice."

Without thinking, Laurel covered his hand with hers.

He looked down. "Or done that without the intent of pulling my arm out of its socket."

When she lifted her hand away, he said, "No, don't. If it's all the same to you." Her hand settled over his again. "Helene."

Her eyes met his.

"I have no intention of hurting you." His mouth lifted at one corner. "Of course. Why would you believe me." He indicated with his chin. "If it makes you feel better, take my .38 while we talk."

"That's all right," she said. "I don't like guns."

She thought of Orfeo. "I've taught you how to play guitar," he had said. "Why should I teach you how to use a gun? You have a gun, you're five times more likely to get shot."

Jimmy Self grimaced. "Smart girl." He fell silent as a woman in a business suit and lacquered nails passed down the aisle, glanced briefly at his stockinged feet, shrugged, and moved on. "Where's the conductor? Anybody know? Where are they when you need them?" she called plaintively. "There's an awful smell in the car I just passed through."

"Which brings me to the subject of this discussion," Jimmy Self continued when she was gone. "Why the hell have you risked everything to return?"

Laurel thought of Gael asking her the same question.

"Richard is dead," Gael had said. "Leave it be."

"I came back to find Bella, his missing daughter," she had told him.

"Richard Mathis, right?" Before she could contradict him, he raced on, needing to tell her. "I did some preliminary digging. From about 2005 on, Mathis's history is what's called twinned."

"Twinned? What does this mean, twinned?"

"Hey, I'm only a lowly foot soldier—less than that now—but I called in some longstanding favors from people you'd rather not know about. They couldn't say for certain, but it seems as if your Richard was leading a double life."

She felt as if she had been punched in the stomach. "You mean he had another family?"

Jimmy Self shook his head. "Not in the sense you mean. He was recruited."

"Recruited?" Laurel was beginning to feel like a parrot. "By whom?"

"Well, that's the sixty-four-thousand-dollar question. It seems he was in Sinai during 9/11. Something happened there—a friend of his was murdered by an Arab jihadi planted in his group. Anyway, shortly thereafter he met with a bunch of Muslim extremists."

"That's imposs—" Recalling how Richard had saved them on the boat, she stopped midsentence. What had actually happened between Richard and the terrorist leader? Had the group really been after drugs? Had he lied to her? All at once, she felt dizzy with unexpected possibilities. Or were they unexpected? Hadn't she suspected he was lying to her that day?

Jimmy Self cocked his head. "You were saying?"

Laurel took a deep breath, let it out. "I'm not going to Dearborn to find out what happened to Richard."

"That's good. You don't want to stick your nose into whatever happened. 'Cause dollars to donuts his death wasn't an accident."

"I'm content to leave it be."

"Frankly, I'm surprised to hear you say that."

"People like us will never find out the truth, Jimmy. And if by some miracle I did, then what?"

"You'd know."

"I have my own secrets. I don't want to know anyone else's."

"You look like the kind of girl to . . . I don't know. You just seem reckless. You came back here when you didn't have to. And here you are on the way to the place where Richard Mathis died."

"Where he lived," she corrected.

His brows knit together as he shook his head. "I don't understand the difference."

"Bella."

"Who's Bella?"

"Richard's daughter. She's been missing for almost three days now. So far I've read nothing about anyone doing squat to find her. It seems the local cops are too busy helping the feds round up Islamics to interrogate."

"I don't know anything about that, but outside of New York the local cops are often, you know, kinda sketchy." Jimmy Self's head swiveled so sharply his neck vertebrae clicked like LEGOs snapping into place. "Do you smell fresh oranges?" Without waiting for a reply, he wiped his forehead with the back of his hand.

"Jimmy, I think we ought to get you to a doctor as soon as we get to Dearborn."

"Why? I'm fine. Never felt better." He shook his head. "What's this kid Bella to you? You ever met her?"

"No."

"Then what? Because she's Mathis's kid, huh."

"That's part of it, I guess. But also I was her once, and now she is me. Her father's dead, and her mother—"

"Her mother committed suicide."

"I read that too. All the more reason I want to find Bella."

Jimmy Self gave her a critical look. "You want to, or you need to?"

"So far as Bella is concerned, it doesn't matter."

"But for you," Jimmy Self said, "I think it matters very much." He gestured with his open hand. "You know best what's important to you. What I know is you're still traveling under an alias. I want to be clear, that could cause you trouble, maybe a lot of trouble, so be careful. Understand me?"

"I do." She said this as a bride answered a priest. She knew she was doubling down on her commitment to Richard and Bella no matter the peril. She felt inside her the combination of excitement and anxiety that came from plunging into the unknown. "In the time we have left before we reach Dearborn, I want you to teach me the basics—how to ferret out clues, how to winkle information out of people. How to be a gumshoe."

Jimmy Self began to unwind inside. "Funny how things work out." After so long in the trenches of the lost, it was a distinct relief. "Gumshoe." He laughed. "Well, it ain't rocket science, especially for someone as clever as you."

His first lesson had begun.

TWENTY-FIVE

The train pulled into the station more or less on time. Beyond, in the gathering dawn: Dearborn. Laurel stepped off the train, realized she was alone, and turned back. Jimmy Self was standing in the open doorway, staring at a point over her head.

"Jimmy?" She had to repeat his name three times, then take his hand. It was cold as ice. "Jimmy, come on. We need to get you a pair of shoes."

He followed her onto the platform. There was grayness everywhere he looked.

"I'm not going to leave you," Laurel said.

"Sure you are. You have promises to keep and miles to go before you sleep."

She made an impatient gesture, shaking off his words. "Jimmy, I'm going to phone for an ambulance."

He shook his head. "No ambulance, Laurel. No doctors. Please." His face brightened. "I could use a coffee, though. Something good—really good, you know. I can't stomach any more shit coffee."

Laurel led him to a bench, and he sank down into it. "I'll see what I can find."

He nodded.

By this time, the passengers had dispersed; car doors slammed; engines coughed to life. Two of the three waiting taxis picked up fares.

"Deadborn," he said, almost to himself.

Laurel turned back, frowning. "What?"

"That's what the kids call it here: Deadborn."

"Jimmy." Her frown deepened. "You won't do anything stupid."

"Worry not." He smiled at her. "All my stupid days are behind me."

"Okay." She held out a hand.

"What?"

"Give me your gun."

He gave her a jaundiced look. "You're joking, right?"

"I couldn't be more serious. Come on."

He grunted. "My gun stays with me. Always has, always will."

"Hand it over, Jimmy."

"Are you crazy? You don't have a carry license."

"No gun, no coffee."

"Christ." He removed the .38 from its holster, its snub nose ugly, sinister, light slipping off it as if being repelled. He rolled the chambers, handed her the bullets. "This is all you get."

She stared down at the bullets, then glanced back at him. "I'll be right back."

"I'll be here. Waiting."

She hurried down the platform, into the station building itself, a modern brick-and-glass affair that these days passed for lovely but was just municipal. The kind of place that helped obliterate what was once the romance of train travel. Just past six thirty in the evening and the newsstand was doing no business. An old woman guarding a pair of string bags gave her a hard stare, as if she owned the place. A soldier on leave leaned against a wall, reading something on his cell phone. Behind him, the wall was covered with Amtrak posters of Tahoe, San Francisco, and Los Angeles. The atmosphere was so ersatz she felt she had arrived in LEGOLAND. The agent pointed her to the vending machine against the far wall. *Something good—really good.* That for sure did not include coffee from a vending machine. *Damn it*, she thought.

She was about to ask the agent where to find the nearest Starbucks when she heard the explosion. It could have been a car backfiring, but she knew better. Jimmy Self had chambered one slug before emptying the rest. Had she even thought to count the bullets? She didn't even know how many that handgun took.

Yanking open the station door, she tore down the platform to where Jimmy Self slumped on the bench, his long wait at a quick and bloody end.

THE BORDER

TWENTY-SIX

Dr. Lionel Pinkus

PATIENT: Margaret Mathis
TRANSCRIPT: 3–3:37 PM, August 15, 20—
EXCERPT BEGINS.
LP: Margaret, have you given any thought as to why you tried to kill yourself.
MM: What? But I didn't! I . . .
LP: Yes? You what?
[*silence*]
MM: I took the pills you prescribed for me.
LP: I see.
MM: [*defensive*] What does that mean?
LP: What do you think it means?
MM: This is all your fault.
LP: My fault.
MM: Yes.
LP: Can you explain that to me?
MM: Sure. You gave me the drugs.

LP: I also prescribed specific doses for each.

MM: That day I guess I needed a little help.

LP: It seems to me that you need to consider the possibility that you tried to kill yourself.

MM: What? No! It was just . . . another day.

LP: It clearly wasn't just another day. Your subconscious made that quite clear.

MM: I didn't try to kill myself.

[*silence*]

MM: I mean, did I?

LP: What aren't you telling me?

MM: Nothing.

LP: You can do better than that, Margaret.

MM: [*becoming agitated again*] Stop climbing inside my head.

LP: Is that what you think I'm doing?

MM: You're telling me what to do.

LP: You seem to want to tell me something.

MM: You see!

LP: I'm simply taking my cues from you.

MM: What cues? There aren't any cues.

LP: Tell me about your husband.

MM: There's nothing to say.

LP: How is his relationship with Bella?

MM: I've no idea.

LP: You have no idea?

MM: Why are you repeating what I just said?

LP: Don't you care what his relationship with your daughter is?

MM: Why should I?

[*3–5 seconds of silence*]

MM: [*patient uncrosses, recrosses legs; shifts from one buttock to another*] I don't want to talk about this anymore. I want to talk about a dream I had.

LP: What do you want to tell me?

MM: I want to tell you about my dream.

LP: I know this is difficult for you.

MM: You don't know shit.

[*another silence, longer this time. Patient looks out the window*]

MM: [*continues to stare out the window, disassociating?*] How do you think it feels to have given birth to a murderer?

[*silence. Patient wipes sweat off upper lip*]

MM: [*patient's gaze swings back*] I don't think I can go on.

[*silence, longest one so far*]

MM: [*abruptly belligerent. Emerging from dissociative state?*] Aren't you going to say something?

LP: What do you imagine me saying?

MM: Something encouraging. For Christ's sake!

LP: I think you should go on. Continue voicing your feelings.
MM: Really. Is that what you think?
[*silence. Patient, disassociating again, looks out window*]
MM: [*voice has a different tenor, floaty*] I didn't want kids. I never . . . I told him over and over again.
[*silence, palpably tense*]
LP: Can you say more about that?
MM: What is there to say? He wouldn't listen. He insisted.
LP: How did he insist?
MM: We fought. Then he said he'd leave me. That ended the argument.
LP: So you got pregnant.
MM: Not just *pregnant*.
LP: Margaret, either you're pregnant, or you're not.
MM: Twins! And I didn't even want one. [*patient bites lower lip*] Oh, God! Oh, shit!
LP: Margaret, it's okay to say it. Nothing bad is going to happen.
MM: [*tight, resigned*] Something bad already happened. My daughter killed her twin.
LP: In vitro. These things happen. They're tragic, but—
MM: [*crying and shouting*] Jesus God, why didn't they both die inside me?! We all would have been better off! So

much grief! So much! You asked why I tried to kill myself.

LP: So you can see this in yourself, this self-destructiveness.

MM: Because of this! *This!* I can't live with what I feel for her, for my daughter, that *thing*. Murderer. I'm so, so better off dead.

LP: Have faith, Margaret. This is progress. Now that you know, you can begin to—

MM: [*dully*] There's nothing *to* do.

[*a longer silence*]

LP: How long have you felt this way?

MM: Too long.

LP: What are you going through, Margaret? It's important you give voice to it.

[*patient gets up and walks out*]

END EXCERPT.

~

"That one there's crazy," Orfeo said. "Don't go near him, even if Dey says to."

"I work for him," Laurel said. "If he asks, how can I . . . ?"

Orfeo gave her the serious stare, the one she used to get when he thought she'd made a wrong move on the chessboard. "Dey doesn't ask; he orders."

"Then—"

"Listen." Orfeo's voice dropped to the level of a stage whisper. "Dey likes to test newbies. And that's what you are at the moment: a newbie.

He'll want to get at you, crack you open, see what's really inside. That's the only way he'll know whether he has use for you."

"So I should refuse."

Orfeo rolled his eyes. "Dear God, yes. Vinny Fish is poison. Especially with girls."

"So . . ."

"If he gives you any kind of trouble, kick him in the nuts."

She laughed. "I can do that."

Orfeo grunted. "Yeah, you can."

That first morning was filled with, as Melville might write, learning the ropes, which was what every shoreline carouser, dragooned or shanghaied shipman had to do in order to raise and lower the sails. Navigating the rigging—the ropes—was a complicated task and a necessary one if the new seaman was to earn his paltry keep. So it was with Laurel, familiarizing herself with the workings of Dey's criminal enterprise.

She was astonished that Orfeo was a criminal working for the boss of a criminal organization, but when she asked him about it, he simply shrugged and said, "It's hard enough to provide for your family in this city, Helene, without ethics tying your hands."

At first, it was pushing papers, for in those days Dey's machine was making a slow and painful transition from paper to electronic files. Of course she tried to make heads or tails of the papers she was given to file, but it was only when she was able to spend stolen moments here and there at the filing cabinets themselves that she began to piece together Dey's business model. She saw right away that it was bloated and inefficient; he was into too many businesses, and for whatever reason, he wasn't keeping track of them. That was even before she found that he was keeping separate financial books, that he was laundering money from the Mulberry Street offices through the business in the Empire State Building. Following that, she created a third set in case the company was audited. Those moments were fraught with all kinds of peril.

People were always checking up on her, so the work she really wanted to do was difficult in the extreme. Nevertheless, she began to ferret out things she was certain Dey's crew didn't know about and Dey himself never wanted her to see.

As for Orfeo, he was more often than not away from the offices on some Dey-related item or other. When he was in, he inhabited a corner of Dey's office he seemed to own. Sitting on a straight-backed wooden chair tilted back against the wall, he lovingly oiled a baseball glove, creating a pocket into which, on occasion, he slammed a baseball. A genuine Louisville Slugger rested in the corner, keeping him company.

Dey's enterprise occupied the second floor of a Mulberry Street building on the northern edge of Chinatown. He owned the building; in fact, as she later discovered, he owned the entire block. This place was a far cry from the dog and pony show offices he maintained in the Empire State Building for prospective buyers of the companies he was selling. She never did see the uptown premises.

Like much of Mulberry Street and its surrounds, the ground floor of Dey's building had been infiltrated by Chinese immigrants—canny businessmen with deep pockets. Their trade was in sports betting, which had grown out of old-school numbers running. The money to be made in sports betting and, especially, the control of fantasy sports leagues had exploded. These two Chinese brothers were all over it. Dey didn't mind, as long as he got his taste of the action, but there were continuing negotiations as to the percentage he was entitled to.

Late one morning five or six weeks after Laurel started working for Dey, she heard him say, "I swear I'm going to kill them!" He strode out of his office, Orfeo a pace behind him. Looking around, his gaze fell on Laurel, and he snapped his fingers. "You. Messer. Take a walk with us."

Falling in behind Orfeo and Dey, she went down the steep flight of wooden stairs, filthy as sin. Dey opened a dented steel door, and they all stepped into the Chinese betting parlor. Fifteen bony men sat bent over three rows of workstations. They looked like workers in old photos of Chinese sweatshops, the computers subbing for sewing machines. They looked up in unison, which would have been amusing except for the grim expression on Dey's face.

Dey headed for the far side of the space, the offices of the two brothers, glassed off from the rest of the business. The brothers looked like twins: thin, medium height, black hair slicked back off their wide foreheads. They even lifted their heads at the same time. At Dey's silent signal, Orfeo went directly to the brother on the left, smashed his fist into his face. He stepped back while his boss commenced to beat the man senseless. When his brother leapt up to intervene, Orfeo, who now guarded the open doorway, hefted his Louisville Slugger. Laurel hadn't seen him carrying it when he'd emerged from Dey's office. He slapped the meat of the barrel several times into the open palm of his left hand, a menacing gesture that shocked Laurel as much as the punch he had delivered. She had never seen this violent side of Orfeo before, had never even been given an inkling of its existence. Could this be the same man who played chess with her, who had bought her a guitar, who had played *Concierto de Aranjuez* with her? It seemed impossible, but here he was. When the brother tried to push Orfeo aside, Orfeo brought the bat down on the top of his head. It was neither a hard nor a soft blow. It was perfectly calibrated to send the man to the floor, eyes blinking slowly and heavily as they tried to focus.

Laurel, scarcely breathing, feeling distinctly nauseated, heard Dey say, "When I tell you it's twenty-five percent, it's twenty-five, not twenty-three, not twenty-one. Now the rate's thirty. Got it?" Bending over, he pulled out the man's shirt and wiped his knuckles on it, streaks of crimson against the starched white sheen.

"Lunch," Dey said as, with a subdued flourish, he led them back across the ground floor and out onto Mulberry Street.

TWENTY-SEVEN

From a distance, Laurel watched Jimmy Self's body being loaded into the back of an EMT ambulance. From a distance, she watched the cops milling around the cordoned-off bench where Jimmy Self had shot himself to death. As if they would find some clue. There was no clue, none at all. From the fringes of the small crowd that had gathered to crane their necks, to gawk, to take photos with their cell phones, to snap selfies at the scene of the crime, she watched. Always watching, always at a distance, always on the edges. At the border. Disengaged, observing as Dey beat the living crap out of the Chinese bookmaker, as Orfeo with perfect betrayal beat down the twin. Orfeo the intellectual chess player, the gentle guitarist with the voice of an angel who cared for his family. Dey's enforcer. She recalled in vivid detail leaving Orfeo's apartment after being taken in by the family, Nonna speaking to her in the church as if she were one of Nonna's grandchildren, how a part of the family she felt even while she knew she was an outsider. How difficult life was sometimes, she thought now. How it mocked your choices, how it shoved impediments in your path just to test your resolve, to see how much it could fuck you up. She had come to Orfeo with only revenge in her heart, but he had taken her in, loved her, protected her. In his apartment, as part of his family, she had been buffeted by so many conflicting emotions. It had taken all her strength, all her courage to hew to her chosen path, to do what in her heart—her very soul—she knew was the right thing.

It was then, in the last moment of remembrance, that her gaze returned to the present, and she saw her suitcase, set against the side of the station. She went and retrieved it, thinking, *Jesus, Jimmy, you thought of everything.*

The ambulance doors slammed closed, the EMTs mounted its running boards and swung inside, and the vehicle drove off. Where would Jimmy Self wind up? On the ME's stainless steel slab, in cold storage like an old fur coat, in an unmarked grave, or scattered at the back of the crematorium. She preferred to think not. Jimmy Self wound up on that bench, waiting for the fine coffee she would seek out and bring to him. If he was anywhere, he was there.

~

The bullets from his .38 seemed to weigh her down all through the cab ride into town, but she was reluctant to rid herself of them. She had nowhere to go, nowhere she wanted to go. She especially did not want to seek the company of others. The taxi let her off at the edge of Thomas A. Edison Park. Within a loose copse of trees she found a wooden picnic table. She sat for a while, doing nothing but listening to the rustle of the wind through the treetops. She tried not to think. But images of Richard and Bella and Jimmy Self reeled through her mind like drunken ghosts. At length, lids drooping, she lay down on the table and cried herself to sleep.

~

It was too early in the morning to know what kind of day it was going to be. The sun, white through the mist rising to meet it, cast a silvery sheen across the trees and rooftops, as if it were the moon, as if it were night for day.

"You hear what happened at the train station, miss?" the cabbie asked.

Laurel stared dully out the window. "What happened?" Was she even listening?

"Man shot himself, so I heard."

He was looking at her in the rearview mirror. She felt sweat break out under her arms, chill the back of her neck. His avid curiosity repelled her.

"First I'm hearing."

His face fell in clear disappointment. "Wow, though. First time we've had something like that at the station, I can tell you." His eyes back on the road. "Girl missing, Muslims being rounded up. A hit-and-run. And all in the same family. Now this suicide." He scratched his head. "Don't know what this world is coming to."

Laurel leaned forward, arms crossed over the top of the front bench seat. "I'm starving," she said to the cabbie. He was wiry, balding, with ears that stuck out like Dumbo's. "Is there anything decent open at this hour?"

"Well, there's a Bob Evans." The years had scraped away much of his flesh, as a sculptor chisels away at a block of marble, leaving only what was essential. "Also an IHOP that's popular with the out-of-town folk."

"No, no, no. I want to go . . . okay, where d'you go for breakfast."

"Me?"

"Yeah."

"No question there. I'd go to Nestors Deli on Michigan and Roemer. They open at five. Mornings, everyone I know stops in there. It's a real mill and swill."

"Now we're talking. Take me there." She settled back in the seat, meager supply of bonhomie used up.

"Are you okay, miss?"

"Sure. Fine. My father just died."

"Condolences, miss. Was he a good man?"

The official cause of death was a stroke, but she knew better. Her father had died of a broken heart. How many nights after her mother had abandoned them had she heard him sobbing in his bedroom, calling his wife's name like a ghost haunting their house? "A good man. To the best of his abilities, yes."

"Yeah. Well, it's good, you know—good you remember him that way. My kids don't get me at all." He laughed, trying to goose the joke along, then shrugged. "I mean, who gets anybody these days—am I right?"

He probably was, but she was suddenly too tired to answer. She'd gone the whole night without sleeping more than twenty minutes at a time, and she was, in fact, starving. For most people tragedy eviscerated their appetite, but for her the reverse was true. She stared out at the row houses, attached like the cars on a toy train that had lost its engine. A police cruiser passed by, the third she'd seen since leaving the station.

A sudden thought occurred to her. She drew out Richard's mobile phone. She had kept the battery fully charged just in case Bella tried to reach her father. She went to the texts, found nothing new. She typed in,

Bella, where are you?

Pressed the send tab, waited. And waited. No reply. She put the phone away but was careful to keep it on. You never knew.

She looked up at the back of the cabbie's head. "Hey, the girl who disappeared . . . whose mother killed herself . . . didn't her father just get killed in a hit-and-run? You know anything about the family—Mathis, right?"

"Heck, everyone in Dearborn knows about them. Damn shame, the suicide, the accident coming right on top of the girl's disappearance."

"They haven't found her yet?"

"Not that I've heard."

"You know anything about the mother?"

"Mrs. Mathis? She—" He broke off abruptly as he pulled up to the curb outside Nestors. Twisted his torso to look at her directly. "Say, what are you, a reporter?"

"That's right. My editor sent me here to do, you know, an in-depth human-interest piece on the aftermath of the double tragedy. That's why I asked about Mrs. Mathis. I'd really like to know more about her."

"Good luck with that," the cabbie said.

"What d'you mean?"

"Story is she went nuts. Started right after the daughter was born, people say." He shrugged. "People say a lotta things—ain't that right. But Mrs. Mathis, there was . . ." He shrugged again. "Let's put it this way: not to speak ill of the dead, but no one was all too surprised when she killed herself, if you catch my meaning."

Maggie obscured, hidden, lost like the figures she and Richard had hoped to find in the tomb guarded by fanged Cul and Culsans; like those figures she was made of darkness and night. All unseen by Laurel; all gone now. Figments, not even ghosts.

"You want to talk to Rosie Menkins," the cabbie went on. "At the hospital." He nodded toward Nestors. "At this hour, chances are she'll be here, though, sucking down coffee like her life depended on it. I suppose if I did what she does, I'd be sucking down coffee by the gallon."

Laurel handed over the fare, plus a generous tip. "What does she do at the hospital?"

"Trauma nurse. The things she sees day in, day out. This town can be quiet, but it can also be violent—know what I mean? Yeah, and because it was Rosie who took care of Mrs. Mathis while she was in the hospital during her first OD attempt." He shook his head, then unfolded the money and gave her a little two-finger salute. "Thanks, miss." He came around, opened the door, handed over her suitcase. "I'm sorry for your loss."

"What?" Halfway out of the cab, Laurel caught herself. "Thanks, yeah."

~

Meals with Dey were lavish affairs. The insider crew invariably repaired to Via Veneto, one of the last remaining authentic Italian restaurants in what Dey half-jokingly, half-bitterly called TIFI—Tiny Fucking Italy. Large and square, it had a black-and-white-checked tile floor; a pressed-tin ceiling from the turn of the nineteenth century, now painted maroon; and dark wood panels that rose halfway up the ocher plaster walls. It was so much like a set out of *The Godfather* that Laurel could imagine Michael Corleone coming out of the toilets with a handgun, grips taped, serial number filed off.

Lighting, from what looked like giant inverted mushrooms, was deliberately dim, curtains drawn across the windows. Unlike the other red-sauce Neapolitan joints sprinkled around it, the food at Via Veneto was Roman, as excellently prepared as it had been forty years ago. Old-fashioned recipes from the time when its namesake had been Rome's main artery for a glittering nightlife led by the gods of that golden era of Italian film: Fellini, Mastroianni, Loren, and Ekberg.

The Bloody Lunch, as Laurel was to call it in memory, lasted well over two hours, Dey ordering course after course. Orfeo sat next to him and she across from him. They were in the right rear corner, Dey's appointed position beneath the watchful gaze of Burt Lancaster as Don Fabrizio Corbera, Prince of Salina. Laurel recognized the prince, having read *The Leopard* in its native Italian. She thought Lancaster a fine choice for the beautiful film version of the novel.

When Dey was in residence, no one was seated at the adjacent tables, no matter how crowded the restaurant got. Regulars who were waiting never complained, and those tourists who did were promptly sent on their way. Dey paid the owner top dollar for those four tops.

Following the antipasti, Dey wiped his greasy lips, impaled Laurel with his dark gaze. "Orfeo here tells me you're quite the genius."

She didn't know how to respond to that, so she kept her mouth shut. She had avoided Orfeo's gaze ever since the incident at the Chinese bookmakers'. "He claims you can do anything."

She kept her gaze steady, unblinking.

"So how about a demonstration."

"What, here?" Orfeo said but kept to himself whatever else he was going to say when his boss's hand cut across the space between them.

Laurel nodded. "Whatever you say." Way down in the pit of her stomach, the serpent of unknowing began to uncoil.

"Under the table, then." Dey smirked. "On your knees." The smirk bloomed into a grin. "Crawl."

Laurel, working hard to keep from blinking, did not move.

"Well?"

"No," she said.

"No?" Dey echoed. "'Whatever you say,' you told me."

"I lied."

"My people don't lie to me."

"Sue me." What had gotten into her? Was she channeling Michael Corleone?

Dey reached into his suit jacket, laid a gleaming silver-plated .22 on the table, its muzzle pointed in her direction.

All of a sudden, Laurel felt the urgent need to urinate. Her heart hammered painfully against the cage of her ribs. "I work for you. I won't blow you."

"Often, with girls, it's one and the same."

You demeaning shit. You'll rue the day we ever met. She stood up. Choosing her words very carefully, she said, "If I walk away, or if you kill me, you'll never find out how useful I can be to you."

"That would be a crime," Orfeo said, as if to himself. But they both heard.

Something akin to an eclipse, silent but powerful, passed across Dey's face. "Sit back down," he said.

"The food is delicious here. But I can't eat with a gun on the table." Out of the corner of her eye, she saw the ghost of a smile on Orfeo's face. She had phrased it just right. If instead she had said, *First, take the gun off the table*, it would have been a challenge, and at that moment a further challenge would have been a mistake.

Without taking his eyes from hers, Dey swept the .22 off the table and back into its hidden shoulder holster. Laurel sat down. Orfeo released the breath he had been holding.

"What, I can't crack a joke now?" Dey lifted an arm, calling for the antipasti to be removed, the pasta course to be served.

"So," he said, after the plates of *strozzapreti al lardo* had been cleared, "what can you do for me?"

He spoke softly, normally, as if they were a pair of friends doing business. It was as if the recent unpleasantness had never occurred. This was Laurel's introduction to Dey's ability to instantly reset his emotions, concentrate on the moment at hand.

"Your electronic books are woefully out of date," she said in a matter-of-fact tone. "Rudimentary, actually. They're so inefficient you need three people to do the work of one."

Dey sat back. "Ah, I see it now. You want more than you deserve. You've overstepped." He shook his head. "I should fire you, but you're Orfeo's reclamation project. I won't disrespect him. Return to your filing." All at once, he launched his torso forward so he was looming over the table, the water glasses shivering, the oversize cutlery chiming. "If you pull a stunt like that again, I guarantee it will be the last thing you do."

And for the next two months and three days, that was how things stood between them, which was to say a kind of cold war, a master who barely took notice of his young, upstart servant. Then, late one Thursday, Silvio, the man who passed for Dey's head of IT, came rushing into his boss's office.

"We're under attack," he cried.

Dey was on his cell, speaking to one of his people in Hong Kong. Putting the call on hold, he said, "What? What are you talking about?"

"Someone's trying to hack into our system."

Dey jumped up. "Well, what the fuck're you doing here? Stop it, shit-for-brains."

Silvio's hands spread, palms up. "I don't know how. The attack is something I haven't heard of, let alone seen before."

Dey spoke a few words into his cell, cutting the call short; came around from behind his desk; and grabbed Silvio by his shirtfront. Then, half frog-marching, half dragging him, he approached the small bank of computer terminals, Orfeo quietly close behind him—only to find Laurel hunched over Silvio's terminal, her fingers flying over the keyboard.

"What the fuck?" Dey bellowed. "Get away from there!"

"Do you want to keep your information safe, or don't you?" Laurel said without turning around or stopping what she was doing.

"Fuck," Dey said to no one in particular. "Fuck, fuck, fuck. What is happening?" But he stood there, the impotent Silvio at his side, open-mouthed because whatever was happening on the screen was happening so fast it was impossible to follow, and even if it had been slowed down, it was all Greek to him anyway.

Tense minutes later, with Laurel's hands finally at rest on the edges of the keyboard, Dey said, "What happened?"

"Someone broke through your insecure firewall."

He sucked in a breath. "What did they get?"

"Three or four files of no real import. Garbage in, garbage out." Laurel chuckled. "Then a whole slew of bogus batch files I created, in among which is an executable file that will crash their system."

Dey wiped his mouth and chin. He would have said, *Good work*, but at the moment he was too distracted. "And who exactly are they?"

"That," she said, starting to work again, "will take a bit more time."

Orfeo stirred after a long silence. "Why don't we leave her to it?"

Dey, engrossed in the figures on the terminal screen, nodded almost absently. He didn't know what he was looking at and didn't care either. No matter how much he pretended otherwise, he was old-school. Then, in his mercurial way, he spun around, said to Orfeo, "Get this moron out of here." Meaning Silvio, who was never seen or heard from again.

From that day on, Laurel became the head of IT. After several years of impeccable work bringing Dey's system into the world of impenetrability, he made her his business manager.

But along the way, something dreadful happened. For Laurel, it was childhood's end; for Dey, it would prove the end, period.

TWENTY-EIGHT

Nestors—the old-school neon sign should have read "Nestor's," but it seemed no one knew how to use an apostrophe—was a homely place, but then Dearborn seemed a homely town, at least on this dreary, misty morning. A chill was in the air and a dankness that went bone-deep, like the inside of an abandoned house or a dungeon.

Laurel found it a relief to come out of the purling gray morning into the buttery warmth, the small clinks of cutlery against plates, the whistle of water boiling in Pyrex pots, the smells of eggs frying, bread toasting, coffee brewing, bacon and breakfast sausages sizzling on the grill. Nestors was filled with the normalcy of small talk, gossip, and friendly conversation among regulars who had known each other for years, if not decades.

She slid into a red vinyl booth overlooking the row of parked cars out front. A small chromium box with a clear face allowed her to pick jukebox songs for a quarter apiece, five for a buck. Sliding in a quarter, she selected "Tears on My Pillow" and immediately felt a pain in her heart start to throb. A waitress in a pink-and-white uniform arrived.

"Such a sad song, hon." She handed Laurel a well-used plastic-coated menu. "But then today's a sad day, isn't it?" Poured her a mug of coffee without asking if Laurel wanted any. Laurel thanked her, identified herself as a reporter, and asked her to point out Rosie Menkins.

"Oh, Rosie's not here today, hon," the waitress said. She had a slab face and hair styled in a manner decades old. "On account of the funeral."

"What funeral?"

"Richard Mathis's funeral's this morning, over at Riverside Church at eleven. Rosie's representing the family." She shook her head, stuck one fist on a sprung hip. "Such a double tragedy. I mean what with Mrs. Mathis killing herself and all." She sighed theatrically. "But, you know, I suppose that's what you get for making friends with those people."

"What people?" Laurel asked.

"Those Islamics," the waitress said, screwing up her face. "Who else?" She pointed to the top of the menu, where a small card had been affixed with a paper clip. "Take the eggs Benny special, hon. That's my advice."

~

The interior of the church was cool and dim. Somewhere funereal organ music was playing softly; people in somber suits and dresses milled about in that slow way people adopted at tragic occasions. Judging by their clothes, makeup, and hairstyles, people had come not just from Michigan but from all over the world. Laurel was abruptly terrified that Kieros would be there, but, craning her neck, she didn't see him. Richard's coffin was up front, pale wood and brass fittings gleaming like satin. As she made her way down the central aisle, Laurel felt the eggs Benny fermenting in her stomach. She touched her fingertips to her forehead, which felt sweaty, feverish. For a moment, she had to stop, hold on to the back of a wooden pew to keep herself from falling over. There seemed to be no air for her lungs to pull in and push out. She might have been standing on the moon, watching herself slowly fold from high above the tops of the stained glass windows. Jesus looked down at her with the sad eyes of a mendicant, and for a moment she thought she heard his voice, whispering in her ear. But it was only air briefly stirred by the passage of three women with stern faces and severely tailored skirt suits. She overheard one of their names—Janet—as a man with deep-set eyes like poached eggs came up to the woman, and the two exchanged a meaningful glance.

The service began before she could approach the coffin, which, in retrospect, was a blessing. She wanted to remember Richard so alive with her on Crete, not as a waxwork dummy, drained of blood and painted with the undertaker's overly rouged makeup. She had made that mistake with her father, had had nightmares for weeks afterward, had wished fervently for the image to be wiped from her memory.

The service was long, made even longer by the number of people who rose to the podium to eulogize Richard. One of them was Janet, last name Margolies. She had been one of Richard's professors at Georgetown when he'd been an undergraduate.

"We come here today to praise Richard Mathis, not to bury him," she began, cleverly reversing the words Shakespeare had put into Mark Antony's mouth, though Laurel was dubious about whether this was a time for cleverness. "For the work Richard was so passionate about will continue, his major contributions to the field already bearing fruit. And those who worked with him, who have come after, will take up his mantle and march forward into the brave new world he was exploring."

She went on in this vein for some minutes more, giving Laurel time to scan the assembled mourners. She had deliberately taken a seat that afforded her a view of the first row on the right, where tradition had it the deceased's family members sat. Bella was missing, and as her taxi driver had said, Maggie had OD'd, vanished down the fatal rabbit hole. That left Rosie Menkins, the woman sitting in the front row, her back straight, her eyes vigilantly, almost fixedly on Janet Margolies.

Rosie Menkins was a heavyset woman with faded blonde hair. But then everything about her was faded, like an old photo exposed to the sun for too long. Her features had settled deeply, sorrowfully into middle age. Her eyes had retreated beneath her wide brow, furrowed now so that she seemed to present a permanent scowl. It was clear she had seen more than her fair share of disease and dying.

At last, Janet was finished. She stepped down off the podium and returned to her place in the second row beside the man with the poached-egg eyes, who seemed to Laurel to be in attendance out of a kind of pained protocol. He looked like he'd rather be anywhere else in the world but here. *Fuck him and the attitude he flew in on*, she thought.

The minister had regained the podium. He was a mousy man with skin as gray as the morning. His smile looked more like a grimace as he thanked Janet. Then he started in on the prayers again.

"Immortal God, Holy Lord, Father and protector of everything thou hast created, we raise our hearts to thee today for Richard Mathis, who has passed out of this mortal life. In thy loving mercy, Father of men, be pleased to receive him into thy heavenly company, and forgive him the failings and faults of human frailty."

There was more, of course, but Laurel had tuned out again. Instead, she thought of her father, of the night she had awoken to discover him about to untie his shoelaces, as he had done every day of his life since he'd been five. For the last time—not even, since the deed had been left undone. She thought of his love for her; she thought of him carrying her in his arms, raising her up from her curled position on the stairs. Had he kissed her cheek as he laid her under the bedcovers? She was sure he had. Wrapped her in the warmth of his love, flickering like a candle's flame.

~

But then her house is invaded by spinning lights, strange men clomping up the stairs, through the rooms, shooing her away, coming between her and her father, when all she wants is to be alone with him. She could have been alone with him if she hadn't gone to church, if she'd left Orfeo's earlier. At this moment *forgiveness* is not a word she recognizes.

They try to be gentle with her, these men—and then, because they called for one, a female police officer takes her down the hallway, asks her questions about her mom, about where she is. Laurel, lying through her teeth, says she has already called her mom, that she is away on a trip, that she'll be home soon enough. In the bedroom, flashbulbs are exploding, lightning shooting out into the hallway, bleaching out all color and definition. A man in latex gloves crawls all over her father, or so it seems. She dekes the female cop, runs full tilt down the hall, into the bedroom, bowling two men aside as she throws herself at her father. They do their best to be gentle with her, but she won't let them. She fights to be with him, fights them all. In this moment, she wants to be punished, needs to be punished.

That night and for six nights thereafter, she sleeps on Orfeo's sofa, while Nonna fusses over her as if she has a fever, which, in a way, she does. She lies curled on the sofa as, years ago, she had curled on the stairs of her house, waiting, falling asleep, being lifted up in strong arms, snuggled under warm covers. And now again under bedcovers for most of that time, dreaming about her father, his eyes burning like coals within sunken pits, his cheeks blotchy with stubble. Making her breakfast. *Hey, Rabbit. Hey!* Her making him dinner. At least, that's her recollection. But over the years that week has receded, hazy as life in a vintage film. On the seventh day she returns home, and no more is said about her father. But for the time of mourning he is all she thinks about.

Hey, Rabbit. Hey!

~

And that house—that damn house—the place of her childhood. She had told the cops that her mother was coming back from a trip, so they'd never checked. Why would they? Her father hadn't filed a missing person report; she hadn't been missing, at least not in that sense. So she had stayed on in the house—that damn house—until the day she'd fled, tasking Gael with the sale. That damn house, that damn anchor.

Now, in another place, she found herself scrutinizing the man with the poached-egg eyes, who was whispering in Janet Margolies's ear. She had the distinct feeling that if he could, he'd get up and walk out. Clearly, he had more important things to do.

At length, the service over, the mourners stood to watch the coffin being carried out through the central aisle. They followed, spreading out across the top steps like a wave rolling into shore, watching in grim silence as the coffin was slid into the rear of the hearse. The moment the door swung down, it was if the assembleds' last connection with Richard Mathis had been severed. A kind of communal shiver passed through the crowd, and then it began to break up into ones, twos, and, in some cases, small groups.

Laurel found Poached-Egg Eyes, his arm through Janet Margolies's as he led her down the steps. They waited as the hearse drove slowly and solemnly away, followed by several cars, then stepped to the curb. A black SUV rolled to a stop in front of them. The driver emerged. He wore a dark-colored suit, sunglasses when there was no need of sunglasses. As his forefinger rose to his ear, Laurel glimpsed the gleam of what she was certain Jimmy Self would call an electronic earwig. Leaning over, Poached-Egg Eyes opened the rear door. Janet climbed in, and he followed. The driver ducked back into the SUV, and it quickly drove off. It took a route opposite to that of the hearse carrying the last remains of Richard Mathis.

On either end of the steps, bees investigated the colorful arrangements of red and white roses. Laurel felt as if she had been stung all over.

TWENTY-NINE

Jimmy Self, sitting beside Laurel on the quiet train, passengers around them swaying gently, nodding off or reading, lost in private thoughts, smiled his wily smile. "What a career you could have had."

She frowned. "What are you talking about? Dey's dead."

"My business, not his."

A lump came into her throat. "Listen, Jimmy. I have a confession to make."

"Just one?" He grinned at her.

"My real name is Laurel Springfield."

"Well, to be honest, you never looked like a Helene Messer."

"Really? What would she look like?"

Jimmy laughed. "Not like you—that's for sure." He shook his head. "Anyway, a rose by any other name is, what, still as sweet. Have I got that right?"

Her heart nearly broke. "You have, indeed." She felt the urge to hug him, but she sensed the gesture would only embarrass him.

Jimmy Self's eyes were clearing. "You know, I never could figure out why you went to work for him. You don't strike me as the criminal type."

"I don't think I'm a type, Jimmy."

"Then what the hell did you think you were you doing?"

"I had a plan."

Jimmy sighed, his eyes alight. "I'll just bet you did."

~

"It is time, Ishmael thinks, to get to sea before he steps into the street, and deliberately knocks people's hats off." Leaving the library, Laurel walks east and enters Washington Square Park. It's a damp and overcast day in late May, the sky low and flannel gray. The plane trees are fully budded out, the ground covered with an undulation of newspaper pages crackling in the wind like sails. She sits on a wood-slatted bench, watching with critical alertness the men play chess on the park's inlaid concrete-aggregate tables. On the other side of her, a junkie, no more than seventeen or eighteen, lies half-sprawled, mouth open, closed eyelids fluttering with dreams of a better life. One of the chess players, an Italian with a natty panama and neat salt-and-pepper goatee, glances up. He has a wandering eye that makes it seem as if he can see everything at once.

"What're you doing here all by your lonesome?" he says, not unkindly.

"Hanging," she says.

"On a school day, huh." He grunts, lifts his hirsute chin toward the junkie. "That there could be you, *piccola*," he says, again not unkindly, "you don't watch yourself."

She grins. "I'm too smart for that."

He eyes her for a moment. "I'll just bet you are." He shoos away his playing partner with a practiced flip of his hand. "This isn't the first time I've seen you here. You know how to play chess, *piccola*?"

She knows how to play chess, all right. From the instant she recognized him six months ago as the man who had driven her mother away that rainy October night, she has planned for this. She knows he's not the one who lured her mother away, but she is sure he will lead her to him.

~

"Orfeo Doloroso? Dey's enforcer?" Jimmy Self was stunned, incredulous. "That's who you played chess with?" He began to laugh. "Moses smell the roses, you're some piece of work." He gestured. "Okay, go on."

~

When Orfeo asks her name, she tells him it's Helene Messer. He doesn't check; he never checks. Why should he? She's far too young to be anything but who she says she is. Besides, she exactly fits the part. He knows street people when he sees them, and she's definitely one of 'em.

When Orfeo introduces her to Dey she's secretly overjoyed. She suspects instantly that he's the man her mother is with. From the great philosophical minds in the library, she has learned a great many things, including patience. She pushes papers for as long as she deems it necessary. Once done, she starts systematizing his books. From there, it's child's play for her to infiltrate Dey's IT firewall. Inside, she finds a list of the illicit payments and their sources. From the library computer she rejuvenated and rejiggered, she plants a virus time bomb inside Dey's software, timed to go off at a certain hour the following Thursday, when everyone works late.

So of course, when the bomb goes off, the virus running rampant through Dey's system, she's standing by to defuse it. Not that she couldn't have done it had it been a legitimate attack from outside. Thus has she simultaneously put herself in Dey's good graces and gained his respect.

For the next three months she labors to keep his files safe and secure from even the most sophisticated outside intrusion. Once done, she starts systematizing his books. And that's when she finds the payments—for an apartment in one of those impossible-to-buy-into brownstones overlooking Gramercy Park, for a woman's diamond-and-white-gold Cartier watch, Hermès scarves, Chanel handbags, Christian Louboutin shoes—and tens of thousands of dollars going to Bergdorf Goodman for dresses, skirts, silk blouses, satin underwear, cashmere sweaters, designer coats, and leather jackets. The list unspools, on and on, confirming her suspicions.

She thinks of her father's love for her mother, broken, destroyed by her mother's selfishness, her greed, her ravenous desire for more, always more. But what had her mother wanted, really? Laurel doesn't know; she's never known. She never will.

~

"Wait a frigging minute," Jimmy Self said. "That was your momma shacking up with Dey?"

"You knew about her? I thought Dey kept her a secret."

"You forget what I am? I don't take on clients I haven't scoped out in detail."

Now. Now she could do it. That same lump formed in her throat again, forcing her to squeeze out her words. "Do you know . . . do you know what happened to my mother?"

"She's alive, if that's what you're asking." Jimmy Self looked at her for a moment. "She's with another guy. Another big shot, flashy dresser, fast-talker. She's modernized, though. He's younger than her. A Wall Street wheeler-dealer this time."

"She must be one great lay, my mother," she said with such vehemence that Jimmy Self's eyebrows shot up. She could see him chewing over what a shit relationship she must have had with her mother.

"You said it. I didn't."

"Huh. Don't tell me you weren't thinking it."

"Well . . ." He gave a little laugh, and in a minute she found herself laughing too. In that moment, she felt their connection tighten.

They sat quietly for a moment then, reveling in the odd, unexpected pleasure of each other's company. After a time, Jimmy said, "So,

Laurel Springfield, is it? Fuck me." He shook his head. "You fooled us all—me, Dey, Orfeo. I'll be goddamned."

Laurel grinned at him.

"Huh, fancy that."

Was it her imagination, or was he looking at her differently all of a sudden?

"So, all right. Back to your story. Why didn't you follow Dey after he left the office?"

"Because I wasn't a detective like you, Jimmy."

"*Then*. This is now. Like you asked, I'm gonna give you a crash course in how to be a good gumshoe. I have a feeling you're gonna need it."

She nodded her appreciation but kept going, had to keep going. The floodgates opened: "Also, I had Orfeo to think of. The last thing I needed was to arouse his suspicions."

"Okay, so now you knew your mother was shacking up with Dey, and you knew where she was. Did you go see her?"

She goes to a movie the day after she finds the information about her mom in Dey's files. *No Country for Old Men*. The Coen brothers can take her mind off anything, transport her to their universe in the space of two scenes. Javier Bardem's haircut makes her laugh out loud, but she is the only one in the movie theater laughing. Woody Harrelson makes her laugh too. But it's the captive bolt gun that transfixes her through the entire film and Chigurh giving his victims a chance at life or death with the flip of a coin. *All chances in life are determined by the flip of a metaphorical coin*, she thinks. She loves the film, but the moment she steps outside the theater, the spell ends. She is back in her life with another choice to make. She takes a quarter out of her pocket, flips it so that it lands on the back of her hand. Heads.

The theater is on West Twenty-Third Street. It takes her thirteen minutes to reach Gramercy Park, a part of old New York where once gentrification actually meant something. She skirts the park itself, peering in through the black-painted wrought iron palisade at the beautiful plantings.

The apartment is on the north side. She walks up the steps, pulls open the outer door, finds herself in a small vestibule. Ahead of her is the locked inner door, to her left a brass plate affixed to the wall on which eight names are printed. Beside each name is a black plastic button, and above these a small grill into which you answer when the person you wish to see speaks to you after you push the appropriate button.

She looks down the list. The unseen hairs on her forearms stir and lift. On the fourth floor: Marie Flowers. Marie is her mother's middle name, Flowers her maiden name. The choice: To push the button, hear her mother's voice, perhaps be allowed into her life again. Or to turn and leave and never look back. But the choice has already been made for her: heads, yes; tails, no. That is the deal she made with herself. A prickling breaks out on the center of her forehead, as if she's facing Chigurh, as if the working end of his captive bolt pistol is pressed into the flesh above her eyes. Life or death.

Tears shimmer in her eyes; her hand reaches out to the brass plaque, her palm cupped over her mother's name, throwing it into darkness. Somewhere on the fourth floor her mother sits or walks or, arched across her bed in rucked Carine Gilson lingerie, fornicates in her frantic efforts to pull herself into life, to understand who she is and why she is here. Then, without another thought or tear shed, Laurel takes her hand away, and the imagined scene winks out, vanishes, fades to black. She turns, opens the front door, and skips down the steps, her gaze on the sparkle of sunlight on the treetops inside Gramercy Park.

~

"And it's at that precise moment," Laurel said, "that I realized what those two words meant for me. Life or death. To press the button, to hear my mother's voice, to tell her I had tracked her down, *that* was, for me, death. She had left without so much as a kiss goodbye. She had given birth to me, but after that, what? She had abandoned me for what? For a luxury apartment, for designer clothes out the yin-yang—for money, in other words. What the fuck. I mean, Jimmy, what the fuck, you know?"

They were both silent until he said, "Well, you did the right thing. You chose life. You destroyed Dey's life."

"I destroyed the false life he had given my mother."

He frowned. "But what about Orfeo?"

"Afterward, when I'd set everything in motion, when I had transferred Dey's money to my own accounts, when I was at the airport just before my flight was about to board, I called him." Laurel looked away for a moment, then back at him. "I said to him, 'I want my life back, Orfeo.'

"'I don't understand,' he said.

"'My name isn't Helene Messer; it's Laurel Springfield. That wandering eye of yours glistening in the streetlight,' I told him. 'I saw you take my mother away,' and I severed the connection."

THIRTY

If there was anyone at Richard's graveside ceremony besides the minister and Rosie Menkins, the nurse who had taken care of Maggie Mathis at the end, Laurel didn't see them. The two of them stood by the open grave, Richard's coffin cradled in the mechanism that would lower it into the ground, the minister at the head, Rosie at the side. As she walked quietly up, Laurel wondered if there would be anyone at all to see Jimmy Self buried. She didn't think so.

The air was somnolent, reluctant to stir. A white sun made its ghostly presence felt through the fog. Far off, the sounds of traffic reverberated like a plucked string, through the trees that dotted the cemetery. Here and there, bunches of flowers lay at the foot of headstones, remembrances of times past but not forgotten.

How much of her past did Laurel want to forget? So much. Memory could be an enemy as well as a friend.

The minister, in the midst of a prayer for the dead, did not raise his eyes from his open scriptures as she neared the grave site, but Rosie Menkins did. For an instant, her gray eyes opened wide, surprised to see another mourner here at Richard Mathis's final resting place, beside his wife. She tried not to look at Maggie's fresh grave.

"You sanctify the homes of the living and make holy the places of the dead," the minister read aloud. "You alone open the gates of righteousness and lead us to the dwellings of the saints."

"Blessed is the Lord our God," Rosie whispered, and with that the priest closed his book, the machine began to lower Richard into his grave, and Laurel's eyes welled up with tears. She was scarcely aware of it until Rosie turned to her and said, "Are you all right, hon?"

"What? No, yes." Felt a tear tickle her cheek as it ran down, swiped it away. "I guess not."

A certain hawkish look left Rosie's face, replaced by an expression of sympathy. "Thank God you're not a reporter."

"Oh, no," Laurel said, her mind making a lightning assessment. Her reporter identity was totally the wrong thing here. "I'm—well, I *was*—one of Professor Mathis's PhD students at Michigan."

"And you made the trip from Ann Arbor."

It wasn't difficult for her to blush shamelessly. "The professor was my mentor. He was going to take me on his next field trip. I don't know how this could happen." She started to cry again. "I mean, why do bad things happen to good people?"

"That's a puzzle I've been trying to solve all my life."

The priest, his work here done, had left without looking at either of them, stepping carefully, his feet raised like a horse in high grass. The men working the machine rolled it to one side, started to shovel in the newly turned earth. It was dark and damp. It looked like clots of old blood.

"With the passing years," Rosie continued, "I've come to the reluctant conclusion that nothing can be done. We're all helpless; we're all in God's hands."

"Do you really believe that?" Laurel said.

"What?"

"About God."

"Of course I do." Her brows drew together. "Don't you?"

Laurel shivered. She was playing a role, and she wasn't, as if she were straddling a border. "I believed in a life out on field digs, unearthing the mysterious past. Now I don't know what I believe."

"What's your name, hon?"

She almost said Angela Chase, which momentarily frightened her. "Jennifer DeAngeles."

"I'm Rosalind Menkins, but everyone calls me Rosie. I'm a trauma nurse at the hospital just down the road."

The two women shook hands hesitantly, awkwardly.

"You really cared about him," Rosie said.

"I did."

Rosie looked around. "Well. It's getting chilly out here. Why don't we find a warm place to have a drink and a talk?"

At that moment, Laurel was startled by the pinging of Richard's mobile phone. Excusing herself, she stepped away several paces, stared at the lit-up screen. A text had come in. A tremor of intent rippled through her. Touched the icon with her fingertip, and this was what came up:

Sept 30: daddy help.

~

Assalamu alaikum, Bella. I salute u 4 ur courage & ur constancy. My name is Akima. I am part of Salim's family. Part of ur family. Here with us in the States u will find genuine camaraderie & sisterhood. A far cry from false & shallow "friendships" u have turned away from. They r part of the subtle corruption of the west. It is so clear that the western model 4 family has failed. It has failed u. But, praise b 2 Allah, all that is at an end. We r ur family now. We will never leave u. We will always take care of u.

As u have discussed w Salim—as u urself have wisely realized—the western model 4 women is a false promise promulgated by Iblis (the devil). Women who go to work take on corrupted ideas & shoddy-minded beliefs instead of religion. The model preferred by infidels in the west failed the minute that women were "liberated" from their place in the house.

The model of the culture of Iblis includes following fashions, having yr body pierced, yr face painted w expensive products, sure signs of the disbelievers of the west. This crass materialism of fashion trends, of more & more ways to spend money, is presented by Iblis in clothes shops & beauty salons, night clubs & concerts where young people congregate to pollute themselves w alcohol & drugs. This is clearly a path away from purity, from religious knowledge, from the teachings of Allah. Allah is good. Allah is great. This we know. This we celebrate 5 times every day of our lives. U will see & rejoice w us when u arrive here & r embraced by me, ur new sister.

Alice's Teacup was just a few blocks past the florists and headstone carvers that lined both sides of the street adjacent to the cemetery. Unlike Nestors, which had been bustling with activity, Alice's Teacup was nearly deserted: only a pair of lonely old women sitting together over their cups, not speaking, their eyes misted over.

Rosie led her to a table near the far end, but excusing herself, Laurel went off to the ladies' room, where, in a vacant stall, she texted Bella back.

Where are you? I'm here. I'll come get you.

No answer.

Bella—she deleted that, started again: Rabbit, please please answer. So curious, like crying out to herself. I will find you wherever you are. I promise.

No answer.

Bella!

Laurel was weeping openly now. *Bella, why won't you answer?* But at least she knew the girl was alive. Wiping her eyes, she flushed the toilet, washed her hands, and returned to the table where Rosie sat patiently. The mobile phone was close. She was waiting.

The café was festooned with *Alice in Wonderland* memorabilia—cells from the Disney film and illustrations from various book editions with, not surprisingly, the emphasis on the Mad Hatter's tea party. The Dormouse always made Laurel laugh, especially on those occasions when he woke up, still half-asleep and bewildered, and came out with the most unintentionally philosophical ideas: "'You might just as well say,' added the Dormouse, who seemed to be talking in his sleep, 'that "I breathe when I sleep" is the same thing as "I sleep when I breathe"!'"

"You're smiling," Rosie said as she ordered them tea and cakes in the English manner from a waitress in a frilly apron and cap. "That's a good thing."

"I love *Alice in Wonderland*."

Rosie laughed, her pillowy cheeks reddened now with the steamy heat. "Who doesn't?"

She waited for their tea and cakes to be served, poured a spot of milk in hers, stirred it with a tiny silver spoon. "I come here sometimes when things get too much on the floor. At the hospital, I mean. I need someplace to unwind, shrug off the responsibility for just a minute—know what I mean?"

"I do," Laurel said, truthfully. She sipped her tea. She'd put a thin wheel of lemon into it. Now it floated like a life preserver in a brown sea. She eyed a raisin scone, undecided as to whether she wanted it. "I have the same issue sometimes."

Rosie nodded. "Academic life can be tough. I'm not too old to remember." She sliced a small cake in two, neatly as a surgeon. "All those tests, one after another. The tension just seems to pile up."

Laurel rubbed her temple with her fingertips. "I just didn't think . . ."

"Well, death, hon." Rosie patted her hand. "No one's prepared for that."

It was the sliver of an opening Laurel had been hoping for. "But you must find it easier, being around it so much at the hospital."

"Easier? No." Rosie shook her head, took a crumb of cake between thumb and forefinger. "But after a while you find a way to deal with it." Her gray eyes regarded Laurel's across the table. "You disconnect from the terrible things happening around you. I mean, you're there, doing all the things you need to do, and curiously, your mind is supersharp, but at the same time, a part of you—the really important part, the part that makes you *you*—has withdrawn to a kind of island where nothing can touch you, nothing can hurt you, where you're alone."

"Yes." Laurel felt a rush of feeling toward this woman she had just met but whom she knew so well. "I've been on that island."

Rosie blinked heavily, as if coming out of a semitrance. "Have you? Fancy that. And you so young, with your whole life ahead of you."

How could it be, Laurel asked herself, that she felt as if she had lived her whole life already and yet had not even begun it.

Rosie leaned across the table. "Hon, you look exhausted. Why don't you get some rest before you head back to Ann Arbor?"

"Where?" Laurel's heart lurched. "Oh, yes." She raised her cup to take another sip, set it down when it was halfway to her mouth. "But, you know, Rosie, I can't help but think of Bella."

"Ah, Professor Mathis's daughter." She clucked her tongue. "It's a dreadful thing. Just disappeared into thin air. No one knows where she went, what happened to her." She sucked in her lower lip. "There was a girl, Gale Fisher, about Bella's age. She disappeared a year or so ago." Her eyes took on a glassy, faraway look. "The police searched for her for weeks. In the end, a hunter found her. Or what was left of her, poor thing. No one should die like that, especially a sheltered child of sixteen."

Laurel, trying to repel the sick feeling in the pit of her stomach, said, "Did the police ever find out who did it?"

"The FBI was called in. I remember what an awful uproar that caused in the community, everyone locking their doors, afraid to let their daughters play outside or go to the mall—or anywhere, really. Just shuttled 'em back and forth to and from school. It's just like now, isn't it?" Her eyes cleared a bit. "But now all everyone talks about is terrorism. Well, I suppose it's no different here than in Ann Arbor or anywhere else in the country."

"Is that the current theory?" Laurel asked, her gut churning. "That Bella wasn't taken by the same person who murdered Gale Fisher?"

"I believe that's the theory that has the most currency now. Well, the FBI thinks so, anyhow. That she was recruited."

"But why would they think that?"

"Because of that neighbor family, the Shehadis. Arabs, you see."

"Don't you mean Arab Americans?"

"The daughter, Elin, was Bella's nanny for years and years," Rosie said, giving no indication she had heard Laurel. "When the girl went missing, they brought the father, Hashim Shehadi, in for questioning, for the second time, I believe. Well, he's in import-export, you see, so he's automatically suspect."

Laurel wondered whether a Caucasian import-exporter would be automatically suspect for anything. She thought not.

"Then the mother was interrogated," Rosie was saying. "Jesus protect anyone from interrogation. Then they hauled in the oldest boy of theirs, Gabriel—he's the troublemaker of the family. Full of hate. I heard he and a bunch of his friends beat up some Christian boys several days ago. Mark my words: if anyone's a suspect, it's him."

"A suspect in what?" Laurel asked.

Rosie made a conciliatory gesture. "Listen—I don't have anything against Muslims per se. We have a lot of them here, and they're mostly model citizens, just the same as you or me." Her face clouded over. "But still, when you hear about these girls being inducted into what amounts to slavery, I mean, you can't help thinking the worst when you see a full beard or a hijab, can you."

She planted her elbows forthrightly on the table. "But if that's what did happen to Bella . . . it's too late, isn't it? More likely than not, she's already on her way to Syria to be with those awful brutes. The things I've read and seen on the nightly news. God alone knows why any Western girl would willingly join them."

"Maybe she had nowhere else to go," Laurel said quietly.

Rosie pursed her lips. "Well, this whole mess is the Shehadis' doing, if you ask me."

No one is, Laurel thought and pushed on with her line of questioning as Jimmy Self had taught her to do. "You took care of her mother, didn't you? At least that's what I heard."

Rosie nodded, remained tight-lipped.

"It was a long slide down, wasn't it?"

"There were reasons."

"There always are." Laurel cracked a sugar cookie in two, its crystals glittering like diamonds. "But do you think those reasons mattered to Bella?"

Rosie regarded her, her hard stare slowly softening. "No," she said. "I don't suppose they did." She turned away for a moment, and it was only the fact of her bosom heaving that Laurel became aware that she was sobbing.

"Excuse me," Rosie said. "I'm sorry." Rummaging in her pocketbook for a package of tissues. She held one to her nose, as if it were an ice pack, as if it would calm her down.

"I'm the one who's sorry," Laurel said. "I obviously overstepped—"

"No, no." Rosie sniffed, waving a hand. "Not at all." She blew her nose, crumpled the tissue into a ball, stuffed it back into her handbag. "It's a terrible thing when people confess to you, a dreadful burden that's difficult to bear alone."

Laurel didn't want her to bear it alone, but she sensed the best thing she could do was to put on a sympathetic face and keep quiet. Neither of those things was difficult for her; she felt once again her false identity slipping, as it had with Richard. This close to Bella, she could no longer ignore the parallels in their lives. Missing. Everyone who meant something to them missing. Laurel had her father, until she hadn't. Bella had her father, until she hadn't. But who would stand up for Bella? Who would care whether she was found? Not her parents, and not the FBI, who seemed more interested in interrogating Muslims than they were in finding her.

Rosie's gray eyes searched Laurel's. "I don't want to bear this secret alone, Jenn."

Her false identity once again reared its head, not to be helped. "You don't have to, Rosie."

Rosie nodded. Bit her lip. Laurel poured her some tea, stirred the milk in. This simple gesture of kindness cleared the final barrier as a jinn cleared the way with smoke and sparking flame.

Rosie took her hand, squeezed it. Then she told Laurel Maggie and Richard's terrible secret: how Maggie had been carrying twins, how one of them had turned in the womb, her elbow pressing against her sister's chest. How Bella had been born alive, her twin dead within seconds of drawing her first gasping breath. "I know how this must sound," Rosie concluded. "Well, to tell you the truth, I don't know how it sounds, but Maggie never wanted kids. Professor Mathis forced her into it, so she said. She was near the end of her tether. People like her, just before they go for good, often experience a moment of absolute lucidity. This is what happened with Maggie. She told me . . . well, she could never get over what Bella did."

"What did Bella do?"

"What did she do? In Maggie's disturbed mind, she murdered her sister."

Laurel looked at her in complete shock. She felt cold down to her bones. An odd kind of keening, animal atavism rose from the core of her. *You have no idea.* "But that's crazy," she said when she found her voice. "Completely insane." Richard had never even hinted at such a horrific tragedy. *Good God, did Bella know? Had her crazy mother told her why she hated her?* Tears stood out, trembling on her lower eyelids. "It was an in vitro accident of nature. Dreadful and tragic, yes. But Bella had no volition. How could her mother blame her?"

"Maggie wished they had both died in her womb." Rosie's hands were trembling. "That was what she was holding on to, what was eating her alive from the inside out."

You have no idea. Now she did. Now she knew why life must have been hell for Bella without Richard, alone in the house with that venomous creature.

Laurel knew what she must ask now, though she very much didn't want to. And yet there was no way around it. She had to know. "And Rich—Professor Mathis. What was his role in all this?"

If Rosie heard Laurel's slip, she gave no indication of it. "He stayed away." The bitterness in her voice was unmistakable. "As far away from his family as he could. That was his solution: to bury himself in his work, polish his image, wash his hands of it all."

And now Laurel understood why Rosie Menkins had chosen her, of all people, to tell this story to. While it was often true that it was easier to unburden yourself to a stranger, this was not her objective. To her, Laurel was a wide-eyed grad student who idolized her professor, a man who, according to the story she told, had mentored her, while turning his back on his own daughter. She might just as well have said to Laurel, *You see, my dear, your darling professor Mathis had feet, boots, and coat of clay. He was a shit, and now you see him in all his muddied glory.*

Abruptly sick to death of Rosie Menkins and her rancid personality, she stood up. "Thank you for your time," she said, dropped a fan of bills on the table. She didn't want to owe this woman. Not one damn thing.

THIRTY-ONE

When Bella retired to her room after school, she read any number of fantasy and science fiction novels, from Frank Herbert's *Dune* to Ursula K. Le Guin's *The Left Hand of Darkness*. She liked these best because they allowed her to travel to different worlds, to get out of her stifled self; the teen fantasies then in vogue were too silly and immature for her. But more often than not, she read chunks of *Moby-Dick*—in the beginning because it was a gift from her father, but eventually, as she used a dictionary, came to understand it better, something about it hooked her deep in her psyche and wouldn't let go.

But that wasn't all she did. Her rage at her situation had incited her to expand her world far beyond the confines of Dearborn, of Michigan, of America. Bella had collected a cadre of friends—almost two dozen, in fact. Or perhaps they had collected her. They were all online; they were spread all over the globe; they were all young, all Muslims, all radical, all oriented toward ISIS and its self-proclaimed homeland, the caliphate in Syria and Iraq. Although she had never met any of them in the flesh, they were real to her in their mind-sets, their dedication, their adherence to the teachings of Allah, the oneness of God.

"Islam is the fastest-growing religion in the world," they told her.

They sent her money, sweets, gift certificates to IslamicBookstore.com and directed her to internet radio stations that played ISIS anthems, twenty-four seven. At first they chatted away for hours on end, talking about anything and everything, but really, when she looked back on it, she realized they were subtly urging her to talk about her loneliness and isolation, her repugnance for the culture of money, cheap fame, the never-ending barrage of sexual explicitness, the shallowness, hypocrisy, and corruption everywhere she looked. But her enmity went far deeper than that. She was an outsider without friends or, other than Elin and Umm, family. But even at the Shehadis' she felt as if she didn't belong. Of course, Elin and Umm did everything they could to make her feel at home—but that house wasn't her home, and being there only heightened her sense of isolation, her conviction that she was no one, that she belonged nowhere.

This was how her friends in ISIS caught her, trapped her, offered her an alternative. And to be truthful, how enticing did an alternative need to be when compared with nothing? When they judged they had drawn her in sufficiently, they little by little began to define the larger group to her. In a sense, they ceased being individuals as they drew back the curtain to show her the infinite blessings of the caliphate, where she, too, could live a life according to God's dictates.

"We came into existence," they told her, "as a response to the American invasion of Iraq in 2003. We began a Sunni uprising against the infidel oppressors and then an insurgency. In those early days, we were part of the Iraqi branch of al-Qaeda led by the sanguinary Abu Musab al-Zarqawi. Have you read your books? Have you heard of him? He was a Jordanian jihadi who, it turned out, had lost his way. His teaching had become obscure, muddled. He had begun to think of himself rather than the group.

"We left him. We left al-Qaeda for much the same reason. We became who we are now, dedicated to eradicating the infidel who blindly attacks us, invades our land, grasping for everything we have, everything we are. The infidel stands in opposition to Islam, to Allah, to our very way of life. So we must act, swiftly, violently, without hesitation, without remorse.

"We fight against great odds, so we provoke here, there, everywhere. Do we want a reaction? This is what we want the infidel to believe. This is, in fact, what he does believe. But no, in point of fact, our aim is to provoke an overreaction."

The battle cry of the harried, the downtrodden, the underdog held immense appeal for Bella, as they strongly suspected it would. Too, they were meticulous in providing her with a clear sense of sisterhood, family, a welcoming home. Through their incessant conversations long into her nighttime hours, they had determined her psychological weaknesses and now were in the process of exploiting them to the fullest extent.

Assalamu alaikum, Salim writes. It is imperative that u tell no 1 of ur conversion to Islam, especially ur family.

Walaikum salaam. I have no family, LOL, Bella replies, typing on her cell. Unless u count my neighbors. They're Islamics. 1 of them gave me the Qur'an. Great, right?

No! These people r a grave danger to u. You must especially stay away from them. Islamics in America r always under surveillance, they r always suspect, they r always a threat to u & me. U must remain true to our online community.

That will be difficult. 1 of them brought me up. She's like my mother. I love her.

What u feel isn't love, Bella. It's dependence. This is how America traps people, by making them dependent on all the decadence, the possessions, the wealth, the soft life that draws them further and further away from themselves. Life is not possessions & wealth—

these r illusions. Life is ideology; r motivation is ideology. Everything else—all the illusion— is stripped away. We r clean, we r pure, we r doing God's duty. Everything u have been taught about the world around u is false. When u are here with us, u will understand. The truth transcends time & space. It is truth that will protect u, it is truth that will save u. Truth will be ur mother, truth will be ur father. Truth will love u as no other. U will bow down to Truth & it will be ur everything.

Listen to me, u must keep a low profile. U must wrest urself from the last bonds of American slavery. This is the present task Allah has set before u as a test of ur faith & devotion. This is how u must think from now on as u have already embarked upon ur rebirth, ur new life.

Yes. I think I understand.

Of course u understand, Bella. Understanding, faith, devotion—these were the reasons u contacted me, these r the reasons we r friends, these r the reasons to undertake hijrah—the necessary & sacred voyage from the land of unbelievers to become 1 with the Islamic State in Syria & Iraq.

I am frightened. I hear stories abt the barbarous atrocities ISIS commits on a daily basis.

Bella, these r all lies ur govt commits abt us. That is why I am here; to set the record straight. To tell u the truth. To assure u not to worry. I will take care of u. I will be waiting for u at the end of ur hijrah. Here u will be loved, here u will be cherished, here u will find and fulfill ur destiny in sight of Allah.

I must confess, Salim. Sometimes I feel I
am betraying Jesus.

O Bella. U must understand that Islam recognizes Jesus as a prophet, along with Abraham, Moses, and Muhammad. In fact, during our prayers, we press our foreheads to the ground because the Bible tells us Jesus & all the prophets before him prayed in that fashion. But Jesus is not God, Bella. In this Christianity is mistaken. Do u understand me?

I'm not sure.

Here is my meaning, put another way. I have invited u to embrace Islam. I am not telling u to leave Christianity. I am informing u that Islam is the correction of Christianity.

THIRTY-TWO

Laurel approached the Shehadi house with a high degree of alertness. She walked at a normal pace. She did not look to the left or the right, did not swing her head around to glance behind her as characters in thrillers did. That kind of behavior might heighten tension, but in a real-life situation it was bound to draw attention.

Having picked up tips from Orfeo and Jimmy Self, she was able to ID two cars parked at either end of the street that seemed suspicious. They were both Chevys that looked as if they had been subtly modified, like detective cruisers.

There was still time to back out. She was not yet in their line of sight. She could turn around now and leave, but once she moved forward from here, they would mark her. She would be of interest to them because she was walking up the steps to the Shehadi house, which they had under surveillance. She did not kid herself. These people were not Dearborn police. They weren't state police either. They were feds. FBI. All at once the full force of Gael's warning smacked her in the face. Considering what had gone down with Dey, she was in no position to walk into the FBI's sights. If they decided to interrogate her, to look into her background, she was pretty sure it would be game over. Gael's work was excellent, but she had to wonder if it could stand up to a small army of feds. On the other hand, Gael worked for the feds; they were in some sense dependent on him for a good portion of their deep-cover work. Could his network save her? Maybe, maybe not. Nothing in life was assured: she knew that better than most.

Here, then, was her border. If she stayed where she was, she would be safe. She could turn around, take a plane to JFK or LAX, and be off to anywhere in the world except here. *Yes, of course*, she thought, *why not keep running away? That's what you've been doing all your so-called life*, which, she bitterly had to admit, wasn't much of a life at all.

Intuition and an admittedly fragile spiderweb of information she had gleaned had led her to the conclusion that Bella had not been abducted. She had run away. Why wouldn't she? She was not only unloved and abandoned; she believed herself despised by her mother, unwanted by Richard. And now here Laurel was, at the epicenter of Richard's life and now her own. That was her choice. Life or no life. That was no choice at all. She was the only one who had a chance to find out what had happened to Bella, to possibly do for her what her parents could not, what Laurel's own parents had failed to do for her. Stand by her, protect her, because no one else was capable of doing so. To go on, to do what she knew she must do, might very well put her in harm's way. But wasn't that what a parent did for her child? Wasn't that called responsibility? Laurel knew, deep down, that if there was any chance at all that by some miracle Bella was here, she had to find her. She had to save her. She was convinced that she was meant to be here. How did she know this? It was faith and faith only. A faith she had never known existed, let alone known she could possess.

How could she walk away? She couldn't. She didn't. It was only later, after it was all over, that she understood that in trying to save Bella, she was saving herself.

She moved forward, stepped across the border into the FBI's range, into the center of their attention as she climbed the steps to the Shehadi house. The front yard she had passed through was a mess, deep tire tracks grinding up the lawn. A mailbox that looked like it had been struck several times with a baseball bat. Around the side of the house, repairs were underway on two windows of the second floor, new panes of glass being hauled up stout ladders and installed.

While all this activity was going on at the side of the house, the front appeared entirely deserted. Ascending the set of steps, Laurel felt an abrupt bout of nerves, and she halted for a moment before the door to catch her breath. Before she could reach out and ring the bell or knock, the door flew inward, and she was confronted by an extremely pretty dark-eyed young woman in her midtwenties, wearing a high-collared, long-sleeved shirt; a charcoal-gray skirt that came down below her knees; and a hijab. It took Laurel a moment to register the fact that her hijab was an American flag pattern. So she wasn't afraid to make a statement in the face of the family's harassment. Good for her.

Behind her: a dim foyer, a jewel-tone Middle Eastern rug, a pair of brass pitchers with long, sinuous spouts and arabesques incised on their bodies residing on a polished fruitwood table. Three matching suitcases were lined up against one wall, a dark-blue coat slung over the top of the largest onc.

"If you've come for an interview," the young woman said, her voice dripping with suspicion, "I must disappoint you."

As she began to swing the door closed, Laurel found her voice. "Are you Elin?"

"No." Eyes narrowed.

"Bella's friend, yes?"

The door began to close again. "I told you—"

"I'm a friend of Richard's, Bella's father."

"I know who Richard is," the young woman said shortly. "I don't know you."

"Richard and I met . . ." Laurel's voice trailed off. Her throat ached. "We met on Crete, his last dig."

Elin—Laurel knew by her reactions that this young woman was Elin Shehadi—regarded her critically. "Are you the one . . . the woman in the photo?"

Laurel's smile was tinged with sorrow. "I'm afraid I am." She held out a hand, but it was not taken. She let her arm drop to her side. *Okay*, she thought. *Fair enough.* "Laurel Springfield." She was not going to lie to this woman. "Yes, I know. I had a different name while I was on Crete." She waved a hand. "It's a long story."

Elin seemed to accept all this at face value. "And you came all this way for his funeral."

"In a sense." Laurel cleared her throat again. So close to Bella she could almost feel her, it seemed she had turned shy. "I also came . . . to find out what happened to Bella."

Elin stared at her, bell-like mouth slightly open so that Laurel could see the tips of her white teeth. After what seemed a very long time, Elin stepped back. "Come in," she said. "Please."

Laurel knew enough to take off her shoes. In stockinged feet she padded after Elin through a comfortably furnished living room. There were books everywhere—novels, biographies, historical and religious texts. Electronic versions of various Transformers at rest in one corner, a couple of laptops open on the coffee table. She paused at a framed photo of the family. Elin turned back, pointed out her mother, father, her four brothers. Laurel was most interested in Gabriel, the firebrand, but she sensed it was too early to ask Elin about him. Could he be the root of the problems the Shehadis were suffering through now?

In a large sunlit kitchen, scents of unfamiliar spices wafted through the air.

"How are your parents?"

"Shaken," Elin said.

Laurel sat down at the wooden table while Elin prepared mint tea. A large carved bowl in the center was mounded with fresh mandarin oranges, fresh figs, dried dates, and colossal pistachios. Laurel waited until Elin set a glass of tea in front of her, then sat at an angle to her. Along with the glasses, she had brought several sheets of creased paper, indicating they had been folded.

"Thank you for taking the time to talk with me," Laurel said. "I was looking for you at the funeral."

Elin gave her a twisted smile. "Well, it wasn't for lack of trying."

"What d'you mean?"

"We were told by the local cops—who I'm sure got their orders from the FBI—not to come, that our presence would be a distraction, that it most likely would cause a disturbance."

To this, Laurel said not a word; she felt too ashamed.

Elin sipped her tea. "Please. Drink." She waited until her guest had taken a sip. "It's to your liking? Not too sweet?"

"It's delicious. Just right."

Elin nodded, clearly pleased.

"May I ask you a question?"

"That's why you've come, isn't it?"

"It's about you. You were very young when you went to work for the Mathises."

"Eleven."

"That seems odd."

Elin smiled. "Yes. I suppose it does. But first, we're talking about Maggie. Every decision she made—or failed to make—was odd. Second, I had what she called the three Rs—I was respectful, responsible, reliable. Third, Bella took to me right away. I was a combination of big sister and mother."

Laurel nodded, feeling once again ashamed. "I understand completely. I didn't mean—"

"Don't worry," Elin said, waving away her words. "I would have done the same thing." She smiled. "It did put a great deal of pressure on my schoolwork. Many nights I hardly slept." A rhythmic banging commenced from somewhere above them. She rose, went to the window behind the sink, tried to look up. "I assume you saw the work going on outside the house."

"Yes. I wondered about that."

Elin, returning to the table, slid the papers across the tabletop. With a quizzical glance at her, Laurel read them with mounting horror: *Go back to the fucking desert ware you belong*, the first one read in an illiterate scrawl. *We HATE you more then niggers.*

"My God!" Laurel exclaimed, then instantly put her hand over her mouth. "Sorry."

"It's all right. We believe in God in this household."

Laurel, shaken to her core, read the second one: *You started this but we'll stop it, sand nigger. We're coming for you.*

"The night my father was first taken away," Elin said as Laurel pushed the hateful mail back at her with disgust, "someone shot out the windows of the bedroom where Bella was sleeping with me. Maggie—her mother—had been hospitalized, you see."

Laurel nodded. "This is sickening, beyond terrifying. Have you notified the feds?"

Elin laughed, but not in a good way. "The feds. Yes, of course, right away. I also gave them the originals of these letters."

"What did they do? Have you heard from them?"

"They came and took Umm—my mother—away for questioning."

"Because she's Lebanese, because she's a Muslim."

"That and because of how close we were—are—to the Mathis family."

"The hit-and-run."

Elin nodded. "No one here believes it was an accident." She sighed. "I'm beginning to think that my father is right. We're not welcome in America any longer."

"Those are frightened bigots talking. You've got to fight—"

"It's fascism, isn't it? What's happened to democracy?"

"When people get frightened, they circle the wagons. They say stupid things. They're terrified."

"Well, but that's just what ISIS wants. It plays into all their propaganda. I don't understand."

"Frightened people are stupid people." Laurel shook her head. "But as far as that goes, I don't fully understand the reaction myself." She reached over, took Elin's hand briefly. It was warm from the tea. How close in age they were, Laurel thought, how distant they were in their experiences. And yet they were two women, and on a fundamental level their empathy for each other was a power not to be denied. "But you can't let these people drive you away. You have as much right to be here as anyone else."

Elin's eyes magnified as tears overflowed them, ran down her cheeks unheeded. "Thank you, Laurel. No one has . . . it's been so long . . ." She took a breath, struggling to come to grips with her emotions. "Sometimes lately I feel as if we're already living in a penal colony. We're spied on all the time, followed wherever we go. Maybe our phone lines are tapped. It would be easy, wouldn't it. Those magic words: *a matter of national security*. Like *open sesame*."

Laurel took Elin's hand again. She knew only too well what it felt like to be constantly on edge, constantly anxious, to feel ghostly footsteps behind you. Only the footsteps Elin heard were real.

"Listen, Elin. I want to help in any way I can, limited though it may be. You know Bella better than anyone. What can you tell me about her disappearance? What do you think happened to her? Do you think she ran away?"

"No, no, I don't think that." She stopped abruptly, as if in midthought.

"Elin?" Laurel squeezed her hand. "What is it?"

Tears overflowed Elin's eyes again. "A week ago we had a terrible fight."

"What about?"

Elin stood up, crossed to the sink, turned on the water. But she just stood there, immobile, her back to Laurel.

"Elin, what did you and Bella fight about?"

When Elin turned, there were more tears in her eyes. She had backed herself against the edge of the sink, hands gripping it, knuckles white. "Yes, all right. Yes. I think she ran away, and it's all my fault."

"Why d'you you think that?"

"She took everything important to her—her laptop, her cell phone, her diaries, books—with her. The police crawled all over the house. They found nothing." She bit her lip, shook her head. "I'm leaving, you see. I'm moving to Chicago; I'm due to be picked up any moment. I met someone, a wonderful man named Matt Kirby. He gave a lecture here just over a month ago, the evening Maggie collapsed. I went with my parents; we followed the ambulance to the hospital. I was waiting down in the lobby when Matt came in. He was worried about the woman who had passed out. He's a very compassionate, caring man. I told him what had happened, and we got to talking. He got a new position in the Division of Social Sciences at the University of Chicago. He's asked me to come with him, and I said yes."

"That seems precipitous."

"To you, maybe. But you see, from that moment on we Skyped every night. We spoke for hours and hours. It's odd, maybe. My parents don't get it, but you have to understand—I've been taking care of Bella since we were both very young. That's all I've known. All I've thought about is how to keep her as happy as I could. And now, well, I'm twenty-eight. It's time I thought about myself."

Laurel thought, *So close in age, but I feel decades older*. "Bella took it badly, I imagine."

"Worse than badly. She pretty much flipped out. I'd never seen her like that, snapping at me, baring her teeth. I tried to calm her, but it was as if I wasn't even in the room. She was frenzied, I guess is the best word to describe it. I mean, it was so crazy, so out of character. I expected her to break down, cry. I was expecting to console her, rock her in my arms like I always did when she was sad or frightened. But this—this explosion of rage and violence—no, that was far beyond anything I had foreseen."

"What exactly did she say? Can you remember?"

"I was so shocked I . . . let me think." She worried her lower lip. "She said things like, 'Don't you see how this country is changing, how it treats you like second-class citizens?' And things like, 'I don't know how you can buy into the falsity and materialism of this culture.'"

"That sounds like pretty sophisticated thinking."

Elin's smile had about it a wistful air of times remembered. "Bella is brilliant. I'm convinced she can do anything she sets her mind to." Her face clouded over.

"Except."

They were interrupted by the front doorbell. Elin excused herself. Laurel heard voices, craned her neck, but could see nothing. Then Elin came in with a tall, good-looking man dressed in a charcoal-gray suit, wing tip shoes, a white shirt, and a polka-dot tie. A serious outfit with a bit of whimsy: perfect. She introduced him as Matt Kirby. With a smile, he nodded deferentially to Laurel, then turned to Elin.

"I'll go upstairs and pay my respects to your parents. I want to hear about their brief incarcerations; maybe I can help. Then I'll take your luggage out to the car."

"Thank you," Elin said, a sweet smile wreathing her face. "I'll be out in a minute."

"Take your time," Kirby said. He turned to Laurel. "A pleasure."

Moments later they heard his tread on the stairs.

Elin came back to the table, but she didn't sit down, instead stood gripping a chairback with the same white-knuckled grip.

"We were speaking about Bella," Laurel said.

Elin nodded. "Bella finds it difficult to believe in herself. Despite how she excels at school, despite what I and my family have tried to give her, she remains wary, terrified of the world at large. She deals with her terror by isolating herself. In a way, she's severed herself from the world around her."

"She's not delusional."

"Oh, no. But she lacks an inner compass. Not surprising, given what her parents . . ." She waved a hand. "But I don't want to get into that, not on the day her father was buried."

Feeling there was no better time, Laurel said, "What can you tell me about your brother, Gabriel?"

At once, Elin's demeanor changed. She stiffened as if Laurel had delivered her a blow. "Why do you ask about Gabriel especially?"

"Did he have any contact with Bella?"

"What? No. Not any more than my other brothers. Bella was closest with me and with Umm—my mother." She sighed. "To be honest, my father wasn't thrilled about having another girl in the house; I was more than enough for him. Praise Allah Umm delivered him four boys. And as for my brothers, they were unfailingly polite to her, Gabriel included, but I don't think they knew what to make of her. They really weren't sure why she was here so much." She cocked her head. "Again, I'd like to understand your interest in Gabriel."

Laurel shrugged. "Along the way, I'd heard some things about him."

"Let me guess. You talked to Rosie Menkins at the funeral."

"Rosie Menkins talked to me, more like it."

Elin's wide mouth twitched. "Yes, that's about right. What did she tell you?"

"That Gabriel and a bunch of his friends beat up a group of Christian boys."

Elin gave a humorless laugh. "I'm assuming she didn't tell you that those boys Gabriel went after attacked Ali, the owner of Ali's All-Night, and beat him very badly. The cops wouldn't do anything, so Gabriel felt he had a responsibility."

"Revenge." Laurel knew more than most people about revenge. Hers had gotten a man—admittedly, a very bad man—killed.

"I don't say what he did was right. My parents punished him. But, you know, he'd had enough of being pushed around. Even Bella felt it."

"It was clear from the outset that Rosie's a bigot."

Elin sighed. "She's not saying anything most of Dearborn isn't thinking right about now. All Muslims are terrorists: that's the hysteria of the moment. Another reason to get out of here."

"Running away?" Laurel was immediately ashamed. She was the last person in the world to accuse someone of running away.

Elin gave her a pained look. "Perhaps some people will think that, Umm among them. But the truth is I think I can do more good elsewhere. I'm transferring universities. I'm going to get a degree in international law. Then I can help my people."

Laurel felt a surge of empathy and respect for this young woman. She had smarts—guts too. She knew what she was about.

"Elin, I know this could be construed as an offensive question. Nevertheless, I have to ask: Have you made any attempt to find Bella?"

Elin drew herself up to her full height. "I've been Bella's substitute mother for fifteen years. So yes, it is an offensive question."

"And yet you're leaving her for good today." Abandoning her, but Laurel knew she had no business even thinking that. This woman had devoted her life to Bella. How long could she be expected to keep it up?

"Listen to me, Laurel. Our family involvement with the Mathises has brought us nothing but persecution and misery, though I have no idea why."

Laurel could make an educated guess that it had everything to do with Richard's twinned life, as Jimmy Self had put it, but she knew it would do no good to tell Elin this. And anyway, how could she be sure? When it came to Richard, how could she be sure of anything?

"She ran," Elin was saying now. "I know she ran away. It's the only explanation."

"But where would she go? Surely she had favorite places."

"Only one," Elin said. "The library."

THIRTY-THREE

The chat room where Bella had met Salim was eight months behind her. It seemed like a lifetime. As she waited here in the safe house, a broken-down apartment above Ali's All-Night, she shivered. She longed to email Salim, to "hear" his reassuring words, the words of Allah, but it was still daylight in Syria; Salim was at work with the other freedom fighters of ISIS, securing a permanent homeland where the true word of Allah could flourish.

It had been four days since she had walked out of her house. She should have made her *hijrah* by now; she should have been with Salim in Syria. But something had gone wrong. The contact who was supposed to pick her up on the first leg of her journey never showed. Salim told her he and his cell had been picked up by the federal police, as he called them. But she needn't worry. Her contact had no knowledge of her, had not yet been given the address of the safe house.

> Have patience. We all must be xtra vigilant now. We will have another contact in place to move u. He is quite near u so it will be very soon.

There was food in the wheezing refrigerator and the cabinets above the sink, whose spout dripped constantly. The toilet, though hideously stained, worked well enough, if she flushed two or three times. There was nothing to do, so she opened the copy of an English translation of the Qur'an Elin had given her and continued to read. But her mind kept drifting toward Salim. She had seen a picture of him: small, slender, eyes as dark as night, rimmed in kohl. He looked at once fierce and tender, though she was at a loss to explain how.

> Now u must make ur Shahada, ur declaration of faith. U will do this in writing. The 1st 2 of our family to read it will be ur witnesses.

~

It is late at night, maybe three in the morning. Through the wall, she can hear the TV in Maggie's bedroom. Maggie, she knows, falls into a drugged sleep with the TV on. Often, she is obliged to steal into Maggie's room to shut it off. Sometimes, she's in and out in fifteen or twenty seconds, hurrying as if the floor is a bed of glowing red coals. Once or twice, though, she stops at the foot of the bed, watching the nonperson lying in unnatural sleep, split off from her by a glass wall. In those moments, she wonders why Maggie cannot look her in the eye, why she speaks to her in monosyllables. She wonders what she has done to arouse such unspeakable enmity in her mother. She wonders why her father is almost never home and when he is, they spend all their time fighting. It's as if he seeks to control her, as if he has a right to tell her what's right, what's wrong.

~

> The real truth of democracy is laid out before you like a poisoned feast. The so-called democratic elections touted by the west are nothing more than a gigantic fraud. Elected officials r all corrupt. This is fact, not fiction. They r all lazy, stupid & bigoted. U see 4 urself how unfairly Arabs & all Muslims r treated in ur

> country. They r spied on, hounded & harassed. Bella, hear me, there can b no justice for Muslims in the west.

❧

And there is her mother, sleeping like a sick baby—or, rather, the nonperson impersonating her mother. A pod person, a nonhuman who is doing a shit job of impersonating a human being. *I don't know where you came from*, she thinks, *but I sure as hell know where you're going. And when you do, I want to be far, far away.*

❧

> I am sending u a prayer rug, Bella. And a hijab, which u must wear when u pray. I think u will treasure both. I picked them out myself. I have also enclosed 2 books that offer u a better interpretation of Islam. U may find the rules more stringent than in the edition of the Qur'an ur neighbor gave u. That 1 has been infected & perverted by western publishers. Pls throw it away. Read the books I send you seriously, eagerly, purposefully. B assured Allah, who loves & protects u, will reward the purity of ur intent.

They knew nothing about the purity of her intent. The world of Dearborn had lived down to its cruel sobriquet of Deadborn. There was nothing for her here—less than nothing. She longed to escape, for something larger than she was, older, wiser—like a jinn to sweep her up in its arms and take her away to adventures, to everything that awaited her outside of this claustrophobic town where she felt drowned, plowed under by its unremitting normalcy, its unchanging small-town ways. She ached for this surcease to her agony the way she imagined a girl ached for her lover every moment they were apart.

Now in her American cell, the darkness her constant companion, emptiness contracted the space within which she existed. She spent the endless hours reading about how ISIS was deliberately emulating the nineteenth-century anarchists, whose philosophy revolved around what they called the "propaganda of the deed"—that is to say, translating the bombing of Wall Street on September 16, 1920, to the bombing of a Russian airliner taking off from Sharm al-Shaykh; the *Charlie Hebdo* killings; the coordinated attacks in Paris, culminating in the Bataclan massacre. At its heart, the strategy took advantage of Newton's third law of motion: an action will elicit an opposite reaction. As bin Laden sought with the 9/11 act of terror to lure the Americans into attacking the Middle East—it chose Iraq—to feed extremist insurgency, so ISIS was provoking a Western boots-on-the-ground reaction in Syria, an invasion of its ever-expanding caliphate, to accelerate the recruitment of the disaffected, the downtrodden, and those, like Bella, whose idealism drew them to a rebellion that echoed their own internal rebellion and discontent.

But now she had read enough. Returning to her phone, she began again to reread her conversations with Salim. Her own personal history.

Bella, I must tell you that the single most significant of Muhammad's hadiths prophesizes the final battle between good and evil, between Muslims—and by Muslims I mean only Sunnis who, like us, adhere to the strictest of Sharia law—and Christians. Muhammad's hadith calls for the battle to be fought in and around Dabiq, which is today in northern Syria, part of our caliphate. This battle, Muhammad predicts, is the precursor to the apocalypse.

I haven't read this hadith, Salim.
What does it say?

> I will read it to you: "The Hour will not be established until the Romans—Christians—land at Dabiq. Then an army from Medina of the best people on the earth at that time will leave for them . . . So they will fight them. Then one third will flee; Allah will never forgive them. One third will be killed; they will be the best martyrs with Allah. And one third will conquer them; they will never be afflicted with sorrow. Then they will conquer Constantinople." Today, that city is Istanbul, the gateway to the west.

Bella wrote back: But what about love, Salim? Surely there must be love where you are, where I'm going.

And this was Salim's reply: There is no room for love when the infidel is rising. In this time the religion of war is the sole imperative.

Gabriel, Elin's eldest brother, in his room in the Shehadi house, read Bella's secret history. He sat cross-legged on his bed, staring intently at his laptop's screen. He had hacked into Bella's email and Twitter accounts. Now he read everything that came her way, all the private, secret conversations she believed inviolable, as people did, despite the numberless stories of hacking and prying into online accounts. The universal mantra of "It won't happen to me" was part of the human condition, hardwired, a natural firewall.

But her conversations with Salim and the other online jihadi weren't private. Her history was not her own. Gabriel followed every word with a studied avidity that would doubtless frighten her were she to be become aware of his ghostly presence hovering just over her shoulder.

Laurel followed the directions Elin had given her to the letter. At some point, though she couldn't gauge precisely when, she became aware that she was being followed. Resisting the urge to turn around and look behind her, she slowed her pace just a bit, glanced in the side mirrors of the parked cars she passed. She expected to see one of the SUVs with the blacked-out windows the FBI used, but in this she was disappointed. She did, however, glimpse a slim male figure slip into a doorway; then, seeing that she had neither stopped nor glanced back over her shoulder, he emerged and continued to pace her step for step. He wore jeans, sneakers, and a hoodie over his head, casting his face in shadow.

From then on, she ignored her tail, as Jimmy Self would no doubt call him, and continued on to the library. The interior held the particular silence and serenity of all libraries. Dust motes danced in the shafts of sunlight streaming through the long windows. Being surrounded by shelves upon shelves of books brought her back to her days and nights in the library in the Village, before she had gone to sea, metaphorically, introducing herself to Orfeo; before she had met Dey, her great white whale, who embodied for her all society's ills and evils.

But now she had set sail on an altogether different sea, as perilous as the one before, perhaps more so. She had more to lose now: Bella's life as well as her own. As she wandered the stacks, something that Elin had told her persisted like a burr under her skin. She knew she would not rest until she had drawn it out, hook by hook. She didn't think Elin had lied to her, at least not after the initial denial. It was something she had said. Laurel paused, stared at the spines of the books at eye level. She was in the philosophy section, titles dealing with ideology, dialectics, doctrines, and rational thought.

Rational thought.

Into her mind came the burr that had been making her so uncomfortable:

"What exactly did she say? Can you remember?"

"I was so shocked I . . . let me think. She said things like, 'Don't you see how this country is changing, how it treats you like second-class citizens?' And things like, 'I don't know how you can buy into the falsity and materialism of this culture.'"

"That sounds like pretty sophisticated thinking."

Laurel stared at the titles of the books again. Philosophy, ideology, dialectics, doctrines. "I don't know how you can buy into the falsity and materialism of this culture." Definitely not rational thought. Well, not for a sixteen-year-old girl from Dearborn, Michigan, anyway.

At that moment, she felt a presence behind her. She spun on her heel. The man in the hoodie confronted her. She flinched as his hands came up. Looking quickly to either side, she saw they were alone. She was trapped.

THIRTY-FOUR

It was a cell that Bella found herself in now, no doubt about it. Unlike the vast majority of girls lured to Syria to become part of ISIS so quickly that they could not have second thoughts, she was stuck in limbo, alone and increasingly afraid. Apart from food, all she had to sustain her were the emails from Salim and Akima—and her father's assistant, Angela. Apart from her, whose correspondence she read over and over, all these people seemed like ghosts, very far away. To be in America—indeed, in her own hometown—and yet to be at the border, ready for days to take that first step away from the West and toward a new life, a new family, a new home that would embrace her fully, that would allow her to be herself, whatever that might be, was excruciating. Right now, at this moment, she belonged nowhere, belonged to no one, and to be honest, she was far too young to be comfortable in such a terrifying position.

Where was Angela? She knew she could easily find out. All it would take would be a single text. But the truth was she was afraid. What if Angela wasn't the Angela she had built up in her mind? What if she was someone different altogether? She didn't think she could bear it. And so she clung to the texts because they were familiar: they were from the Angela she wanted but was not sure actually existed.

Even so. Even she, disaffected, easily turned, thinking herself ready for the adventure of a lifetime, at long last free of Deadborn, at long last belonging somewhere, being part of something larger—though she had no clear idea of what that meant; she was simply parroting what Salim and Akima had offered her—Angela's texts made her suspect that she might have inadvertently taken the path of least resistance, the wrong path, that she had wandered into the fathomless deep. A shiver of fear passed through her. Now at the very end, when the gate had opened and she was about to step through, she wasn't sure she wanted to go on. But she was terrified to go back, because there was nothing to go back to, no one to save her from herself. The thought that she was lost in every way she could be lost only frightened her all the more.

Pulling out her father's dog-eared copy of *Moby-Dick*, she opened it almost reverently. She was almost at the end, for the second or third time, but this time, when Captain Ahab, tangled up in the harpoon's rope, was stuck fast to his titanic nemesis, Bella saw herself bound to her anger and rage, on the verge of drowning.

Closing her eyes, she imagined a jinn coming to rescue her, a swirl of hot sand and smoke coalescing in front of her, wiping out the turbulent sea that was about to take her down. The jinn held out its hand, taking her away from the constant anxiety of unknowing, back to its crystal palace of certainty that only she could see. A place of magic where she would be safe, where she wouldn't be alone. And there she would be loved and protected. What an idiot she had been! What a stupid little girl!

Thinking of her own rage caused her to think of Gabriel, Elin's oldest brother, so rageful, so ready to fight. Who knew what he was capable of? Maybe he was the backup; maybe he was the one coming for her. *If that's true . . .* , she thought and shivered as if with a fever. Her split with Elin had been awful and, she knew, irrevocable. She had been systematically culled out of the herd like a bewildered calf, and now here she was paralyzed in no-man's-land until she heard from—

Her cell buzzed, making her start. Her heart pounded. She had disabled the GPS, as Salim had instructed. Her cell buzzed again. It slipped in her sweaty hand. Then the screen lit up with the text icon. She navigated to it. The text was short: two words.

Prepare urself.

That was when, shaking like a leaf in a storm, she texted her father—daddy help—and got a series of replies. She wanted to text back, but she was terrified that she was under surveillance, that somehow ISIS not only knew where she was but was watching every move she made, monitoring her cell phone. Well, why not? It was being done all the time, by everyone, everywhere. She wanted to leave; she wanted to stay. She didn't know what she wanted and, as a consequence, did nothing but metaphorically fold into herself. Her mind folded like an accordion, shutting down in an attempt to protect herself from decision overload.

And then the message she had been waiting for and now dreaded with every fiber of her being: I'm coming 4 u.

Bella shivered until her teeth chattered. Then she began to cry.

THIRTY-FIVE

His fingers curled around the edges of the hoodie, drew it back off his face. He was a boy of maybe seventeen, not a man, despite the beard. She recognized him from the family photo in the Shehadis' living room.

"Gabriel." Her voice verged on being hoarse.

"We need to talk." He had a man's voice, not a boy's. And there was something in his dark eyes that made him seem older than her first fright-skewed impression of him.

"Go on," she said, her voice just above a whisper.

"You're looking for Bella."

For an instant, Laurel's tongue stuck to the roof of her mouth. "That's right," she finally managed. "How—"

"I overheard your conversation with my sister."

Laurel had nothing to say to that, though his admission chilled her. Everyone was listening to everything, it seemed. Now it was Gabriel's turn to glance from side to side. An older woman had entered their stack, and he led Laurel away, farther into the library.

He wet his lips. "I need to ask you why." He was dark and handsome, with his sister's wide, sensual lips. They made him look somehow cruel.

"I want to help Bella." And because she did not know what else to say, because her friendship with Richard was complex and also profoundly private, because all her feelings were bound up in this line of questions—because, she had to face it, she was closer to Bella than she had ever been and, therefore, desperate, she said, "I promised her father I would find her."

He regarded her with a stony expression.

Involuntarily, she took a step toward him. "Do you know where she is?"

"No." But he was young, after all, and his expression told her he was lying.

"I want to help her." Laurel could hear herself begging him, but she didn't care. "Please. If you know where she's gone, you must tell me."

There was a long silence during which she felt Gabriel's scrutiny of her in a physical, MRI kind of way. Like God, it seemed, he was weighing her, holding her in the balance, trying to determine if she was worthy.

Please, she begged silently. *Please.*

"All right." He nodded. "Come with me."

"I think something very bad is about to happen," Gabriel said as they hurried along the street. "My sister told you about the incident at Ali's. During the fight, I happened to glance up and glimpsed a light in the second floor corner window. It was just a sliver through pulled blinds; then it went off, and I forgot all about it until I began monitoring Bella's online conversations."

Laurel was taken aback. She stopped him in the middle of the sidewalk. "Why would you do that?"

"Just what the cops would have asked me had I told them. I didn't say a word. They would've locked me up for the kind of hacking they do all the time. And they probably would've accused me of being ISIS." He shook his head. "No, I couldn't afford to tell them anything. But you—you're like a jinni sent from Allah. I know you can help."

The afternoon was lengthening, reaching out toward its end. The western sun was copper, turning the shadows a strange, unnamable color. Newspaper leaves skittered across the sidewalk, along the street, caught in the corners of car windshields, house stoops. The day was unseasonably warm. Time seemed to slow down, to sigh, as if nearing its end. They started walking again at a more hurried pace.

"Over the past several weeks, maybe as much as a month, I felt a change in Bella," Gabriel said. "Elin's too close to her, loves her too much to admit it. But I could tell. She started talking the way some of the guys I hang with talk. Ideology, hatred, the perversion of the Prophet's teachings, peace be with him. As I began to pull away from them, she seemed to be moving into that orbit. It was just a sense at first, but it wouldn't go away. I stayed up nights thinking about it. That's when I hacked in." His dark eyes searched Laurel's. "She'd been corresponding with a cabal of ISIS recruiters. They have her head spun around—she doesn't know whether she's coming or going."

Laurel immediately thought of Elin's comment that Bella lacked an inner compass. And now the words Bella had used in her terminal argument with Elin came back to her with an entirely new and sinister cast: "I don't know how you can buy into the falsity and materialism of this culture." That hadn't sounded like her, Elin had said, and she was right.

"That's when I remembered the light I'd seen above Ali's All-Night, and I began to wonder."

"Wonder what? Has this Ali been radicalized?"

"Probably not. But I've seen some funny things around there at night."

"What kind of funny things?"

"There are kids around here—kids like me. Only not at all like me."

"Radicalized, you mean?"

He nodded. "Ali used to live in the apartment above his store, but when he moved out six months ago, after buying a small house, the rats moved in. Radicalized rats."

"And you told no one about this?" The moment she said it, Laurel knew she had made a mistake. Responding to the return of Gabriel's stony expression, she said, "Of course. Not after the way you and your family have been treated. I'm sorry." She pitched her voice low and soft, as Jimmy Self had told her to do when the end of the interrogation came into view. "So the apartment above Ali's . . ."

"I think that's where Bella is hiding, waiting for her ISIS contact."

Laurel frowned. "But from all I've read, they fetch the recruit as soon as they deem she's ripe; they don't allow time for second thoughts. You're saying Bella's been up there for days."

"The FBI has had a local jihadi cell under surveillance. They picked them up in a sweep four days ago."

"So she was left on her own."

"They won't do that," Gabriel said. "They don't want to let her go." He took a breath, let it slowly out. "They've arranged for a backup to come and take her."

It was at this point that she showed him the text for help from Bella from earlier in the day. "This is Richard's phone," she said. "She's had second thoughts. She wants out."

"Her new contact has told her he's coming now."

They rounded a corner, and Gabriel stopped them, pulling her back into the shadow of a doorway catty-corner across the street from Ali's All-Night. It inhabited the ground floor of a two-story yellow brick building on the corner. Plate glass windows at the front and around the side. To the left a narrow wooden door with a glass diamond at head height that presumably led to the living quarters on the floor above.

"This is where the street fight happened," Laurel said.

"You should've seen what they did to Ali, an old man who never had a bad word to say about anyone. He used to give Bella candies when she came in with Elin or Umm."

She was just behind him, and when he twisted to check out the street, she saw the soft metallic glimmer just above his waistband.

"Gabriel," she said slowly and carefully, "what are you doing with a gun?"

"It's just an old Police .38 Special, easiest handgun to get here." He turned back to her. "Don't worry; it isn't loaded. I got it from a friend after the street fight. I show it around so no one screws with me." He shrugged. "It's a fact of life now, Laurel."

She held out a hand. "Give it to me."

His brows drew together. "No. Why?"

"Just do it."

Reluctantly, he handed it over. "I hate guns," she said as she took from her pocket the bullets Jimmy Self had given her and, one by one, loaded them into the .38. "But there are times when it pays to protect yourself." She glanced up at the second floor of Ali's All-Night. "If, as you say, someone's coming for her, this seems to be one of them."

There was a peculiar languidness to the late afternoon, the torpor of midsummer past that belied their heightened sense of urgency and danger.

"The street's all but empty," he said. "We'll never have a better chance."

"Wait," Laurel called as he stepped out into the street. "Gabriel, come back."

There was some traffic, but he easily sidestepped the vehicles like a matador evading an oncoming bull. Except for one angry honk of an SUV horn, the cars passed him by without notice. He was on the opposite sidewalk. With a muttered curse, Laurel hurried across the street to join him. At that moment, a group of six boys appeared from around the far side of Ali's All-Night, almost as if they had been lying in wait.

They all had cuts, bruises, and abrasions. By this, Laurel intuited they were the ones on whom Gabriel and his friends had exacted revenge. *Newton's third law*, she thought: *For every action there is an equal and opposite reaction.*

"Hey, raghead," they called. "Fucking sand nigger." They held open gravity knives, hammers, and crowbars. Weapons of the street.

What Newton didn't express was that each pair of action and reaction bred escalation.

Laurel grabbed at Gabriel's arm. "Come away. You don't want this." At the same time, she glimpsed one of the boys hanging back behind the others. He was neither timid nor afraid; he was using them as a screen. When she saw the gun in his hand, she stepped smartly in front of Gabriel, her gun hand coming up. But Gabriel was ready for her, ready for this moment. Later, she was to think that from the moment he had overhead her conversation with his sister, most everything that had come after had been part of his plan.

He grabbed the .38 out of her hand, stepped forward, and straight-arm aimed at the gang. At once, they shouted, scattering. All except the other boy with the gun. He smiled at Gabriel. "What a disappointment you are. How America has subverted you, made you weak and lazy. Now you want all the comforts of this life. You have turned yourself from Allah's will. I don't know how you can buy into the falsity and materialism of this culture. Say goodbye to your luxuries, betrayer."

With the hyperreal clarity of extraordinary circumstances, Laurel could see his finger tighten on the trigger just as Gabriel took another step toward him and fired, another step, fired again, another step, fired again, though the boy was already down, jerking involuntarily.

An instant later, Gabriel went down in a hail of crossfire. Immediately, men poured out of several SUVs. Laurel tried to run to him, but the feds and the local cops barked at her to step back, to keep quiet, that the area was not secured, though traffic in either direction had been stopped.

They were right. Something—perhaps a homemade bomb—was thrown by one of the boys, who'd momentarily returned before racing off. It crashed through the side window of Ali's All-Night. An explosion shattered glass. Flames shot out of the broken windows. The feds took off around the side of the building. The cops—those who hadn't been close enough to be knocked down or injured—stood in shock. Had anyone called the fire department? No matter, not enough time. No one knew what was going on except Laurel. And at that moment no one besides Laurel knew that the boy Gabriel had shot was the local ISIS contact coming for Bella. But all that would become known soon enough.

~

After the shots fired, after the dreadful explosion, smoke began to filter up through the old floorboards from below. Bella could feel the heat. Fists over her ears, she was screaming so loudly, so wildly, that her throat was already raw.

Running to one window after another, she pushed aside the blinds, tried to open the windows, but they were locked. She might have swung her backpack at a pane of glass, but alas, panic had buried all rational thought. Instead, she collapsed against her backpack, all she had in the world, all she loved, reduced to this spot. But not for long. Heat and smoke drove her to her feet, but not before she snatched up her father's copy of *Moby-Dick*. Some survival instinct deep in her lizard brain made her put the book up in front of her face like a shield as she ran to the door, but when she pulled it open, she was greeted by swirling clouds of smoke and a heat that might have singed her lashes and brows were it not for the thick book.

She recoiled. She would have screamed more, but every time she opened her mouth, smoke billowed in. Involuntarily, she inhaled, choked, and coughed. She sank to her knees, the book held tightly to her breast. A terrible despair broke over her then, and she felt as if she were Ahab, tied to his terrible monster, drowning with each roll of the great beast's body. Pulling her hands over her face, she wept, sobs racking her thin shoulders.

It was then she heard her name.

"Bella."

Her name being called from someplace unknown to her.

"Bella!"

Hands falling away from her tear-streaked face, she saw her jinni emerging out of smoke and fire, ash and embers. "Are you here to take me away to your crystal palace?"

Her jinni smiled a smile so beautiful Bella started to sob all over again. And she must be a jinni because she started to sing the song her father used to sing to her, which, unknown to him, she had memorized:

> "The Owl and the Rabbit went to sea
> In a beautiful pea-green boat,
> They took some honey, and plenty of money,
> Wrapped up in a five-pound note.
> The Owl looked up to the stars above,
> And sang to a small guitar,
> 'O lovely Rabbit! O Rabbit, my love,
> What a beautiful Rabbit you are,
> You are,
> You are!
> What a beautiful Rabbit you are!'"

And in this blissful state, she was scooped up in strong, feminine arms. In this state Laurel, her jinni, singing to her, brought her out of the furnace and into the cool twilight of Dearborn. Into salvation.

THE WATERY PART OF THE WORLD

Gael Luzon took care of everything, including clearing the misdeeds of Laurel's past. How he managed it Laurel was never to know. Perhaps he used his DOD contacts; perhaps he had called upon others. Some things, as she had come to learn, did not bear knowing. But certainly what greased the wheels was the FBI rounding up a large ISIS sleeper cell using the identity of the boy Gabriel had shot and the contacts on his cell phone.

Gabriel was a hero, though Laurel could not help but think of what Gael had told her: "It's the innocent who get caught in the crossfire. The innocents always pay for the sinners' transgressions; the sinners see to that."

It seemed half of Dearborn attended Gabriel's funeral, the mosque filled with Muslim mourners, the Christians on the sidewalk and street. Laurel and Bella, who in her heart of hearts had never converted, were the only two non-Muslims allowed inside.

Gabriel's body lay washed and wrapped in a clean winding cloth. The three eldest Shehadis rose, one by one: Hashim spoke of fear, ignorance, and the courage to do the right thing under adverse conditions. Umm spoke of devotion to one's faith, to one's family, to one's country. Elin spoke of friendship and childhood's end.

To everyone's surprise, save Laurel's, Bella spoke next. As she stepped to the podium, she clutched her father's copy of *Moby-Dick*, the smell of ash and smoke now forever a part of it. She did not speak at length; she allowed Melville to speak for her.

In a voice clotted with emotion, she opened the book and read from the beginning of chapter 37. "I leave a white and turbid wake; pale waters, paler cheeks; where'er I sail. The envious sidelong swell to whelm my track; let them; but first I pass."

That was it; that was all she said. Laurel knew that she was speaking as much about her father as she was about Gabriel.

Outside, a man on the street was selling miniature American flags made of stiff paper attached to minuscule wooden staffs. Everyone, it seemed, bought one. As the body was carried out, they laid them upon it until Gabriel was covered, like a war hero, in American bunting. He was laid to rest on his side, his head pointed toward Mecca. Laurel looked for Rosie Menkins but in the swarm of people couldn't find her. Perhaps she hadn't come.

On another day, Laurel asked Bella if she wanted to see where her father was buried. She shook her head. "He's not there. I know it."

On another day, forty-eight hours after the Shehadis' lawyer filed suit against the Dearborn Police Department and the state of Michigan for defamation and wrongful arrest and imprisonment, a Town Car drew up to the Shehadi residence. A man in a charcoal-gray tweed overcoat stepped out. Laurel knew him as the man with poached-egg eyes. Richard had known him as Perry White. He introduced himself to the Shehadis and their lawyer by another pseudonym. He stayed with them for just under an hour, at the end of which a settlement, including an ironclad gag order, was agreed to and signed.

On yet another day that heralded the coming of autumn, after Gael the *brujo*, the sorcerer, had worked his magic; after all the requisite official forms had been signed, stamped, and filed away in the bowels of the vast federal bureaucracy, Laurel took Bella to Chicago, where she could finish high school, start therapy, and also be close to Elin. The first time Laurel met with the therapist on her own, the therapist said, "Bella needs three things from you, Laurel: unconditional love, understanding, patience." The second time she said, "Think of Bella's recovery as a pendulum. She's been given a mighty push, so the pendulum swings wildly from one side to another, but the anchor you provide works like gravity, slowing those swings back and forth until, finally, the pendulum reaches equilibrium and ceases to swing altogether."

When they had first arrived in Chicago, Laurel had given Bella her father's cell phone, and for a while the girl had been obsessed with reading their texts, though of course she had them on her own phone. The therapist told Laurel this was a normal part of the healing process, and she was right. The therapist was a specialist in deprogramming, and she turned out to be excellent. One day, Bella put her father's phone away, and Laurel knew that she was reaching for equilibrium. Evenings were spent at home—a small but comfortable two-bedroom apartment overlooking the lake—and weekends walking lakeside. Always they spoke of Richard, sharing memories, each one filling in blanks for the other. There were so many blanks! Many of them, mysterious to both, never got filled in. But gradually, Richard rose to walk and sit beside them, doubtless a different Richard than the living one but Richard all the same. Their Richard. And in the end, that was comfort enough. His temporary resurrection was another rite they both had to pass through, and it made them even closer. Not surprisingly, Bella had an intense interest in everything Laurel, but what did astonish Laurel was Bella's curiosity about Laurel's father. Mourning was a lonely business at best, and Laurel found comfort in talking to Bella about Eddie Springfield. Of their mothers not much was said, but perhaps that was to be expected. Laurel did not know whether Bella knew the origin of her mother's enmity toward her, and she was very much inclined to let that particular sleeping dog lie.

Bella was now Laurel's daughter, by way of adoption, a situation that, as time went on, suited them both more and more. Two years after Bella was freed, on the day of her eighteenth birthday, Laurel took her to see Gael in Manhattan, where Bella, breathless, goggled at the view and traded jokes with one of Gael's young male workers. Gael took them out to the finest restaurants, but Bella loved the pizza parlors, of which there seemed to be an endless supply, best. After a week, they flew to Washington, DC. At Bella's request, they went to the White House, the Capitol, the monuments, and spent an entire afternoon on a private tour of the Smithsonian that Laurel had arranged. More than once, Bella wept bitter tears. Laurel wisely kept her own counsel. Then it was on to San Diego, where, Gael had informed her, Orfeo had retired with his family. Nonna was gone, and the kids were all grown up; she scarcely recognized them. But curiously, Orfeo seemed much the same. Perhaps a bit older, definitely wiser. He greeted them both with open arms and a full heart. There was no tension between him and Laurel. Whatever black mark had been on their books had been expunged with extreme prejudice. It was not only time that healed all wounds; it was the people who suffered them.

She watched him teach Bella how to play chess, and Bella stared spellbound as she and Orfeo played *Concierto de Aranjuez* on guitars—he had kept hers all these years. Laurel had forgotten nothing, her fingers as nimble as ever. Orfeo beamed like a proud papa.

Despite all this, or perhaps because of it, the two women tacitly accepted the startling fact of their parallel lives. It was too obvious to speak of—or too intimate. Possibly both.

Then, because Bella had chosen it as her birthday gift, they flew back to New York, and some days later—after evenings at the theater, the ballet, and one glorious night at the Museum of Modern Art—they set off for Crete, not the fastest way by jet but by boat. They both were desirous to see the watery part of the world, as Melville put it, and, further, experience it together. Upon their return, whenever that might be, Bella had expressed the desire to follow in her father's footsteps, to learn to uncover the truth about ancient civilizations.

They had long since discovered their shared love of *Moby-Dick*, although, as Bella remarked at the outset of the voyage, "I've always been afraid of whales, and *Moby-Dick* made me terrified of them."

"And yet?" Laurel prompted, because she knew there was more and because she was thinking how different this was from Richard's last anxiety-laden trip home.

"And yet my fascination with them, with the book, with Melville's point of view only intensified. I was repulsed and drawn at the same time."

"That much size," Laurel said, "signaling that much anger and rage. I think we both understand, don't we?"

"We do," Bella said, soberly. "I thought about this while I was alone, waiting for . . ." Her voice shut down for a moment, then started up again with a lighter tone. "But at some point you have to let it go or be caught up in it till you drown."

Laurel put her arm around the girl, fast becoming a young woman. She felt the salt wind in her face, watched the gray-green water ahead, aware of the land falling away behind them, Manhattan as miniature as if it were inside a snow globe. A fierce elation gripped her, as if she were running as fast as she could toward a horizon already visible, rising up from unknown waters, its contours, its beautiful features familiar to her. Her heart thrumming in her chest, her hair flying free behind her. The world before her, expanding. *No*, she thought with the shock of revelation, *not me*—us.

"I used to be in love with rage," she said as she kissed Bella's cheek. "But that was a long time ago."

ABOUT THE AUTHOR

Leslie Archer is the nom de plume of a *New York Times* bestselling author of more than twenty-five novels.